THE SAFEHAVEN COMPLEX

CHASING MERCURY
BOOK THREE

Paul Phillips

I QUATERNI BOOKS

*In memory of my parents, who are both in this book,
one way or another.*

*And my uncle, John Cresswell, who got 'Lucky' Luciano
and Odette Sansom to tell their stories, among many others.*

CHASING MERCURY:
A NOTE ABOUT THE SERIES

The Safehaven Complex is the third and final book in the Chasing Mercury series.

It is a continuation of the story that began in *The Borodino Sacrifice* and developed in *The Herrenhaus Forfeit.*

However, it is also designed to stand alone as a self-contained adventure and, as such, it recaps key plot points and reintroduces recurring characters for first-time readers.

I hope you enjoy it!

Paul Phillips

PROLOGUE

They had launched their rockets from here. The surviving woodland still bore traces of their subterfuge. Areas of what would soon become dense tree cover, mysteriously left untouched by the construction of the Atlantic Wall and the ravages of the *Hongerwinter*, hid at their centre points a series of circular clearings for the mobile V-2 launchers.

The old man tapped at the ground with the tip of his furled umbrella. It was a habit of his – an unfortunate habit, he would have told his recruits, in a business where any habit was unfortunate and potentially fatal. But it was a long time since anyone had been required to listen to anything he said. And if, at fifty-six, he was not really so old, well… he was unlikely to get much older.

In addition to creating the camouflaged launch sites and the bunkers that surrounded them, the Germans had cut the Haagse Bos in two with an anti-tank ditch. This had filled with water, of course, and now looked much like any other canal in the country. Strolling along its edge, seemingly without a care in this world without war, were the two figures he had been watching.

A man and a boy. The man looked well-dressed and well-fed, which even in the spring of 1947 was remarkable enough for The Hague or most other parts of the Netherlands. He was about forty. His young companion – somehow, despite the fair hair, 'son' did not quite fit – was more plainly dressed in shirt and shorts and as skinny as any of the children one saw roaming Europe's overgrown battlefields. With the years of poor nutrition and the prematurely drawn faces, it could be hard to

1

pin down young people's ages nowadays, but the lad appeared to be eight or nine.

Colonel (Ret'd) Richard Campbell Smith, CBE, DSO, MC planted his brolly among last year's acorns and bent awkwardly to retrieve the much-chewed tennis ball. At his heels, his borrowed Lakeland Terrier showed teeth and tongue in renewed interest.

"Fetch!" he wheezed, pitching the ball underarm; with an embarrassed groan as it faded towards the pair by the anti-tank ditch, he added: "Blast! Sorry!"

Nursing his game leg, he hurried after the terrier, all too aware from his brief acquaintance with it that it would soon lose interest in the ball when it met human prey.

By the time he caught up, the over-friendly dog was making a proper nuisance of itself, jumping up and leaving dirty paw-prints on the man's suit trousers and the boy's bare knees.

"I really am most dreadfully sorry," Smith told them, searching for the leash in his coat pockets. Interestingly, the man appeared to understand while the boy only frowned. The reply was delivered in English with a hint of an American as well as a Dutch or German accent.

"No matter. No apologies necessary."

"That's jolly decent of you – here, Susie, damn you!"

With the infuriating animal leashed at last, he had time to spare the boy an avuncular smile.

"Do you like dogs?"

An uncertain expression, with a glance to his guardian for direction. Smith felt the grin dying on his own face. And a growing pressure like a giant's fist in his breast.

"He has not much experience of pets," the man said. "The war, you understand."

"Of course..." And suddenly, with the shock, with the fist, it was all Smith could do not to gasp in pain and sink to his knees. Instead he bit at his moustache and tipped his hat. "Well… good afternoon. I'll leave you to your, your…"

Unable to think of the words, he wrenched the dog away,

tripping over it, heart thundering, chest constricting. Already he was fumbling in his inside pocket for the confounded little brown bottle of nitro-glycerine tablets.

Crime, he thought, in the absence of anything more nuanced – or indeed any further intelligence which even the most incompetent of his old recruits would have been able to extract from the seemingly casual encounter. Your rotten, rotten *crime...* As he tipped the bottle, his hands shaking, he pictured the look on the boy's face.

The look of the boy's face.

And whose it looked like, not just a little but a lot. A face both defiantly young and marked with a knowledge beyond its age. A face he had not seen for nearly five long years.

As he reached the path back towards Clingendael and his car, Smith heard the dog growl. Two youngish men had stepped out from behind an oak tree and were heading obliquely towards him, hands deep in the pockets of their unseasonably heavy coats. They did not look like the sort of men who spent time behind trees in parks. Nor was it like Roger's dog to take against humans so suddenly. Smith had learned when to trust an instinctive reaction, however it might manifest itself.

He changed his grip on his umbrella and pressed on.

PART ONE

EUROPE

CHAPTER ONE

When the time came to file through, it was all too evident there would be precious few mourners in attendance. Perhaps this was the reason for holding the memorial service in the chapel that was tucked away at the east end of the crypt and not above in the cathedral proper.

After all was said and done – and so much more not said, or barely alluded to – an even more exclusive group gathered by the outsized red marble sarcophagus that all but blocked the entrance to St. Faith's chapel.

Grim nods were exchanged, a hip flask passed, cigarettes shared and lit. One of their number, a lanky American with a moneyed manner and unsettling eyes, rapped on the marble and winced theatrically.

"Who's this guy? 'Duke Wellington'? Hey Mike, I think we caught his act at the Cotton Club!"

With an All-American crew-cut and a sports jacket that was failing spectacularly to blend in, his stocky companion chuckled. A dowdy-suited mourner, passing by, paused to look scandalised.

"I say, sir!" the gentleman puffed, and said no more.

The taller Yank waited until they were alone again and then scoffed.

"Look at all of us! Wasn't it this very fella here who said something like 'nothing is so melancholy as a battle won'? Boy was he right!"

"Next to a battle lost, Sloane," protested a more imposing military type in what passed for a well-bred English accent and actually hid a very different background.

"OK, Jones, you got me there. But lighten up a little, for crying out loud!"

Having uttered these words, Sloane made a show of flinching, as though anticipating a bawling out or even a physical assault from the only female in their group, whose furious glare flashed in the candlelight beneath her little black suiter hat and veil.

"'Oo gave you the right to stick yer oar in, if you don't mind me asking? You only met him the once and he weren't that impressed and I know it 'cause I was there!"

Seeing his feigned unease turn to genuine puzzlement, the fierce young woman stepped out from the murk of mouldering banners to press home her advantage.

"Corporal Jenny Simmonds of the Auxiliary Territorial Service. Least I was then... I was 'is driver."

The strangely washed-out-yellow eyes opened wide.

"That day in Berlin, on the Rubble Mountain! Oh ma'am I apologise. Relationships like his and yours, in our business, are closer than anything. You may hit me if you wish."

"Well it weren't no 'relationship' neither, I'll have you know, and I ain't in the business no more, if I ever was, so I'll just say thanks but no thanks."

Sloane grinned and gave Mike a nudge, shaking his head in admiration.

"'Fanks but no fanks' – Adolf never stood a chance with these folks, nor Boney before him!"

By now the other mourners, all ancient brass hats or grey men from the ministry, had finished their respectful study of military memorials and exited the central vault. Sloane led their group past timber shoring and the dust sheeting that all but obscured the other huge tomb, a black bathtub of a sarcophagus emblazoned HORATIO VISC. Above them, a crude patch, braced with planks, marked where a German bomb had detonated in the North Transept and opened up the crypt.

Following dutifully, limping a little in the clutch of so much cold stone, the third American peered behind each pillar, scanned every shadowy alcove and searched the obfuscating patterns of ornamental ironwork for a familiar silhouette. Surely she would have come, if only to see who…?

It was Jones who put him out of his misery.

"Sent word. Officially I mean. She didn't tell you?"

He sounded almost sympathetic. Bradley couldn't bear that.

"We're not really in touch anymore."

"No?" 'Mr Jones' – real name Rastislav Zajíček, post-war occupation uncertain – looked as if he might know better. But then, as former assistant to the late Colonel Smith, he always had. "Well, I gather MERCURY decided that playing the grieving widow would be a bit much. Not that she isn't grieving, in her own way, and she did attend the private interment – but I mean it was *pre-eminently* a marriage of convenience, wasn't it?"

"All I know is what you told me when you bullied me into working for you," Bradley said, recalling Jones' first arrival at the Munich stockade and, after the Limeys had sprung him, the combined blackmail threat and mission briefing in the Parisian cemetery. "Smith took her under his wing when she escaped from Czechoslovakia at the start of the war. Later he gave her the means to go back in as a secret agent."

"The real secret being that it was to look for her child." Jones nodded. "I must say that took us by surprise."

"Must you?" Bradley pulled a face, more in disgust than amusement.

"Now let's not start all that again. I know you think you were sent in after her as bait or something, but it all worked out in the end and this is hardly the time…"

"Too right it ain't!" Jenny Simmonds had wormed between Sloane, Lord Nelson and a precarious-looking arrangement of cement-plastered ladders to stick her own oar in. "What it's time for is to find out what happened to the 'old man'!"

Jones's genial expression hardened.

"His heart gave out. In The Hague of all places."

"What was he doing there?" Bradley wanted to know.

"Setting up an international court of justice, in the vain hope that the next tinpot expansionist might not drag all of humanity down with him."

"I thought he had retired."

"So did I." Jones looked almost sincere for a moment. "But I suppose if it's suggested that one's advice might go to save a hundred million lives, or a thousand million…"

"You know there's a word for that? Billion," interjected Sloane. "Me, I'd choose watercolours and breeding roses."

Still rocked by Jones' revelation about Mila, Bradley struggled to focus his thoughts. It was like this load-bearing nexus of vaulted caverns and rounded-off stone: nothing comforting, nothing to get hold of. He regarded Jenny.

"Did you not know what had happened to Colonel Smith?"

"I knew what *they* said had happened." She cocked her head at Jones and Sloane in turn, as exemplars he supposed. "But that's what they deal in, ain't it – stories?"

"And you think there's more to this one."

A churchwarden was hovering on the far side of the battered mosaic floor, no doubt eager to clear the way for the workmen to return. Bradley saw Sloane tip a wink to Major Mike Murphy, who detached unobtrusively to meet the threat on their flank.

"It may be the time, Miss Simmonds, but it is hardly the place," said Jones. He checked his wristwatch. "I suggest we all go for a pint."

*   *   *

Watling Street was an ancient route from Canterbury through London which had first been paved by the Romans. The City that flourished around it had almost subsumed it, but thanks to the archaeological exploits of the Luftwaffe it had regained a pristine simplicity. Between the east face of the cathedral and the blackened three-storey corner pub more than two hundred yards along the old thoroughfare, little remained save brick-dust and foundation walls. It was the same in most directions. The great domed edifice of St Paul's was the miracle of the Blitz.

As an honorary Englishman and Londoner, Jones took charge. Bradley didn't spot whether he paid, browbeat or simply commanded the trio of labourers to vacate their table, but in no time he had everyone seated, a many-paned, many-cracked window prised open to let out the fog of pipe smoke and a fawning landlord offering to fetch them their drinks. Bradley was impressed. Usually he spent half his time in these godforsaken places just trying to catch the attention of the barman and the other half pondering how they had managed to magic his beer into a few lukewarm suds.

Once the girl had brought the glasses and a fresh ashtray, Jones produced his familiar cigarette case, tapping with the end of a king-size Pall Mall to bring the meeting to order.

"Now... the old man had ischaemic heart disease, which led to a heart attack while out walking. That isn't a cover story, Miss Simmonds, but nor is it the whole truth. A significant contributing factor would be the fight he got into directly before he died."

"A fight!" Jenny's wide open mouth was mirrored to varying degrees around the table. As they had only just heard an hour ago, Smith had certainly shown vigour and valour in his youth, but he had never been a field operative in the branch of the intelligence service he ran.

"A knife fight. Well, more of a sword in Richard's case. That damn trick brolly of his. When the Dutch police worked out what it was, it helped them enormously with two mysterious cases of unsavoury characters who had staggered into hospital with nasty lacerations."

At which point and, as Bradley reflected, not for the first time, Sloane revealed himself to be less of the clubbable diplomat on the side-lines and more a co-conspirator.

"Between Jones and my people, we persuaded the folks over there to sit on the details while we looked into it. The two hoods were petty criminals, housebreakers, who had gotten rather good at acquiring the art collections of wealthy Dutch Jews when they went into hiding from the Nazis. In more than one case, it seems that the same intermediary who knew where the loot was stashed also tipped off the Gestapo about the owners' hiding places. A neat business plan that leaves no prior claims or plaintiffs."

"And Smith was investigating this intermediary?"

Sloane gave Bradley a pained look.

"Not officially, but we just don't know, sport. And if he was, we don't know why. The two housebreakers were eager to cooperate once it was explained to them that their wartime activities would see them up against a wall. They pointed us towards their boss, one Maximiliaan Hubertus de Klerk. I'm afraid he was known to us already."

"What do you mean, afraid?" Jenny demanded. Bradley could tell how she was putting on a brave face but was actually close to tears.

"What I mean, Miss Simmonds, is that he's untouchable." Sloane glanced at Major Mike before continuing. "You see there's something called Operation SAFEHAVEN. It was launched at the Bretton Woods conference in '44 and falls at least partly under my area of the State Department – let's call it Research."

"Funny way to spell Strategic Services…" Bradley grunted, but Sloane was not biting.

"Gone, sport, in all its exotic permutations, apart from some hidebound central agency that Truman will be unveiling to little effect later this summer… SAFEHAVEN, though, was and is an economic operation, designed to prevent the Nazis from stockpiling all their ill-gotten gains in neutral countries and potentially bankrolling the Fourth Reich. Now that threat has proved as hollow as the rest of their beliefs, the mission has shifted to getting people's gold and other stuff back."

Further lowering his voice, Sloane adopted a less self-satisfied tone as he met Jenny's gaze.

"M.H. de Klerk, we discovered, is untouchable because it turns out he has already cooperated with SAFEHAVEN. Having acquired a significant slice of Netherlandish heritage, including works by Rembrandt, Van Dyck and Vermeer, he fled to Spain before the war's end. Did a deal with us and the Dutch government. Immunity in return for the pictures."

"They let a Nazi collaborator go! Someone who'd informed on Jews…"

Jones stubbed out his cigarette and laid a placatory hand upon Jenny's.

"That part was never proven. De Klerk is a well-travelled mongrel of a man and in fact his wife is Jewish. Probably how he found out about the poor souls and their art collections in the first place, but it muddies the waters and lets him claim he was keeping the Nazis off his own back. At any rate, finding himself in The Hague, and feeling justifiably nervous, he paid his old housebreakers to frighten off anyone who got too close. Unfortunately for everyone, Richard didn't frighten. He fought back."

And now the tears did come.

"Poor bugger… fighting for his life, all alone!"

"Apparently he had a dog with him, belonging to a colleague he was staying with. The animal must have run off and led the police back to where he died – a rather bare bit of woodland on the edge of the Haagse Bos, but quite peaceful. I visited the spot when I went out to bring him home."

It was a side of Jones that Bradley had not seen before. Jenny must have felt something similar. She squeezed his hand and said, softly: "Thank you."

"I'm afraid that is the extent of official interest. De Klerk is out of bounds and in the wind. Whatever Richard wanted with him, if indeed it wasn't all a dreadful coincidence, he left no record of it."

For the moment no one, not even Sloane, had anything else to say. They sipped their watered-down beers – in Sloane's case, wisely, a whisky – and smoked their cigarettes, lost in their own thoughts.

Absent friends, Bradley mused. He caught Jones' eye.

"Does she know?"

"I thought you could be the one to tell her."

And there it was, the burn and kick in his throat and chest, the quickening of the pulse, as though he was the one knocking back whisky instead of soapy British beer. The feeling, again, of being manoeuvred to the brink of the first drop on the Coney Island Cyclone: exhilaration, inevitability.

"I bet you did," he said.

If Jones had not told Mila the truth about her husband's death – assuming it was the truth – then he wanted to use the timing and delivery of that information to particular effect. Had he told her himself, earlier, she would have persuaded him to redouble his investigations. Mila had a way of getting what she wanted from people. So to leave it to Bradley, now, after several months and this apparently impromptu reunion at the memorial service… Clearly Jones expected Mila to press him into investigating unofficially, with her. Clearly he expected Bradley to be happy to go along with it.

He was as cunning as ever, as cunning as his boss had been. And he was right.

It was a year now since Bradley had helped her locate the boy on the North German bombsite, the boy who might have been the son she'd had stolen from her by the Nazis. And nine months since they'd followed another lead to another child, with the same inconclusive outcome. Europe was full of lost children with little or no memory of their lives before the war. Time and time again one met with blank faces – apprehension gradually turning to hope, not that they had found again their long-lost parent but simply that someone might play that role and at least take care of them. For the real parents, like Mila, it was soul-destroying. Everything was rejection. The child's rejection of the certainty of recognition, in forgotten names and language, in blighted features and those blank, traumatised stares. And the rejection that was required in return of the searching parent: to abandon every unsatisfactory candidate, one after the other, even as that glimmer of hope kindled in their eyes.

Eventually, neither of them had been able to stand it anymore. Mila had all but adopted two, then three, then four orphans at Bradley's last count, teaming up with her contacts in the Control Commission for Germany to run some kind of boarding school in the British Zone. And Bradley had drawn on his own contacts too, Sloane among them, to find work in the American Zone supervising Disarmed Enemy Forces on mine clearing and reconstruction projects. By the time the brutal winter brought everything to a standstill and placed the whole continent on a crisis footing once more, he and Mila had hardly been communicating. A Christmas message, delivered through a third party, had been their last. Seven months ago.

Blame the winter, blame the work, he told himself. But you know what it really is that has driven you apart.

And what might bring you back together.

"She's in Scotland," Jones said, for all the world as though he had been following Bradley's thoughts. "That's why she didn't come today. Richard left her his estate on the Cowal peninsula. I believe she has moved her children's refuge there."

Bradley shook his head in wonder. Or perhaps to clear it, in preparation for the long slide that was coming. Twice before they had forced him to mount that scaffold, only to blindly launch himself into the chaotic fray: the first time at the very end of the war, when Smith's department had borrowed him from the US Army to track down their missing agent MERCURY, who had gone rogue behind Soviet lines; the second when Sloane's Strategic Services boys – or others in the shadows – had sent him after her again to prevent her causing further trouble. In neither case had they let him in on their real intentions, trusting him and Mila only to stir up the right hornet's nest in the right place and, if they were lucky, to get out in one piece. Replaying them in his head, Bradley detected the same equivocation in Jones' words this time.

Tuning back in, he was aware of Major Mike asking a question of Jenny Simmonds. *And what do you do, ma'am?*

"I work at a department store in Clapham Junction, Ardin' & 'obbs," she raised her eyes comically through her veil and instantly her pinched face became charming. "Be'ind the 'at counter."

Jones had been listening too. He turned to her abruptly and

the military manner was back.

"Take a leave of absence. Get pregnant."

"I'm gettin' *married*, sir…"

"Later. You're needed first, for coordination and liaison. Perhaps a spot of driving too."

She was doing her best to look affronted, you could tell, but Bradley recognised the other signs: the colour in the cheeks, the quickness of calculation behind the eyes, the tightness in the throat that fell somewhere between apprehension and the urge to hoot.

"I don't follow…"

"Heavens, woman, it's staring you in the face. I can't draw on official resources – as a matter of fact I am not even in the service of this country anymore. Sloane and Major Murphy are only passing through. Due back in Washington, isn't it? That leaves Bradley here, sorely in need of logistical support."

"But… for what?"

"For getting to the bottom of this, of course. For continuing the old man's inquiries, whatever they were and wherever they might lead. And for catching the bastard who did for him. Drink up, all of you – chop chop. We have work to do!"

CHAPTER TWO

"Hänschen klein,
ging allein
in die weite Welt hinein..."

The boy on the terrace was indeed by himself, as was his custom. But unlike 'little Hans' in the nursery rhyme, he had not ventured out into the wide world alone.

Trying to elicit a smile as she came up to him, Mila Suková sang the next lines to an exaggerated marching beat.

"Stock – und – Hut
stehn – ihm – gut,
ist gar wohlgemut."

This Hans had no staff or hat to suit him well, nor did he look remotely happy. She ruffled his hair.

"How was your evening meal? Good?"

The blank look again.

"But missing your *Wohlgemut* a bit, *ne*?"

Mila swore inwardly, knowing that her ability to see the world through a young child's eyes, or lack of it, had let her down as much as her German. As best as anyone could tell, Hans was originally from the US Zone, near Frankfurt – hence her poor attempt to allude to a local dish, 'Green Sauce', with its herbal ingredients including 'cheerful' or *Wohlgemut*. But all that was beyond him. Whoever had kept him alive, before his unexplained appearance, naked, upon the moonscape of Dortmund, would more likely have used a recipe for boiled weeds and wallpaper.

And there was the next line of the song, which she was never going to sing. *But mother cries sorely, for she has Hänschen no more…*

"Nearly bed-time. Won't you come in with the others? We are going to have a story."

The boy frowned across the gardens to the gleaming loch and the humpback whales of silhouetted hills beyond. Although the sun was low now, its glow would linger, dusted with insects and thistledown, for hours. The boys and girls who'd shyly request of her an *Appel* not an *Apfel* were more used to northern midsummer evenings, but even for them, Scotland at this latitude could be disorienting.

Let me get them settled while the darkness stays away, she thought.

Including the pair she had picked up in Hanover before leaving Germany, she had six of these damaged, vacant children in her charge now, four boys and two girls. They included her first, soul-shattering disappointment, 'Paul', whom she had tried so hard to convince herself was Pavel, even to the extent of doubting her own memories and the unresolved ache, deep within her, that Kafka had called *the knife I turn inside myself*.

None of them would benefit psychologically from being uprooted like this and all would need to be repatriated as soon as possible, but for the moment, and especially after that winter, what else was she to do? Her Mil.Gov contacts in the British Zone of Occupation were stretched to breaking point. Her former underground network was scattered across Germany and Czechoslovakia, scratching a living on the black market. A return to what remained of her family in Prague was impossible with the communists in the ascendant. Only Richard's undeserved generosity in leaving her this place – and the Mayfair flat which she had promptly sold to provide funds – had given her the means to save the children's lives. With luck their spirits could wait until she found them a better mentor.

One who knew how to talk to them, would be a start.

"Well, come on now, Hänschen. I really think you should…"

With a mixture of dread and relief she noticed the long shadow of the housekeeper coming around the corner of the terrace, loaded down with baskets from the clothes line.

"May I be of assistance, My Lady?"

As always, knowing Richard and his ways, Mila was moved to wonder how much here was fusty tradition and how much fine-drawn mockery.

"Thank you, Mrs Macrae. I was just, um…"

"Should I take Master Hans upstairs and see he gets a braw *hot chocolate*?"

Somehow, despite speaking only her version of English, and that with a strong accent that Mila often found indecipherable, the stout, unsmiling woman had won Hans' attention. Life returned to the eyes. The pout twitched. He got up, ready to take the corner of Mrs Macrae's apron.

"It's good of you to…" Mila rolled her eyes. Now it was her own English letting her down as well as her German. "Make such an effort."

"Och, they're nae bother, the wee'uns. Colonel Smith had us put up all sorts. Commandos. Submariners – *midget* submariners! After those, these midgets are a doddle. Come on you…" She cocked her head for Hans, clicking as she might for a pony. "Let's get ye up to Miss Robinson and snuggled in. Then I'll be after fetching Rolli's bicycle from the front gate where he thought to leave it out on the road."

"Oh, let me do that," Mila said, glad to bring something to the table, even if it were a humble offering alongside the housekeeper's unflappable facility and the authority of Miss Robinson, their new governess.

"Very kind, My Lady," Mrs Macrae called out as she rolled away with Hans in tow.

Watching them go, Mila nodded to herself.

"That's put me in my place."

She stooped to tidy away the playthings Hans had been tinkering with, a few stone and whalebone chessmen that might even have entertained Richard in his own childhood. The mismatched pawns were reminiscent of the weather-beaten Pictish stones one found growing out of the ancient landscape like surviving teeth in mouldering skulls. Hans had been acting out some battle, remembered or imagined, or half-remembered, half-imagined. Perhaps that explained why he had descended again into his brooding.

Mila felt a familiar jostle of shame. She could never quite silence the inner voice reminding her that however blameless their broken souls, however sincerely she had shouldered the burden of their welfare and however much, if by some miracle he was still alive, Pavel must resemble them now, these were the children of the enemy. It was their parents' childless friends who had acquired abductees via the Lebensborn foundation – and might therefore have 'adopted' Pavel. It was the adults for whom they wept every night who had made the war and committed its atrocities. And in each young face, in a certain uncharitable light, there lay the blueprint for another generation of the grey- and black-clad brutes.

And then there was the other voice, of course. The voice that nagged ceaselessly and had ever since she'd taken the decision to pause her search and come to Scotland. The voice insisting that she had abandoned Pavel in his hour of greatest need, that the next child, in the next ruined town, would surely – *surely* – have been him. The voice screaming that unless she abandoned these orphans instead and got back out to Germany this *instant*, she'd be a worse mother than any of those barren Nazi wives who had come shopping for the blondest, bluest-eyed children from the east to change them beyond recognition.

But how, of all the crazy missions she had taken on, was she to complete this one? She selected a fallen pawn and stood it up. The little featureless stalagmite didn't really look like a Pictish stone. It looked like every town in Germany.

ZECO first, the Zonal Executive Control Office at Lübbecke, she told herself. The next pawn followed. Bunde, for the Control Commission's Education Branch, from where Marjorie Jessop had put her onto 'Paul' before her recall to England. Then UNRRA in Spenge. Plus, of course, the British Army of the Rhine at Bad Oeynhausen, especially for liaison with the increasingly uncooperative Soviets. After which it would be

Frankfurt again for USFET, now European Command or EUCOM, and OMGUS, the US Office for Military Government, which also covered their sector of Berlin. And, repeatedly, like a poor move considered, rejected and in desperation considered again, the overwhelmed Central Tracing Bureau at the Buchenwald sub-camp in Arolson.

Too many squares, too few pieces now, and those too mismatched to combine as a dominant force. Stalemate. No way to draw the enemy out. No way to compel him to move.

Or was it that there might be a way, but she could not see it – as she had not seen, and as Mrs Macrae had, with Hans…?

She found herself holding the stumpy, seated figure of a queen. Although the strange medieval face looked mournful, the way she pressed one palm to her cheek suggested something else. *Zahnweh*, Hans had proclaimed on one of his better days. Toothache. But to Mila she looked like she was planning her next move.

Best of luck with that, you stupid bitch…

She brushed off her hands and headed up the driveway towards the main gate.

*   *   *

Doon the watter, was what they called it, this journey out from Glasgow. First by train to Wemyss Bay and then by paddle steamer to Rothesay on the Isle of Bute. Here, he was informed, it was necessary to negotiate transfer to a single masted 'puffer' to go around to Tighnabruaich on the Cowal peninsula.

And all, Bradley mused, to reach a place that was itself on the mainland. Short of going into obvious exile on one of the more distant islands, she had isolated herself about as well as she might.

Here on the east side of the peninsula, the sun had already gone down behind the rocky woodland and there was a chill in the air that matched the choppiness on the Kyles of Bute as he stepped from the little cargo vessel onto the wooden pier at Tighnabruaich. The skipper had told him to ask at the hotel for a local man, name of Darroch, who might be persuaded to drive him, provided he wasn't already *blootered* by this time of day, in which case he would never find his car, much less the road to Kilfinan.

And if he was?

"Whit's fur ye'll no go by ye!"

Whatever that meant, it seemed the final word on the subject.

Hefting his kitbag as he made for the centre of the village, Bradley knew he was drawing looks. His civilian wardrobe had stretched no further than the Victory suit he'd worn in Germany as a phony Treasury Department official and only slightly more authentic Special Agent of the Counter Intelligence Corps, so before leaving London he had visited Jenny Simmonds' store to acquire a tweed jacket and flannel trousers. The girl proved to be as capable as Jones had suggested and, unfazed by his lack of clothing coupons, had produced the key to a basement room where they kept the outfits ordered and paid for by gentlemen who had not returned from the war.

Even so, being of military age and build (though nowhere near as scrawny as the average British squaddie, nor as toothless), with a fedora clamped to his head rather than a newsie and a stiff knee he was doing a less than perfect job of disguising, he stood out among the fishermen and the day trippers homeward bound to the Clyde. The hell with it. He stopped to light an American cigarette. A couple of local lads began to circle eagerly.

"Know if Mr Darroch's in the hotel bar?"

"Aye he will be, sir."

"Know if he's sober?"

"As he gets, sir. You're American!"

"I believe I am." They were watching for his Luckies but he drew out a couple of coins instead. Scottish Shillings. The lads' eyes widened.

"Go fetch him for me would you. Tell him he and his car are needed, if he can find it."

"Aye, sir!"

He set down his bag, toying with the other loose change in his pocket. There was a telephone box on the quayside. Would it be better to call ahead? He decided against it. He was uncertain how she'd react to his arrival, and then to his news. Better to present the first as a done deal and the second in person, otherwise he might yet be hurrying back to the puffer with the shipyard workers in their 'bunnets'.

While he waited, he found himself watching for interlopers as closely as the locals were watching him. From past experience, he knew that when the likes of Jones and Sloane sent you someplace, all you could be certain of was that they weren't telling you everything. Either the situation was more dangerous than they were letting on and they were trusting you to improvise when trouble started, or they had actually painted a target on your back, invisibly, like the bomber boys with their beams. Perhaps it wasn't just that Jones aimed to set the pair of them investigating the circumstances leading up to Smith's death. Perhaps that itself was another phony pretext and he wanted Bradley at her side because she was already in danger. Perhaps he knew that her self-imposed isolation had in fact made her a sitting duck.

And, he reflected grimly, despite buying his ticket and climbing aboard, perhaps he hadn't chosen to travel 'down the water' at all. Perhaps that was just another of the secret world's confidence tricks – and instead he was being sold down the river again.

The doors to the public bar crashed open.

Mr Darroch, it appeared, was well and truly *blootered*.

*   *   *

In the shade of the drystone wall and the overhanging firs, the lane outside the front gate was darker than she had expected. Colder too, if you were wearing only a thin summer dress and even thinner cardigan. Mila's eyes took a moment to adjust. When they did, she spotted Rolli's ancient bicycle lying in the ditch. And the man lurking behind a patch of ferns that had burst through the wall.

Instinctively, she bent down and fumbled for the bicycle.

"Hello? Who's there?"

Her first thought was that the silhouette belonged to the housekeeper's husband, who was employed as a caretaker and gamekeeper on the estate. A man of few words, Macrae kept himself to himself and might well have been quietly mending walls out here. He might even have ignored her when she first came out. But he would not have refused to answer her point blank. Nor would he have settled into a pugnacious crouch like this, brandishing a heavy, hooked stick of the kind the Scots called a 'kebbie'.

She swung up the nickel-plated bicycle pump, one hand supporting the end that pointed towards the man and her other clenched to suggest a vertical grip that wasn't there. In spite of everything – the surprise, alarm and frustration – she felt an ironic smile tug at the corner of her mouth. The silenced pistols she had been trained to use as an agent behind enemy lines were designed to look like innocent bicycle pumps. If the intruder proved to be more sinister than a local robber or poacher, he might even make the association himself.

"On your knees," she hissed, choosing her footing carefully as she circled round behind him. Since it wasn't really holding a pistol grip or trigger, and as the man could no longer see her, she snatched the cudgel from him with her right hand. "Now – face down!"

She didn't make the mistake of putting a foot in his back, which would have unbalanced her and invited a blind sweep. But she would have to get down and restrain him before he turned his head and discovered that she was unarmed. How was she going to do that? What could she use?

What did it signify that he had still not uttered a word?

Her dress was cinched at the waist with a thin bow of matching cotton print. She doubted it would stand up to a desperate man wrenching his wrists apart but during her training, not far from here, a formidable lady had shown her how to make use of the most modest means and methods to fulfil their mission of setting Europe ablaze. She pulled the belt out from its loops and got it ready.

"Keep your face down!" A jab in the nape of the neck with the silenced 'muzzle' for good measure, then, as she sank onto his legs: "Left hand behind your back, fingers spread. Now the right."

She was no longer holding the bicycle pump but her captive didn't know that. Quickly she slipped the double-knotted strip of material around the base of one thumb, then the other, and pulled it tight. The rest of its length she wound around and between the thumbs, again knotting it so tight she felt the cotton start to give. Given time, he might work out how to combine his fingers to loosen the binds, if the sweat of the exertion did not make them unpickable, but he would not be pulling his hands apart with brute force. The pain in his thumbs, she knew, would be so extreme that his first attempt at that would also be his last.

Anyway, time was not a luxury that either of them would have. Not until she got him back to the house and away from its darkened perimeter, where any number of his accomplices might be about to come to his aid. She needed Macrae and his wife. And the telephone, if the line had not been cut.

Just for a moment, she permitted herself to consider the simpler option of dropping one of the tumbled capstones on his head. She even picked up his kebbie and tried its weight. But the war was over.

Instead, using one hand with the other on her 'gun', she felt under the collars of his rain coat and jacket. Sure enough, he was wearing a necktie – the second modest item she'd be needing. Pressing his head down, she twisted the tie around to the back and pulled it tighter. Then she hoisted him by his thumbs, impressed with how immediately the pain made him scramble to his feet. While he was still finding his balance, she forced the hooked end of the kebbie under the tie at his neck and gave it a turn. The man grunted and tautened. Now she had him yoked in a rigid driving harness.

She pushed him ahead of her with the stick.

"Any tricks and I'll put a bullet in your spine. Do you hear me?"

He had not yet uttered a word and it was important that he did. She needed to judge the seriousness of this predicament, which meant getting an idea of what he wanted and who he was working for. Her activities during the war and after it had made her many enemies: ex-Nazis, communists, rival black marketeers and gangsters. The latter two groups certainly included vengeful individuals with a presence in Britain. But what about the first two? Might they have the resources to send someone after her?

The reply when it came stopped her in her tracks.

"With a bicycle pump, Miss Slavík? I admit you got me at the start there but, yah, I worked out some time ago that it's not a Welrod."

The cultured English voice was brought up short by the pressure on his throat as she hesitated. But he had got enough words out, in a sufficiently snotty tone, for her to recognise the type. She had been briefed by them, trained by them – even if her sneakier tricks had been inspired by someone without the privileged masculine overconfidence.

And he had called her by her old *nom de guerre*, Slavík. Nightingale.

"Who are you?"

"Someone who was asked to keep an eye on you, by a mutual friend."

They were nearly at the house. Any minute now they might be seen by the Macraes, Miss Robinson or one of the children. That would leave an awful lot of explaining to do. Mila untwisted and unhooked the stick.

"And who would that be?"

He turned to face her and swallowed, wincing. To go with the unruly dark hair escaping from the pomade, he had a naturally swarthy complexion that was most likely masking the effects of being half-choked. His voice came in a relieved gasp.

"Your husband. The late Colonel Smith."

She looked at the heavy stick and brass pump in her hands, as though debating which one to hit him with.

"So… if he ever died of a heart attack, he asked you to wait three months and then lurk around outside his childhood home one evening?"

"Ha bloody ha. Fact is he suspected that a hostile party would come after you, wherever you might be. He charged me with making sure I was present when they did."

"And I'm supposed to believe that's why you were hiding by my gate?"

"Someone is coming."

"So you say."

Looking agitated for the first time, he swung his hands awkwardly into view. The late sun still skimmed the slopes here; enough to show that his thumbs were discoloured and swollen.

"No, I mean someone's coming, right now. Can't you hear it? For God's sake cut me free!"

Mila cocked her head. A vehicle was approaching, engine racing, stones popping on the unmade lane and shrapnelling off the *drystane*. At that speed it would be unlikely to make the bend and would come crashing through the gate virtually on top of them.

"There's a commando knife on my right hip and a .32 Webley self-loading under my left shoulder!"

Is there now, she thought.

Hazel eyes, not pleading, not even trustworthy, but solicitous. In the golden light, framed by dark lashes, their colour was astonishing, like something tantalizing trapped in Sambian amber. Mila sensed how they had disarmed other young women over the years. Dozens, even hundreds. Solicitous and duplicitous, that was the thing. Captivating, one might almost say, but not quite, or not for certain women. For certain women, such as those who had loosened their dresses for the first time in ages and could feel the fresh evening breeze off the heather and the sea, the effect was the opposite.

Liberation.

CHAPTER THREE

It was a bright, if blustery, summer's morning, not a chilly afternoon. There was no sign of sombre cloud or (for the moment) of penetrating rain, though it would take a fool to bet against the latter. The shrubbery – if that was the word for the battle between cultivated plants and prehistoric fronds that marked the garden's borders – was very far from leafless. Yet there was indeed no possibility of taking a walk today. Curiosity precluded it.

Ava Robinson, twenty-two, spinster, allowed her gaze to lift above the visitors at breakfast on the patio to the view across Loch Fyne and Knapdale. What was it in the book? Something about the Northern Ocean, boiling round the naked, melancholy isles?

But who was she kidding? She was not Jane Eyre.

For starters, one of the outcomes of which there was no possibility was that of marrying the master, for there was no master here, only the mysterious mistress.

And then there were the children. Motherless, certainly, and foreign. But there the resemblance with her favourite story ended, unless these were monstrous replications of the piteous creature in Jane's dream of a ruined world. Although she had been retained as their governess on the basis of her grasp of their language, in practice her position would have been better filled by a psychiatrist.

With a shiver, she turned and peered through the balustrade at the top of the terrace. There, matching the growth-encrusted face of the nearby Aquarius, gleamed another eroded visage. It was that of the terribly burned little girl whom the others called *die Made*, Maggot. And at the next gap, also trained on the adults, the sharp features of Maggot's only friend, the one they called *die Ratte*.

Watching, always watching. Those two in particular, but the others as well. Watching for danger. Watching for weakness. Watching for openings.

Mrs Macrae knew by now to keep the cupboards padlocked. The adults had all learned where to search about the house and grounds should anything go missing. Ava herself, having mislaid soon after her arrival here and in quick succession her handkerchief, purse, grandmother's ring and father's watch, had been forced to commence her relations with the children by means of a humiliating and counterproductive confrontation that had left everyone, herself included, in floods of tears. And even then, when the purse had been 'found', it had been empty.

This, she guessed, would be a red letter day for the habitual scavengers. The al fresco breakfast, though seemingly composed predominantly of steam and smoke and things unsaid, would present opportunities for cigarette butts and the leavings of toast and eggs. The two visitors would be targeted for the full repertoire of begging tricks at the first available chance, no doubt with Maggot thrust to the fore. And given the slightest provocation – an overly distracting conversation, an unbuttoned pocket – the more light-fingered would descend like the vermin they were named for.

In most cases they had lived an atavistic existence in the ruins of their towns, preying on the occupation forces, or being preyed upon. Rat and Maggot, according to the mistress, had survived three occupying armies in four different cities, for at least two years. It would take more than a few games of croquet and a book at bedtime to work that out of them.

And more than a Leith girl who'd learned of life from the Brontës to rise to it.

Seated in her customary position, alongside the grown-ups and yet apart from them, she raised her teacup and studied the newcomers over its brim. They had arrived at dusk yesterday and had created something of a stir. Mrs Macrae, who could now be heard clattering dishes through the kitchen windows, had expressed dissatisfaction at the lack of forewarning, which had left her unprepared. It was not how things were done. And although of course she had improvised without a hitch, rustling up food, drink and bedding for the two men, who appeared not to know one another, and a balm for the English one, who had somehow injured his thumbs, the effort, tellingly, had not been dismissed as *nae bother*. It was, by inference, *bother*, and of the kind that would not have occurred in the master's day.

Not that the mistress of the house looked much as though she gave a damn. From the scraps of idle conversation she had caught, Ava gathered that last night's commotion (including, as it had done, the Vandalous arrival, forced sobering up and swift dismissal of a local taxi driver) was little more than a source of mild amusement for her. Even the veiled warnings she had detected from the two men, the repeated suggestions that everyone should keep their eyes peeled and their wits about them, appeared as insignificant to her as a persistent wasp and were as breezily brushed away. Composed and elegant, like a big cat with her short fair hair and lithe limbs, and with that white scar on her suntanned cheek so suggestive of past battles won, she just sat there pouring the tea – *shall I be mother?* – and switching her attention between the pair of them, as though she were their equal, if not their superior.

In the case of the American, Ava suspected that the latter might very well be the case. She had not been told who he was to the mistress and was in no position to ask, but it was apparent that the man was a little cowed by her, or more than a little in awe. Certainly he hung on her every word like some apprentice or amanuensis, or even (and here she was not certain) an admirer. Although she had never met one before, she had been given to understand that Americans did not behave like that. Yet this one did.

The other one (it was not that Mr Bradley was unattractive, in his rugged, faltering way, but she really could not help it) – the handsome one – had been introduced to her as Mr Pendleton. ("Pat, please," he had said, and she had wanted to!) He looked somewhat like a tramp and even more like a matinee idol, with that dark stubble and greasy hair and that stare – those deep, deep eyes. Despite his posh ways, there was more of Heathcliff's half-civilised ferocity in there than Mr Rochester's harshness, she thought, before telling herself never to think like that again.

She found she had adopted the tone that Mrs Macrae took sometimes with the children, or a pot-boiler's version of it, to berate herself in her own head.

Such a mucky mind, young lassie! And with poor sweet Alec only missing these three year and not yet declared *deid*.

But the mistress – *call me Mila* – was addressing her directly.

"Miss Robinson, the children, if you'd be so kind..." The uncomfortable formal tone, made ambiguous by that slight, lilting Eastern European accent, was tempered suddenly by a smile of kinship and collusion. "I have to speak to these gentlemen on matters of business."

"Of course, Miss…"

'Pat' rose promptly, Mr Bradley less confidently. Although the stiff knee that he'd been massaging might explain the momentary delay, his self-admonishing grimace told her no, he was just unused to polite society, and her heart warmed to him.

But what warmth could there be, with her fiancé three years out from Tiree, still strapped upright in his broken Sunderland, on the bottom of the cold and ghastly ocean?

Steeling herself as she mounted the steps to the top terrace where the orphans were enacting their own endless re-examination of life and death, she let the mask and mantle of the plain, Quakerish governess settle over her again.

*   *   *

"Who." Mila said when Miss Robinson had left them. "Who is coming?"

Pat Pendleton glanced back at the kitchen window, then at

Sam Bradley.

Mila met his harrumph with a disapproving tut. It was one of the first mannerisms she had learned in her dealings with the British and remained one of the most useful.

"If you can say it to me, you can say it in front of Sam. Otherwise… goodbye Mr Pendleton, let's not waste any more of anyone's time."

"Pat, please," he said tetchily. "Fact is I can't say it in front of you either. But what I can say, by way of a security check if you like, is that when my employers took over yours they also acquired your poem. You see, Bradley…"

"I know about the poem codes," Sam said. "And I know hers."

Pendleton pursed full lips.

"She's not joking about you two being thick as thieves! Fine. Your poem was *When You Are Old*. 'One man loved the pilgrim soul in you…' and so on. Yah? And now that you know I'm not making it all up, let me quote you some more W. B. Yeats: '*The broken wall, the burning roof and tower*'…"

Richard had lent her his book; committing poems to memory had been as much about learning the rhythms and resonances of English as preparing for her mission.

"'*And Agamemnon dead*'."

"Exactly, Miss Slavík. Zeus rapes Leda in the form of a swan and conceives not only Helen but the fall of Troy. A turning point in history."

"Are you going to *get* to the point, Mr Pendleton?"

"Pat, please. And I already have. History is about to be changed. Our Zeus may still be disguising himself as a cuddly animal, but it won't be for much longer. To continue my frankly tedious Yeats analogy, we need to put on his knowledge with his power – and feel 'the strange heart beating where it lies'."

"You're talking about Stalin," Sam said.

"Give the boy a coconut! I'm trying to explain that our *priorities*, as your people would say, have shifted to understanding his knowledge, his power and his heart. As a matter of urgency, in fact. So please believe me when I say that someone is coming, because we have that on very good authority."

Mila frowned.

"You said this came from Richard. That means it's hardly current intel, or a matter of urgency. Unless you're going to tell me he's still alive."

She looked pointedly at Sam. During all the fuss last night, after Darroch's 'Flying Fifteen' had demolished her gatepost, they had managed only the briefest exchange, amounting to *why are you here?* and *Jones told me something important about your husband's death.* But now, with a long-faced look, he shook his head fractionally.

Was she entirely sorry that he did?

"Richard's concerns weren't specific," Pendleton explained without explaining, as though addressing a child. "He just worried about you."

"Enough to tell a busy spy engaged on urgent work to watch over his strange foreign wife?"

"Enough to ask a friend in the Foreign Office to keep an eye on a former British agent, should certain less-than-friendly players renew their interest in her. Which they have. And I think the word is 'estranged'."

"Why would they renew their interest?"

"You embarrassed them, once over that Czech affair, once more when you pinched the Hanoverian crown from under their noses at Schloss Blankenburg. They lost people that night."

"Since you're so well informed in the 'Foreign Office', you're bound to know that their losses were caused by a band of Jewish avengers in the British Army, not me."

"Loss of face is more important to them. It can be fatal in Moscow these days and facts don't come into it. Since SMERSh was disbanded, Abakumov and Beria have been scampering around each other like they've joined the bloody Bolshoi. Either might want to be seen to be tough on past troublemakers."

"Meaning it could be MGB or MVD." Sam was looking sick all of a sudden.

"Mmm. State Security or Internal Affairs. Or your old foreign intelligence friends GRU for that matter." Pendleton shrugged. "Might even be some new, unholy alliance, formed to protect themselves from Stalin or, just as likely, thrown together by Stalin to consume each other. All we got was a reliable tip-off that something was imminent, probably involving hired muscle."

"Why just her?" Sam demanded. "I was there too, in Czechoslovakia and at Blankenburg."

"And now you're here. Isn't that a rum coincidence?"

Mila knew better than to press Pendleton on that. One way or another, he was toying with them. What she really wanted was to be alone with Sam, to find out what he had heard and what he was thinking. But there were other, more pressing matters.

"If what you say is true and they know about this place, the children are in danger. I can't allow that."

She looked at Sam.

"There's somewhere else we could go," he said. "Something else we could do."

"Would that work?" she asked Pendleton. "Would the children be safe if I weren't here?"

For several seconds he returned her look without speaking. Reining in his short temper for once. Considering.

"I'd say so. Not that they don't go after children, whole bloody families… but that tends to be reserved for punishing their own. Making an example, as they see it."

"So these children, and the Macraes, and Miss Robinson…"

"…will be safe. For the time being. After that, it depends."

"On what?" Sam asked. It was Mila who answered him.

"On how far we run and how well we disappear. Too well and they'll come back here to question everyone."

"So how do we disappear just-far-enough?"

"We keep moving. We keep one step ahead of them." She fixed Pendleton with a challenging glare. "And we have someone to help us make sure it stays like that."

Again the delay for processing.

"I suppose that falls within the bounds of what I promised

Richard, as long as it doesn't enter the neighbouring territory."

"The things you can't talk about." When he dropped the sneer and gave her that smile, the one that lit in his eyes like Becherovka bitters, she felt her resolve weaken, but she wasn't about to let it show on her face. "Now, I'm going for a walk with Sam and you're staying here with your commando knife and your .32 Webley self-loading. If you're nice to her, you may find Mrs Macrae will make you another pot of tea."

She got to her feet, waiting for Sam to join her.

Pat Pendleton held up a thumb, partly to show her that the swelling had subsided. He broadened the grin and ran his hand over his hair to tame a wayward lock.

Oh, Mrs Macrae would make him another pot all right!

*   *   *

By the time he had told her all that had transpired at St Paul's and afterwards, Bradley found they had walked down the hill through the woods to a snaky little estuary and a secluded bay. Not far out, a red-rusted wreck or blockship was lined with cormorants.

Mila picked up a flat pebble and sent it skimming over the waves.

"Poor Richard."

Her eyes were bright and moist. But there was a fresh, salty breeze off the loch.

"Yeah, I'm sorry."

She turned to him with the briefest of smiles.

"I had already... *reconciled?*"

Bradley shrugged. "I guess."

"I had already reconciled myself with his dying. Can that be right? It is a strange language you speak, Sergeant Bradley."

That was something she had said to him, the first time they had spoken in earnest, on a pleasant stroll on another summer's day, in the midst of danger. It had been the beginning of their opening up to one another. And she had remembered.

Reconciliation.

He bent and picked his own pebble, pitching it smoothly. He was aware of the girl watching him.

"How is your shoulder?"

"It hasn't slipped out again, since Blankenburg."

"That's good."

"Hurts some though."

"Yes," she said, vaguely, as if agreeing with something else.

"Can you think why Colonel Smith might have been investigating this character, de Klerk?"

She put a hand to her head, pressing down a few strands of fine, fair hair. Bradley knew why she'd had to cut it short, after it had burned in the back-blast of an anti-tank weapon that her partisan group was using to ambush a Nazi patrol. Why she kept it short was a mystery. Someone had said it was to make it easier to wear wigs and other disguises, but those days were past, weren't they? Someone else, who knew her as well as anyone might, had suggested that it was to draw a line between the young woman she had been before the war and the woman she became – and to make it clear to everyone, herself included, that she had not yet completed her wartime mission. All Bradley knew for sure was that he liked it well.

"I barely knew him," she said. "Zajíček knew him."

"Jones."

"So if he couldn't tell you…"

"Yeah, if."

"And now there's this Mr Pendleton…"

"Pat, please."

She laughed, properly this time.

"Yes, Pat. Who was he to Richard?"

"I assume he's MI6."

"That's the assumption. Because of its links with Czech Intelligence – through Zajíček – Richard's department was kept at arm's length from both SOE and MI6, but in practice our missions were organised through one or the other, sometimes both."

"So he might have worked with you."

"Not me, but I was sent into the field in early '43. I don't know what happened after that. Now he appears to be claiming that MI6 has gained control of all remaining SOE assets. From what I've heard on the grapevine, that rings true. Certainly he must have had access to Richard's files to discover the poem he assigned me. Unless…"

Their eyes met. She rolled hers.

Bradley bit back on a curse.

"Jones again."

"Potentially."

"He damn well told us to our faces that he wasn't in the service of this country anymore!"

"Which probably means he is."

"So do we do what he seems to want us to do – go out to Holland and track down de Klerk?"

"It would keep us out of the way. And, I don't know…"

"You want to anyway."

Her face, not grieving but customarily severe, seemed to come alive.

"Not to avenge him – we have both seen where that leads. But I think I owe him a debt."

Remembering the day in Paris at the war's end, when Smith and Jones had dragged him from his drunken decline and coerced him into chasing her down, Bradley nodded.

"OK."

She searched his eyes and he felt his cheeks begin to prickle.

"You're sure, Sam? This is nothing to do with you, really."

"Are you crazy? It's everything – and like Pendleton said, I'm mixed up in it, one way or another."

They had sat side by side on the shingle rise. Mila nudged him with her shoulder.

"Thank you."

The sun still danced on the water but now it looked like bad weather was coming down fast from the mountains up the loch. After what seemed several hours and was probably a couple of minutes, she lifted the hand that he had been hoping would creep the last inch towards his own.

"They trained people on the landing craft here, for D-Day."

Bradley looked at the cormorants drying their wings in the freshening breeze. Remembering.

"A turning point in history."

"'And Agamemnon dead'."

He blushed again. He knew nothing about poetry. Or Greek mythology. Zeus had turned himself into a swan to rape Leda? Why the hell had he done that?

"I guess some girls you mess with at your peril."

Her reply meant even less to him. Except, in its menace, its resignation and impenetrability, it meant so much.

"Some girls get caught up in some pretty dark webs." And with that she glanced at the murky purple clouds descending over the hillside. "We should head back."

It was only drizzle, but the dense, humid woods were soon saturated. Bradley took her hand to help her over slippery rocks and sudden streams. By the time they were climbing out of the undergrowth towards the lower wall of the property, visibility had shrunk to less than fifty yards and it was more like twilight than mid-morning.

That was how they saw rather than heard the shots up by the house.

*   *   *

Ava stood behind her bedroom door on the top floor. Though the *Gandiegow* had plunged the whole house into near darkness and the upstairs rooms most of all, she could see her pale hand on the latch. It was trembling.

She had been so intent on listening for the intruders, for so long, that she realised she must make a conscious effort to breathe, or else she would collapse in a faint. Yet even after one desperate gulp, her breast froze again, her heart thundering.

Glaikit lassie, she berated herself in that pastiche of Mrs Macrae's voice. Waiting for the demonic goblin-laughter, is it? When ye ken full well there's men in the hoose.

She was right, the mockery in her head. This was no madwoman in the attic – *she* was in the attic! Nor could the terrifying sounds be attributed to some modern-day Grace Poole. Unlike in *Jane Eyre* there were no secret staff, no other staff at all. The local girl had turned up for work this morning to be promptly sent away again. The only other people at home were the children and Mrs Macrae who, while Ava had dithered, had taken charge of them and locked them in the nursery. Mr Macrae himself had gone for timber earlier to fix the gate.

And Mr Pendleton? He must be dead!

It had all started just as the wind had got up and the cloud had come down. She and the housekeeper had been hurrying the children back inside. The mistress and her American visitor were still out walking. With the mist already at eye-level, no one had spotted the furniture van above the wall until it rocked precariously into the unbarred driveway. G. STEWART & SONS. REMOVERS & STORERS. SPRINGBURN, GLASGOW. It must have come the long way through the mountains.

And here Ava's memory had to be playing tricks on her, because what she recalled – what she *pictured* and always would – was Mr Pendleton sweeping her off the patio after Mrs Macrae, with one smooth, batsman-like movement that somehow brought him round again with a *pistol* in his hand.

"Get upstairs! Lock the doors!"

And four bangs. The door behind her. Three more.

She had arrived, breathless, on the second floor in time to see Mrs Macrae shutting and locking the nursery door on her – with a glare through the gap and a hiss of *up there!* And up she had gone, to her little turret room with its flimsy latch and the sounds of breaking diamond glazing.

Were they in the house now? Or was that a fight in the kitchen areaway, with a body crashing against the windows? If so, whose body?

All of a sudden she wasn't afraid anymore. Or if the fear was still there – which it must be – it was an old fear from a thousand nightmares, sublimated by a ferocious waking anger. These were familiar, half-remembered terrors. Of furniture vans. And uninvited thugs. Of having to hide. And having to flee. They were from a time when she had been not much older than these poor defenceless children – a shy, bookish Leipzig girl with English pretensions, whose name had been Eva Rabinowitz. But this time she could do something about them.

She had not saved her grandparents, her aunts and uncles, nor all her cousins. She had not saved Alec from the pitiless wave. But she could save Mr Pendleton, just as Jane had saved Mr Rochester from the burning bed.

She could save Pat.

Before she knew it she had gone down the back stairs again. The stable door at the end of the kitchen passageway was ajar and the sulphurous light on the flagstones drew her towards it.

And there (her mind almost saw it before her eyes registered it), Mr Pendleton lay slumped against the wall.

In the midst of blaze and vapour, she thought.

He raised his head and their eyes met. But then his wince of agony turned to a deeper frown and he shook his head. His voice, too, was strained.

"Get back…"

She looked. There were two other bodies in the yard and neither was motionless. In fact one, bare-headed now but clad in a removal man's brown coat, was getting to his feet. Like Pat, he had dropped both hat and gun and was fumbling for the latter.

And then, in a sudden rush – for all the world like that big cat – a lithe female figure sprang from the terrace above and landed lightly, bare-footed, behind the man. Before he could react – before, really, Ava even realised that it was the mistress, drenched, with a carved chess piece protruding from her fist – the bare arm had swung and made contact.

As her mind caught up with what she had been watching, Ava thought for a moment that the animal shriek must have come from the man, who was now toppling unconscious to the flags. Then, as the mistress came momentarily to rest and she saw the

40

expression on her face, she understood.

And even as this wild creature's eyes slid to the second injured intruder, assessing his fitness to fight on, there was another incomprehensible disturbance in the rain and Mr Bradley was there, a rusty croquet hoop clutched in his hand like a twin-bladed misericorde, poised to deliver the 'mercy stroke'.

Ava felt abruptly ashamed that she alone was standing bolt upright when everyone else, glistening in the uncanny light like bronzes of ancient wrestlers, was so athletically crouched or fallen. She turned to Mr Pendleton and knelt beside him. When she saw the colour of his face she let out a cry of her own.

"Pat!"

The mistress was at her side and trying to push her out of the way. Ava fought back. She lifted his chin, judging how pale he was, then helped him sit up and shrug off his jacket to examine the wound in his arm. The rain had diluted the blood on his shirt.

"Bugger only winged me," he grunted. "Drop of Scotch and I'll be fine."

The mistress nudged Ava.

"Miss Robinson…"

"Fetch it yourself!" she hissed.

She didn't see or hear the reaction. For the moment, helping him to tear off his ruined shirt and bind its other sleeve around the gouge in his upper arm, her attention was only on Pat. And it was to her, with a wry smile, that he reported:

"These two came crashing in like old Darroch last night. I got both of them, but they had on thick coats and this .32's a bloody pea-shooter. Then one of them got me."

Mr Bradley must have been listening. She heard him call out unintelligible words.

"They had Tokarevs with double that power. He's lucky."

"That's me," Pat said.

"He also needs to get to hospital," the mistress said behind her. "Whisky or not, that isn't going to fix itself."

"And these two need a doctor," said Mr Bradley. "Well… this one probably needs a priest."

Ava exploded.

"Them! Don't worry about them, rotten swine!"

She tensed at the touch of the mistress's hand on her shoulder, but instead of pulling her away, it gave a comforting squeeze.

"It must have been terrifying. I'm so sorry we weren't here. Is everybody all right?"

She sniffed and nodded.

"But I don't understand…"

And then the hand did pull at her, but only to enlist her help in getting the half-naked Pat to his feet and indoors.

"I'll try to explain, after we've patched up Mr Pendleton properly. Then we can decide what to do with the others."

"Surely there's only one thing to do and that's to call the police!"

Leaning against her, letting her take some of his weight – and his dampness, and his astonishing warmth – Mr Pendleton gave an approving grunt.

"Miss Robinson clearly has good sense to go with her looks. And when you've patched me up, you can let me drive them down to the village in their van. I'll make sure they're safely under lock and key."

Flushed, flustered, Ava barely caught his next words and found it hard to make sense of them. The poor dear must have been growing delirious.

"…under the lock anyway."

CHAPTER FOUR

It was no wonder, thought the Broker, that the man he had been sent here to meet had chosen the dingiest corner of the half-ruined coffee house, tucked away behind a shrapnel-scarred pillar and a partition of shattered multicoloured glass. Even with his hat tilted down, coat collar up and a thick scarf wrapped high around his neck, the reason for his shyness was all too apparent. He had no face.

What was not so certain, especially if one balked at looking closely, was whether the shiny, somewhat flesh-toned mask, with its rudimentary bump for a nose and crude eye-holes, was a temporary shield for the horrors beneath or the latest in surgical transplants.

He was a nonperson and was known only as the Omitted.

The lamplight glinted on bloodshot eyes moving inside the holes. These followed the hands as they lifted the *Häferlkaffee* to the gash of mouth that showed above the scarf, below the mask.

The hands! They were certainly artificial and seemed barely articulated. The effect was that of a mannequin being forced to ape a human pose for which it was ill designed.

The Broker found himself holding his breath. When the chipped china met what passed for lips, he could not tell if the sigh of relief was his own or the Omitted's.

And then the tension of the mug being set down on the marble tabletop...

But the eyes were moving again, even if the face – *the face!* – was not. The gash turned up at one side in what might even have been a smile. And the voice, speaking educated Russian, was firm and melodious. Whatever had done this to him, the Broker knew instinctively that it had not been a fire; there was nothing wrong with his lungs.

"You see the mirror, there? See the decoration?"

The Broker looked. One wall of the coffee house was dominated by a huge mirror which made the place appear twice its size – or would have done, without the prominent crack from floor to ceiling and the wild intrusions of *art nouveau* engravings. Swirls of vines and so forth, intertwining with the steam and cigarette smoke.

"To hide the bullet holes. One of our fellows had too many 'coffees' and got careless with his *peh-peh-sha*." A puppet-hand raised and swung in a way that left you searching for the strings. "But look at the reflection, between those pillars. Out there, beyond the park, you can just see the 'golden cabbage'? That's all that remains of the Secession Building, where Klimt's Beethoven Frieze was once installed. Before the war, there used to be a motto above its doors: 'To the Age its Art.' Well… *that* is the art of our age."

A puppet, perhaps; that was what he looked like. But he spoke like a puppet master, one tired of his creations. The Broker swallowed and took the plunge.

"I'm afraid you won't like my news very much either. That snatch operation in Scotland – there were complications."

"Complications?"

"The contractors' transport was found burned-out below the Rest and Be Thankful Pass. It is unclear whether they were in it, or even if they reached their target."

"Rest and Be Thankful?"

"It is the old military road linking Loch Long and Loch Fyne, cut by the English to subjugate the rebels."

"Then that was their mistake – as it is ours."

"I beg your pardon?"

"To 'rest and be thankful'. One must always go forward or go back." Again the sweeping gesture, but this time the Broker had to catch the little vase on their table as with a chink the hand made oblique contact. "It is like this place – people were starving, freezing, so we had a food riot. Good. But now the weather is fine. The edelweiss is flowering. We must have another."

And who exactly, the Broker wondered, were 'we'? Despite his penchant for quoting Lenin, as an unrehabilitated nonperson the Omitted could hardly claim to represent the Party, or any of its organs. Yet he was clearly playing an active part in advancing the interests of one or more of the above. In the Soviet Union, an unofficial blind eye could be of more benefit than official blessing; was that it? Did he have *carte blanche* to go with that blank face? Or did his past connections – for surely only bonds or dirt of the most indelible kind could have enabled him to retain or regain his freedom – stretch just far enough to give the impression it was so?

More to the point, what did communist-led protests against the western occupying powers in Austria have to do with the attempted seizure of a Czech dissident in Scotland? How many irons could those puppet's hands hold in the fire?

"It is possible that the contractors I was instructed to employ did not take their target seriously enough," the Broker probed. "I questioned their choice at the time. If I had been free to use different resources…"

"'While the state exists there can be no freedom.' The selection of those particular criminals was part of a larger stratagem and far more important than the success of their mission." What control he had left of what remained of his lips forced them into that twist of a smile; but a smile with its upper half absent was as lifeless as the rest of the face and there was no humour in what he ventured next. "Have you ever had to catch rats, to eat?"

"I can't say I have."

"Well, you can imagine, or try to. If you have a tiny piece of barley bread – hardly enough to keep you alive another night – you must invest it, yes? The capitalists have that correct. So you throw it on the floor of the hut and wait for the rat. But the rat is fast and you have been digging all day. Now you have nothing,

45

not even your morsel of bread. So next time you pin down the bread and, sure enough, you catch your rat. One rat! To feed all your bunkmates, and you last in line, because you are *Parasha.*"

Digging all day, the Broker was thinking. At Kolyma probably, in the Arctic Circle. The lowest of the low, sleeping by the slop-bucket, in the worst place on Earth. That would be what had taken his face and hands, as they turned white, then black. In the Gulag.

"Are you listening? The day may come when you need to know this. One rat is not enough. But to get more, you must set things in motion. You fasten the bread to a line and work together, leading it around the hut. The rats, you see, are just like these two-legged pricks here. What draws them out is competition. They cannot bear to let one of their own triumph in their place. The capitalists were right about that too. What is it that they say in the west? It's a dog eat dog world?"

"As it happens, I believe that's a perversion of a more natural rule. The original Latin phrase is *canis caninam non est.* A dog does not eat the flesh of a dog."

Deep in the holes, the drowned eyes blinked as though in pain. Or remembered pain. Or something else, beyond remembered pain. Shame.

"That is Nature's rule. But what do you suppose we were eating when we ate our rats? How do you think our rats grew so fat? It wasn't the barley bread – or other rats."

The Broker said nothing. What more was there to say? And correcting a man like this, quoting *Latin* to him…? He would have to be much more careful. Nor least because he still could not see the point of the analogy. If the MERCURY woman was the morsel of barley bread, was the Omitted not one of the pursuing rats?

"Dogs may or may not eat dogs," the latter said. "And rats may have fleas that have lesser fleas. But what concerns us here is that criminals conspire with other criminals. Believe me, there is nothing so efficient as a criminal grapevine. We have set things in motion. We have started the chase. Our requirement now is to be kept informed about all those who join it. And when I say informed, I mean of everything they do – you'll have to stick to their arses like bathhouse birch-leaves!"

This poetic instruction had an air of finality. The Broker nodded. Reaching inside his coat pocket for his wallet, he asked in the manner of parting small talk:

"With what objective, by the way?"

Both mask and puppet hand moved swiftly, immediately catching the waiter's attention. How could they not?

"Keep your little *pizda* buttoned up, we are not finished." The Omitted spoke quietly to the waiter, who removed their coffee cups, the vase and sugar bowl, to return a moment later with a chess board and a box of old, elaborate pieces. "Aren't you up for a game? If it was good enough for Stalin and another nonperson, it is good enough for you and this one, although you will have to make his moves for him. Come on, set it up! White and red – how appropriate!"

"Who will play white? Shall we toss a coin, or…?"

The Omitted turned over his hand to look at the unarticulated palm, perhaps recalling when he had been able to hide a pawn in his fist – or much else besides, equally unarticulated.

"You take the advantage. I want to illustrate something while we play."

"And what is that?"

"Something called a colour complex. Have you heard of that? It is a theory in chess that I have spent a lot of time considering. A lot of time. Yes, you may make the conventional response for me. And there, and there – ah, how appropriate, the Vienna Variation!"

What could be more natural, indeed, than two shady gentlemen ensconced in the back of a coffee house in the *Innere Stadt*, playing chess? Lasker had done so, before a certain Austrian corporal had sent him packing. Freud had done so. And as the robotic-looking creature across from him had just alluded to, Stalin and Trotsky had done so. The only thing that had changed was that this part of town was now the Inter-allied

Zone. Even when frowning over one's next move, it was important to keep an eye out for the 'four in a jeep', the international patrol comprising one MP from each of the occupying powers, who would barge in without warning to check that nothing more sordid than pride was staked on the game.

Not that pride wasn't sordid enough around here, of course.

Peering at the board, the Broker was conscious of the pale mask looming above him. Was he even looking down, or simply impelling his opponent to play against himself? Or, in the manner of that infamous 18th Century illusion, the 'Mechanical Turk', was the apparent automaton in fact being operated by another, hidden master?

"The idea behind the colour complex is that certain pieces can only attack and defend certain squares, of either light or dark, but not both. Failing to appreciate this can leave an apparently strong position surrounded by weak squares, as I hope to demonstrate."

When he looked up, the Broker saw that severed smile again. Despite everything, there was a residue of knowing confidence to it, suggesting that whoever this man had been in his past life, he had been blessed with good looks. The Broker's eye was drawn to the brass-tipped gentleman's cane propped against the kaleidoscopic partition and he noted for the first time how one of the artificial hands was shaped to fit its head.

Now the same hand nudged a pawn in an unexpected area of the board.

"You asked what our objective was. Revenge, of course. That's our endgame here."

*   *   *

"And it was *'er*, definite? The MERCURY bird, with 'er tame Septic?"

A passer-by, peering inquisitively, might just have observed three dim silhouettes through the overgrown screen surrounded the veranda: one man standing, almost to attention; another, larger, figure, seated regally; a third almost invisible, if observed at all. It was the enthroned figure that had asked the question, in deep, gravelly tones, and the words would have meant nothing to the passer-by, had he been brave or foolhardy enough to eavesdrop. But that was irrelevant. Save itinerant workers and the women with the bundles on their heads, who all knew better than to stray to this side of the road, nobody passed by here.

True, this was hardly the *bundu*, as the locals called it, but neither was the house located anywhere exactly civilised. The nearest link to civilisation was Banket Junction, ten miles away, and that was never going to be mistaken for Liverpool Street. In fact the large, rather shabby colonial house sat on a dirt farm road surrounded by nothing but flame trees and sweetgums. Its lonely situation was beneficial only for being within equal striking distance of Salisbury and the Mutorashanga mines on the Great Dyke.

The upright figure placed its hat on a table, the better to gesticulate with two open hands.

"That's what I'm 'earing, guv. You know them nutters from the Glasgow mob, the San-Toys? Someone put 'em up to it – give 'em Bolshie shooters an' all. They was seen, heading out to this estate what she in'erited. And then they wasn't seen no more."

Perched in the erratically padded peacock chair, enrobed in some kind of embroidered sheepskin he'd taken off the divan, Jimmy Lonsdale gave a pensive nod, before shuddering, violently. Of course, he did everything violently, that was the whole point of being Jimmy Lonsdale, but now his head was pounding violently too and he felt suddenly sick to his stomach. He wrestled with the conflicting urges to double forward onto the rattan matting or to shrink back into the shadows and dissolve away to nothing, like the ghost in the corner.

Although he didn't like to acknowledge it, much less broadcast the affliction, he was coming down with another bout of it. Even the word sounded like it had gone bad, like the name of a putrid great aunt you had to suck up to on her death bed or an airy-fairy princedom full of prancing nobs who ought to have got the chop a hundred years ago.

Malaria.

The ghost caught his eye, looked confused, looked away.

"'*Oo* put them up to it?"

Parsons drew out his hankie to mop his face and neck, dropping his soggy ticket from England in the process. Although it wasn't summer down here, and the dry season to boot, thanks to the three-bar fire the servants had brought out, it was still a sweatbox on the shuttered and netted veranda. If you weren't shivering like a Billingsgate porter.

"Well… A Bolshie, guv. That's what I'm 'earing. An' now she and 'er Yank 'ave 'ad it away on their toes."

"Yeah? Where?"

"The Continent…" For a moment, Parsons' disorientation matched the ghost's. The thought processes were written on his face: could you even call it that, when you were on a *whole nuther continent* yourself now?

"Meaning Europe."

"Yeah, guv. They come down from Scotland, met some other bird in South London – we was going to find out who she was but we lost her – then departed Victoria on the Night Ferry, what was running a sort of test prior to starting up the regular service again. They was in the first class sleeping cars all the way, so we couldn't get close to them, but we managed to follow them from Paris to Brussels, where they was met at the station by some geezer with a motor, chauffeur-driven…"

The last words were muttered emphatically, almost accusingly, as if to say *so what were we supposed to do?*

"An' that's where you lost them too."

"Yeah, but they 'ad someone sorting some pretty nifty travel arrangements, 'cause you can't just up and take a Continental tour like the old days."

Gravely, Lonsdale shook his head, though not in agreement. Parsons meant before the war, of course, but there'd been other good old days, right in the thick of it, when he and his brother had ridden roughshod over any restrictions and under the cover of the occupying army had treated liberated Europe as their private fiefdom, ripe for profit and plunder. Those days were gone now.

"So remind me, Vic, why exac'ly I'm shelling out to have your boys – *my* boys – tail them?"

"Well… I thought…"

"What did you think, Vic?"

"You'd want us to go after her. For Gerry, and everyfink."

Bringing out his own 'widow', an altogether fancier bit of cloth, Lonsdale braced himself and began to cough. Great heaving coughs that hit like a bodyshot combination and left a bitter taste in your throat. If it went on like this, he'd probably see blood again. At last, he fell back into the cane fan of the chair, exhausted.

To meet another shifty glance from the grey-faced spectre in the corner.

Gasping, desperate for air, and warmth, he thought: *A shadow of your former self.*

His sometime associate, Jack Penny, had put a curse on him alright. Not the Ikey mumbo-jumbo he'd dished out from the condemned cell at Wandsworth before he'd swung for killing Gerry: despite his gypsy ancestry, Jimmy had no time for superstition. But in foiling and exposing his and his brother's smuggling operations, that little Whitechapel back-stabber had put him to flight for real. He'd had to leave London and his mob behind and ship out sharpish to the colonies, with their poncy airs and graces and their stifling rooms, their endless nights with nobody passing and nothing going on except their teeming, always-fucking-chirping insects. A son of Seven Dials to the soot under his nails, the change of air and light and hours had nearly done for him.

Still, there were compensations…

Like a tart on the squint for tomfoolery, he opened the cotton clamshell he was clutching. No pearls or sparklers here. Something nasty, but no blood neither, which was a result. Being more or less a fully paid-up colonial ponce himself now, he registered that he'd folded his crisply laundered widow neatly before *ahem*-ing into it. He clocked the embroidered monogram on one corner. JJL. James Joshua Lonsdale. Chromium Magnate. Or magnet, as Gerry would have said, the berk.

"An' I thought…"

"Going for a accumulator, are yer? Come on then, what yer think this time?"

"Well, we know your next visitors 'ave an interest too."

"The Septics."

"That's right guv. In *'er* Septic. They might want to go after 'em an' all."

Give me strength, Lonsdale thought. With a bubbling groan like a spent carthorse stretched out quivering on the cobbles, he forced himself to his feet, which was enough to make him a danger to the mosquito coils smouldering in their hanging baskets. Now he was towering over both of them, especially the ghost of 'Dickie' Daylesford, slumped in its customary corner, a stain on the front of its trousers, watching dreamily. The previous owners had been smaller people, in every sense.

"First and foremos', Vic, since it looks like we're going into business with our American cousins – even if most of them do seem to come from Italy – I reckon it might be a halfway clever notion to stop referring to them all as Septic Tanks, yeah?"

"Right, guv."

"Second… *Nah.*"

"Nah, guv?"

"Nah. We ain't going after her and her… American. Nor encouraging *our* Americans to do nothing like that neither. It weren't her fault she got mixed up with us. That was Jack's doing, and Gerry's, same as everything else. She and that Bradley were just bloody good at getting out of it. Bloody good."

He hadn't been there to see it for himself, but he'd pictured it, over and over. The filthy great cargo ship coming out of the mist to lay waste to their base at the sea fort. The weapons they'd been smuggling on behalf of several different parties all going to the bottom of the Thames Estuary. The German crown they'd almost-promised to His Majesty's Government, in a beautifully planned double cross, disappearing like a magic trick – to reappear months later in the Mediterranean, to the embarrassment of His Majesty's Government and everyone else involved.

Oh, he'd pictured it. It was enough to make your blood boil.

If it wasn't proper chilled already.

Causing Daylesford to pull up his legs – it was that or walk right through them – he ducked and dived along the veranda and spotted the houseboy hovering. This time of the afternoon, Dickie and most of his fellow expats would have had them fetching gins and flapping flipping fans, but that wasn't Jimmy's style neither.

He shook his head.

People thought him ruthless, and he was. He'd learned that early, when little more than a Covent Garden cutpurse. Jimmy the Shiv, he'd got called back then, and that sort of carnage really did leave the bright red on your Widow Twankey. Jack had reckoned he enjoyed it too and perhaps he did, but not the way Jack meant. The dodgy stuff – striping people permanent, hurting women, sucking the life out of so-called innocents like Dickie here – was never personal, just business. You put your reputation out there so you didn't have to go yourself. In time, when you'd made your mark with embroidered tales not snot-rags, you found you didn't even have to work on the rep.

"Nah. Not worth the aggro. Not worth the cost. And what I'm 'oping, Vic, is our Americans see it the same."

"But, from what I'm 'earing, guv, this Bradley geezer crossed them before, couple of years ago…"

Jimmy sneered.

"You told me. Bradley had the job of minding an official, in Sicily. Some silly-bollocks got a bit previous and tried to whack him. So Bradley done it, his job – and them. Now there's a father or an uncle who's after his head for it. But he ain't no big wheel. The rest are businessmen, like us. They're coming to talk opportunities, not bloody *vendetta* – so long as no one does nothing stupid like reminding them. Least not till someone decides that's the right move. Meaning *me*."

He was piss-weak and tipped the scales two thirds what he'd been in his fighting days. Still, the single finger he prodded into Parsons' sweaty breastbone sent his lieutenant stumbling backwards into one of the lesser wicker chairs. A cloud of dust and God-knows-what rose in the dappled golden light. Another spectre.

"Oi! Alright guv – I got the message!"

Jimmy returned to the chair opposite, his head buzzing something rotten. Or had another of the little blighters got in again? Not the mozzies. With the rainy season fast approaching, they'd be scrambling soon enough at sundown. But there were plenty of other creepy-crawlies that wanted a piece of you in supposedly temperate Southern Rhodesia, regardless of how much you proclaimed the place a white man's paradise. The thing, he had to remind himself, was not to take it personal. Until you had to.

That was the question, though. When did you have to? When was it no longer the smart move to keep your cool and think exclusively of business? Because one of those nagging little bastards always circling his bonce was the suspicion that he could have saved everything back in England, Gerry included, if he hadn't gone off to take care of other enterprises and left his hot-headed kid brother in charge. If he'd only stuck around, taken care of Jack Penny instead, and that Bradley and the MERCURY bird…

Or wouldn't they have nabbed him bang to rights, to face the hangman in place of Jack? Wouldn't it be Jack here now, moving up from his beloved copper to chromium, to reap the rewards of ramped-up wartime production and the advent of the shiny new age? And wouldn't it be Jack, instead, rebuilding old contacts and shipping arms to that tribe of his who were about to launch another bloody war in Palestine? A nice little earner that, if you didn't fall foul of the customers and their middle-men…

"You alright, guv? You gone a funny colour."

"I'll turn you a funny colour, you cunt." But instead of throwing his customary look – a look like a bone-crushing counter – he found himself watching the washed-out Daylesford, who was so wicker-toned and wicker-textured now he was almost transparent. He hadn't coped so well with what had happened to his missus, even after he'd signed over title deed on this place and his controlling shares in the chrome mine. Which was a lesson, really, in the need to separate the business and the personal. Though not, perhaps, to take your eye off either.

Jimmy switched to a softer tone himself.

"No you done good, Vic. When you get back, have someone find out where they went in Brussels, and after. Keep tabs on 'em, don't worry 'bout the dosh. Just 'cause we don't want to start nothing don't mean they won't, eh? Best be certain."

"Right, guv."

"Now I know you been flying for four days and you need a wash and brush-up, but first let's run over the plans for our guests next month. They'll 'ave been in the air even longer, some of 'em, so we better make sure we ain't left no loose ends. From what *I'm* 'earing, their boss-man don't like to leave nothing to chance neither – even if they do call him Lucky!"

CHAPTER FIVE

"Down, Susie!"

Roger Hemsby pulled an apologetic face and jerked at the dog's lead to drag it away from Mila, who it appeared to have forgotten greeting with great enthusiasm only five minutes previously, not to mention countless times before that.

"It's quite alright, she's a dear!" Mila laughed, crouching again to pat and pamper the thing. Bradley marvelled at her patience. He had begun and ended his relationship with it by means of a forceful shove and a refusal to make further eye contact.

There was an infuriating springiness to Hemsby too. He was one of those men the British seemed able to churn out on a production line: far older, close up, than his gawky boyish deportment first suggested; difficult to pin down in all sorts of ways.

When first he'd picked them up, and then put them up, in Brussels – where he was engaged in 'frightfully dreary' work transforming the Dunkirk Treaty between France and Britain into a wider western union of military, political, economic and cultural interests that included the Benelux countries – he had come across as thoughtful, consoling and quite plausibly a sober acquaintance, even friend, of Smith's. Yet, soon after, he had lapsed into a breezy, inattentive manner which appeared to be his normal temperament, although Mila, who could read the Limeys far better than Bradley, swore that it was still an act.

Since bringing them by official car to The Hague and introducing them to his 'bolthole' on the sea front at Scheveningen, and his dog, he had become as bouncy and absent-minded as the animal itself. Bradley couldn't wait to get away from him.

But first there was the matter of retracing Smith's footsteps and piecing together his final days. Hemsby had taken them to the location where the police said that it had happened: the assault, the fight, the killing (in Jones' unforgiving interpretation). He had reprised his sympathetic act there, until Mila made plain it was not needed. Now they were leaving the woods via a waste-ground that skirted a stretch of squared-away ruins every bit as grim as anything Bradley had encountered in Germany.

"The Bezuidenhout district," Hemsby grunted. "Residential area, or at least it was, poor devils. Apparently, we were aiming for the V-2 sites in the Haagse Bos, but our chaps' targeting was a little out of whack."

"People here must have been very angry," Bradley said.

"Well, the ones who weren't dead, they were pretty miffed, yes. Still, they all came out and thanked us when our Lancs dropped food instead a couple of months later. The Dutch are good like that."

"Food is good like that," Mila said.

"Oh, absolutely. And after what happened this May in France and Italy – Vienna too – we know that's going to be our battleground with the communists."

Maybe it was that word, battleground, or the man, or his dog. Bradley couldn't help it.

"And we all know who's gonna pay for that!"

But Hemsby only shrugged distractedly.

"Hmm. Well of course these people did, with their lives. Now… let's move on to something prettier."

Clicking for his dog to keep up, he bounded off between two further rubble stacks and disappeared. Bradley looked at Mila. She rolled her eyes.

She was wearing a smart skirt and blouse, with a light, loose raincoat. Her hat looked much like his own, albeit with a feather in it, but then Bradley knew he was not an expert in ladies' fashions and ought to have paid more attention to what Jenny

Simmonds had been saying. He did know, because she had shown it to him, that she had a pistol in her handbag, and not a ladies' gun either: it was one of the Russian Tokarevs the 'removals men' had been carrying. The other was in the back of his waistband, under his tweed jacket.

The junction of the ruined Korte Voorhout and the crossing onto the Nieuwe Uitleg was a construction site. Beyond lay Hemsby's 'something prettier' – a typical inner-city canal quayside, lined with trees and tall, old merchant's houses. Similar high-gabled facades ran along the facing bank, reflected in the still water, until Susie chased a brace of ducks into it.

"Why are we here, Roger?" Mila said.

"Two reasons. Firstly it's more or less on our way to the Mauritshuis, the museum collection that Richard visited shortly before… popping off. You did say you wanted to retrace his movements?"

"Yes. And the second reason?"

Hemsby set Susie's lead down on the cobblestones and planted a foot on it, freeing both hands to rummage through his jacket pockets. At length – and with a self-amused grin – he produced a large key on a string.

"I've found you a base for while you're in town. Number 16, right here. It's being refurbished and I know the people. I thought it might suit you down to the ground. The funny thing is, it used to be Mata Hari's house."

*　　*　　*

"I suppose it could be handy," she said when Hemsby had left them alone. "Having somewhere central to use as a safe house."

"If Hemsby knows about it, I'd say that's stretching the definition."

"Yes, quite. But if we were detaining someone for questioning, or calling on reinforcements, without wanting to fill in police forms at the hotels…"

She registered his dubious expression and shrugged. Who could they call? With no transmitter or signal plan, contacting anyone from the former MERCURY network would be time-consuming at best, and from what she had heard of the prevailing mood in Czechoslovakia, getting out would be difficult, getting back harder still. Sam's old contacts were simply not to be trusted; he said so himself. So who did that leave? Jenny Simmonds, a shopgirl from South London.

And 'Pat' Pendleton, she acknowledged ruefully. Assuming he had recovered from his wound – and could be trusted any more than Sam's people, which of course he could not.

Sam was regarding her with a curious look, almost tentative.

"But… Mata Hari? I saw the movie. Us kids snuck in back of the Fabian Theatre on Newark Street to watch Garbo get her clothes off. Am I missing something?"

"I don't think so. It seems to amuse Roger Hemsby to compare me with an exotic spy who was entrapped and executed for her sins."

And with that, tucking the key to Nieuwe Uitleg 16 in her bag with her Russian automatic, she put the matter from her mind. Having strolled the short distance to the Gothic parliament complex and the Hofvijver lake, she and Sam were soon loitering in front of a far grander residence which, with its iron railings and Dutch flags, had obviously been transformed into another public building.

Mila frowned. There was nothing inherently suspicious in Richard's visiting a newly reopened art museum two days before his confrontation with de Klerk's men. He had been a cultured man and during the London Blitz had even taken her to a lunchtime concert at the National Gallery, where contemporary war art had replaced the evacuated collection. If one had no particular desire to return to the Scheveningen flat and its overfriendly terrier, one might very well choose to kill time at the Mauritshuis.

But what if one were, presumably, on the trail of one's quarry: close enough to start tailing him through the woods? There was something that didn't fit.

Had Richard been tailing de Klerk when he came here?

Sam, no slouch at tailing things himself, must have been following her thoughts.

"We oughta check with Sloane. Send a telegram to Jenny. Maybe those paintings de Klerk had to give back to SAFEHAVEN in return for his freedom…"

"Are here? Sloane said his speciality was private Jewish collections but yes, perhaps there's something in that."

"If we're lucky, he comes back to see them, for old times' sake."

"I'd settle for an attendant who remembers Richard and what he was doing here. But I suppose we won't know what we're looking for until we've found it."

"I've snuck into a few movie theatres over the years. Never been in an art museum though."

She threw him a wink as she set off for the entrance.

"What a sheltered life you've led, Sergeant Bradley. I've stolen treasures from several."

Having not long been reopened, and this being a Saturday, the museum was busy. Local folk and foreign diplomats alike had flocked to view the newly reassembled collection which, the guide book promised, included the Royal Cabinet of Paintings, spanning the Dutch Golden Age. Yet for all the pomp, this was no National Gallery or Louvre – nor, of course, the Sternberg Palace. The Mauritshuis was conspicuously a former family residence, and the exhibition spaces followed the layout of a conventional, if generously proportioned, townhouse. The downstairs rooms left and right of the entrance hall and its double staircase contained a dingy selection of the Flemish Masters, as well as several portraits of the former owner, Johan Maurits, Count of Nassau-Siegen, prodigious slave-trader and great-nephew of William of Orange. She recognised a Rogier van der Weyden and Vermeer's *View of Delft*. When they moved on to the prize of the collection, the marble-floored, red silk-walled room crammed frame-to-frame with the master's works, even Sam said he had heard of Rembrandt.

Had the Nazis looted – and de Klerk returned – any of these?

The former was more than likely, the latter possible, but the cheaply mimeoed guide offered no insight into those dark days. Unless Richard had been shown round by an expert, he would not have known either. So what had he been doing here? Where had he lingered?

Tiring of musty interiors and dusty light through half-curtained windows, they proceeded upstairs. Here the collection was better lit and appeared more haphazardly thrown together, perhaps because the acquisitions – or reacquisitions – were newer. Mila found herself captivated by another Vermeer, a young woman in a turban, looking over her shoulder, in vibrant lapis lazuli and yellow.

But it was in a lesser upstairs room, one with alcoves around an ornate fireplace, creaking floorboards and several busts displayed on tables, that she found Sam similarly captivated. The painting he had stopped at was in one of the alcoves and might easily have been overlooked. It was a circular panel of about a metre diameter depicting the faces of three rosy-cheeked laughing boys. No, the same boy from three different angles, but always tousle-haired and naughtily vivacious. *Lachende Jongens, Frans Hals, 1625*, the pamphlet said.

"This is pointless. We need to find an attendant to talk to," she said.

Sam looked at her and then back at the painting.

"You can't see it?" he said, in a strange, flat tone.

Her heart jumped. She recognised that tone. It was the one in which he had called her over from her search through the cellars of that mountaintop sanitorium at the war's end, when he had first come upon the evidence that her son had not died as a baby, as she had been told, but might still be alive.

But what evidence could be hidden in a three hundred year-old painting?

Three boys' faces – one boy, laughing three different ways. Perhaps eight years old. Fair-haired, full-lipped. In a loose lace collar. Sketched in age-cracked oils on a dark, neutral background, on wood. The features were alive, the brush-strokes broad and free, quite unlike the bulk of the Flemish works on the floor below. It was what was known as a 'tronie', the notes explained. Not a portrait but a study, to demonstrate the artist's ability to capture a mood, an emotion. And he had captured it masterfully, with a rare modern spontaneity.

But why was her heart pounding? Why did she stagger then from foot to foot – and put her hand out to support herself on Sam's arm?

"I suppose you don't look at yourself much, and if you do it's a mirror-image, reversed…"

"What do you mean?"

He took her shoulders then, gently, to steady her, and to position her directly in front of the painting.

"Mila it's *you*. Your look, your smile, your laugh."

"I rarely smile. And never laugh."

"No, you do. And you're right, it's very rare. That's why…"

Even staring straight ahead at the painting, at the boy and his rosy cheeks, she could sense the blush on Sam's.

"OK… you're saying I look a little like this 17th Century boy. That's flattering, I suppose, in a way…"

And then she knew that she was resisting it, in the same way as her shoulders were tightening within his loose grasp. Because underneath she understood what he was saying.

"You think…?"

"I do," Sam said. "And I think Colonel Smith saw it too. Because he… he…"

One man loved the pilgrim soul in you.

Time itself turned a somersault. She let go. With all her resistance gone, she accepted what Sam was telling her and fainted in his arms.

*   *   *

It was three quarters of an hour later and they had found a bench across the lake in the shade of the trees. From a street vendor, who'd been only too glad to take Roger's diplomatic food vouchers, they had bought deep-fried seafood and vegetables, slathered in mustard and wrapped in newspaper. By the time Bradley returned with two bottles of *gruit* beer from a café across the Lange Vijverberg, Mila had nearly finished hers.

"I even told Roger how important food was," she said, wiping her lips. "I feel such a fool."

"You haven't been eating?"

"Not properly. I've had so much on my mind."

Bradley nodded. Since Scotland they had spent more time together than ever before, but he had tried to give her as much privacy as he could. Even when they'd had to share a sleeping compartment aboard the Night Ferry, out of instinct he had allowed her to go to the dining car alone. Theirs was a professional relationship, after all, and she was not the kind of woman who needed a man beside her to guide her choices or make her feel comfortable, nor to deter unwanted attention: she could do that quite well enough via her withdrawn manner, if need be with the glacial force of her gaze.

And the snarky voice in his head that whispered *professional relationship?* That was all the round-the-clock company he needed.

"Are you feeling better now?"

A goofy smile. That smile.

"Yes, quite recovered!"

"Able to talk about what we saw over there?" As though they hadn't both been staring at it, he indicated where the square mass of the Mauritshuis backed onto the lake.

"I think so."

"Incidentally, I thought throwing a faint like that was a genius stroke – getting us into the Director's office for a look around…"

She took a pull on her beer.

"Deputy Director. And yes, Dr van Gelder was very helpful. But I wasn't putting it on."

"No. I figured."

"It was just all too much. If that is Pavel, as you seem to think…"

"We both think it, Mila. And of course it's not just because he looks like you. It's that de Klerk is linked to the painting – like Dr van Gelder confirmed, it was one of those he returned – and that's got to make it the trigger for Colonel Smith tracking him."

"Yes, that's what I mean."

For a second he failed to comprehend the look of dread on her face. He thought it must still be the shock of suspecting – and not knowing, which was worse – that she had just had her first glimpse of her grown child. Then it struck him.

"You think this makes you responsible for his death?"

"It appears that he was doing it for me. Even after all these years. And even with so many more important things…"

She bit back on tears. Bradley couldn't help it: his lip curled.

"So now you're going to take the blame for his not setting up an international court and saving, what was it, a billion lives? You're being ridiculous."

"Am I, Sam?"

And there it was, that unguarded appeal. Like when they had paused on that mountaintop in the midst of danger and she had first told him her story. When she had wept on his shoulder and he had stroked her unruly crest of feathers.

He yearned to say again what he had said then. *Poor nightingale.* But he couldn't. That was not who he was to her. That was not what she needed from him, now.

"No, you're being a decent person. That's in short supply."

"I am not a decent person," she said.

"Then good. Because right now that's the last thing we need."

She sat up straight and took another swig.

"True. We need the person who painted that fake. He's the one who can point us towards de Klerk – and Pavel."

"When you were playing up the grieving widow act for Dr van Gelder just now, he told you something. I was kind of distracted. Plus, his English wasn't great and he kept using Dutch words, but I thought with your German…"

"He said he remembered Richard because Richard had asked him about the van Meegeren case, which was in all the papers. Van Meegeren was another supposed Nazi collaborator, plundering Dutch culture, and he was involved in selling a Vermeer to none other than Hermann Göring, for his private collection, possibly in cahoots with de Klerk. After the war, when he was charged with treason and facing the death penalty, van Meegeren came clean and confessed to having forged the Vermeer, among many others. He became something of a national hero. Whether or not he played any part in it, this probably helped de Klerk to muddy the waters, as Zajíček – Jones – said."

"I think I read something about it."

"But Dr van Gelder says he told Richard about another case, similar, but less well known. A van Gogh, this time, and a Nazi who was not nearly as newsworthy as Göring. In fact, van Gelder could not remember his name, only that his tastes must have tended towards what the Nazis deemed 'degenerate' art and therefore he needed to keep his dealings in the shadows. The forger went by the name of 'Schim'. He failed to convince people that his actions were a sophisticated form of resistance against the Nazi occupiers, and the van Gogh, real or fake, was never recovered, which did not help his cause. He was sent to prison."

"You think he was the guy who made the painting of your son? Maybe because de Klerk didn't want to hand the real one back?"

"It seems ridiculous, as you'd say. Why would he have Pavel? And why would anyone in possession of the original need a model to pose for the forgery, instead of just copying it?"

"Still, Colonel Smith must have figured it that way."

"It would seem so."

Bradley shook his head in bewilderment, and not just at the strange turn their investigations were taking. At everything. He felt out of place in this world of art galleries and art aficionados, of folks who looked like they slept soundly all night and couples strolling arm-in-arm under the trees. He had noticed a man and woman watching them, the man skinny and pallid in suit trousers and shirtsleeves, the woman fit and tanned in a flouncy summer dress. Mismatched, perhaps. But their hands were clasped tight down low between them and their eyes soon returned to one another's. They had looked straight through him and Mila because to each of them there was no one else in the world.

He pulled out his smokes. Thought about offering her one. Didn't.

Something was nagging at him…

"Say, if this forger is in jail, how could he have painted the forgery?"

"I don't know," Mila shrugged. "But he was Richard's only lead and now he is ours. I think we need to go and visit Mijnheer Schim."

CHAPTER SIX

Entry to the 'Orange Hotel' was via an arched gate in a weather-beaten brick wall running along the edge of the east dunes in Scheveningen. It was through this same gate that the hotel's 'guests' had been marched to their final outing on the dunes. The police prison had been the detention centre for all those who resisted the German occupation.

Now it played host to those who had profited from it.

Mila and Bradley were shown into a cell complex in the ground floor barracks. Barred skylights gave plenty of illumination, and the cell doors had been freshly painted, in bright orange, of course. It would have been considerably gloomier in Nazi times.

The warden ordered his guard to unlock the cell, then gave a formal nod to take his leave of them. The guard stood back obediently. After two days of official negotiations, Roger Hemsby's Foreign Office letterhead still worked wonders, even if his fingers had gone nowhere near the typewriter keys.

Inside the cell stood a high-sided bunk and a simple table and chair. At the table sat the forger 'Schim', real name Willem de Hoog.

And on the table? Mila looked. Sketches. Self-portraits, she realised. At his table, in his mirror, lying asleep. He had made himself look a lot like Vincent van Gogh – in reality, as well as in the drawings. Red-bearded, crop-haired, gaunt, his weary, knowing eyes fixed on hers.

"Mr de Hoog…"

"Schim, please." His English was better than Dr van Gelder's had been. "That is my professional name. I presume you wish to interrogate me in that capacity."

"Schim."

"A translation would be 'shady'."

Mila indicated the sketches.

"May I? These are wonderful."

"Derivative, my son calls them."

"I have a son," Mila said. "He's why I'm here."

The eyes played over her and then went dead. It was as though someone had shot him with an anaesthetic dart.

"No. I would remember," he said, turning back to his work.

"Remember what?"

"If we had slept together. Lately I have had to admit to several of my creations, but not this one, madam. You will have to try your luck elsewhere."

"Her *luck!*" Before she could stop him, Sam had kicked Schim's chair legs from under him. The forger was forced to stagger backwards onto his bunk to avoid falling to the stone floor.

"And who's this brute? Did I damage his career as a curator? You must join the queue, my good fellow."

"You know who you look like," Mila said.

"Of course. I find the observation banal. If people would *really* look…"

"And you know what happened to him."

Sam had picked up on her lead. The jack knife he stabbed down into the table, piercing several of the drawings, was his own improvisation.

Mila checked over her shoulder. If he had heard anything, the guard leaning against the wall on the far side of the door had been briefed not to intervene.

"I shan't cut off your ear just yet, Schim. I want you to hear me."

Sam picked up the chair and replaced the forger upon it.

"I am listening."

"Good. I was going to tell you about my son. The thing is, I have just seen a picture of him, for the first time in over seven years. It was signed by Frans Hals."

For several seconds, she was conscious of watching Vincent van Gogh wrestle with his emotions.

"If I might venture it, you hardly seem old enough." The dour face cracked open in a grin. "To have a son of at least seven years of age, I mean – not one who was painted by Master Hals!"

"Thank you. He is nine now. If he is still alive."

"And how old is he in the painting?"

She looked at Sam, receiving only an uncertain look that matched her own.

"No less than eight, I'd say. I'm afraid I'm no expert in children. Mine or anyone else's."

Schim stroked his beard. In thought, all animation paused, his features took on a cadaverous quality. Van Gogh, seeing it in himself, had called it the face of death.

"Painted since the war, then. But not by me."

"We supposed not."

"Nor by van Meegeren. If it has fooled the great Dr van Gelder, it's not his style at all."

"How do you know it fooled Dr van Gelder?"

"Madam, practically everything fools Dr van Gelder. And I could spin you a line about how I knew that a certain Mijnheer de Klerk returned Frans Hals' *Laughing Boys* to the Mauritshuis and have just now deduced the rest of it. But the fact of the matter is that I've been asked about this painting before, earlier this year." He looked her up and down, then switched to Sam. "Another *English* visitor."

"That would have been my husband. He passed away shortly after seeing you."

Schim raised his eyebrows, furrowing his high forehead with its distinctive widow's peak. Then he turned to his table and began scribbling furiously. For a moment Mila supposed that he was writing down their next clue – an address where de Klerk or even Pavel might be found hiding – and her heart leapt again. But despite their energy those were free, flowing movements with the pencil and when he turned back to present her with the paper she saw that it was a simple likeness of a stern-faced middle-aged gentleman with a military moustache and, magically captured, a kind of righteous fury in his gaze. Richard.

She gave a gasp that almost turned into a sob.

Schim looked momentarily ashamed of himself.

"I can't tell you who painted your Hals. Not without seeing it up close – and the back of it, what it's painted on, that's the key."

"A helluva lot of use that's gonna be," Sam grunted.

"An American. I thought so! I knew de Klerk. He was in America for a time and he speaks English a bit like you."

"What was he doing in America?" Mila asked. "Trading in art?"

"Among more illicit activities. I believe he was known to his criminal confederates over there as 'Dutch' or 'Dutchie'. I don't know if that is relevant. But I do think I might know who his client was, for the Hals, if we are to assume that someone has absconded with the original painting. A big Nazi bastard named Anselm Kuhlmann, who worked closely with Seyss-Inquart in robbing the Netherlands and murdering its people."

"And how would you know that, Mr Schim?"

"I tried to sell him my van Gogh, but the deal went sour and I only just escaped with my life. He was a great admirer of *Entartete Kunst* – 'degenerate art', or what you and I would call modern art. When that psychotic watercolourist with a goat's-hair mottler on his lip ordered it all to be purged, Kuhlmann acquired a substantial collection of his own. Van Gogh falls broadly into that category. And so, in a funny way, might Frans Hals. An admirer might see him as a progenitor of impressionism."

"Enough to want him in his private collection, wherever he might have fled?"

"Exactly, madam. They hanged Seyss-Inquart at Nuremburg, but they never got Kuhlmann."

Sam went to sit on the bunk, either to affect a more friendly air or because his knee was bothering him. The bunk creaked.

"Everybody's got teams hunting ex-Nazis, or hiding them. Believe me, I know. We won't pick up that guy's trail. Our only good lead is the phony painting."

Schim let out a sigh of apparent resignation: the kind of resignation that was also an acceptance.

"Ah, but here, my good fellow, is something that you do not know. A forgery is not a 'phony'. To convince people, it has to be painted as fluidly and delicately as the original. Even this requires interpretation, every bit as inventive as the master's. And then there is the art of which the master had no need or knowledge…"

He looked up at the door, beyond which they could see the epauletted shoulder of the lurking warder, and lowered his voice to a whisper.

"If you can get the painting, my son can examine it. He was always good at checking my work to ensure I used the right historic techniques and materials. He might identify your forger."

"Get the painting?" She and Sam said it as one.

Schim – or Vincent van Gogh – grimaced sheepishly. Then he grinned again.

"There is a further benefit in doing so which you may not have considered. If you can prove to the world that de Klerk did not return the real painting, might that not invalidate the preposterous immunity deal he made with the Dutch government and your people, the Americans? He would be exposed. If you are looking for him, it might flush him out."

"Or send him deeper into hiding," Sam said. He looked at her and she pulled a helpless face.

"Get the painting," she muttered, almost to herself.

"Get the painting," Sam echoed grimly.

Schim nodded.

"Get the painting."

*   *   *

The sightseer who was not a sightseer stepped softly backward and let the dim light and the early morning mist off the canal merge his outline with that of the tree trunk where it burst through the cobbles. A lone caller was coming along the quayside of the Nieuwe Uitleg. A slight figure in scruffy woollens, wearing a peaked barge cap. He held a scrap of paper which he checked before knocking at the door to Number 16.

The watcher was about to ease forward again to a more convenient vantage point when he froze – or would have done, had he not already made himself immobile. In the corner of his eye, he had spotted movement behind one of the trees further along the quay. A kissing couple who were not a kissing couple, revolving fractionally in their lovemaking to grant the woman a better view over her man's shoulder. And what of? Of the front door opening to reveal an unlit hallway and someone female in a cap and apron – a maid, a housekeeper? – questioning the young arrival on the step.

He drew back carefully and his hand began its unhurried progress towards the pistol under his armpit.

*   *   *

"Impossible!"

'Pep' de Hoog, clean-shaven yet somehow even more ferrety than his father, gave a lemon-sucking wince and waved his hands back and forth as though he was marshalling torpedo bombers on a flat-top. Obviously one for theatrics, he turned his back and went to gaze down at the Smidswater from the second storey windows.

Perched alongside Bradley on the edge of the large dressing table in the spare bedroom, Mila let out an indulgent sigh.

"What is impossible, Pep?"

They could see his glum face distorted on the old glass.

"Getting away with it, of course! Oh, it's no great challenge to pull the thing down off the wall and run out of the room with it. One old fart of an attendant to dodge or stick up. But in the next room, another, forewarned, and on the stairs more of them, ready for you now. Another at the front doors – all he has to do is make sure that they are closed – and of course that's your only option because the building juts out into the lake and has no back entrance. But say you can do all that. What then?"

Having invited the forger's son to the Mata Hari house to pass on the message from his father, Mila had asked him, at the end of a long, involved examination of the insurmountable obstacles to a night-time break-in – chief among these the layout of the Mauritshuis, which allowed for no lengthy intervals between the patrolling watchmen – whether it might be more feasible to snatch the painting during opening hours. Already, Bradley could tell that his response was testing her restraint.

"What then, Pep?"

The young man turned back, signalling helplessly. Bradley pictured confused aviators toppling off the deck either side.

"You are in the centre of town, in a public space, clasping a heavy ninety-five centimetre wooden disc. The staff of the museum are hard on your heels." Abruptly, he returned to the map that lay amid the building plans fanned out on the bedspread. "There… and you want to get it back here, yes? Should be easy – not much more than half a kilometre. But it's only just September and still daylight until late. Police are everywhere. Witnesses are everywhere. So you run here, onto the Korte Voorhout, or you are clever and you pass it to someone else. But you're seen. They're seen. 'Where did they go?' 'Over there, officer – the bloody Mata Hari house!' Or you aim to stash it until later, here in the park – but there's no way out. Get onto the canal? It goes under the road, the building site, goes nowhere… So instead you have a car waiting to rush the painting out of town, yes – not near the museum, you can't drive there, but here maybe, or here… Only where do you go now? There are no main roads. Not until you get to here, past the waste ground, by which time, again, you've been seen, followed. It won't take long for the police to set up road blocks. *That* is what is impossible!"

For a second, Bradley thought he was going to fling himself face-down on the bed like a thwarted child, soggy-looking sweater, maps, blueprints and all. He didn't think Mila would appreciate that, not with all the hard work that Roger's letterhead had been doing. Pep, presumably, came to the same conclusion just in time. He pulled a face that was much like his father's sudden expression of remorse.

Bradley wondered what his life had been like, coming to manhood during the Nazi occupation, walking a tightrope between collaborating and resisting, ever fearful of deportation as a slave labourer, or worse. Not to mention nearly starving to death, as every surviving Dutchman had nearly done, at the end. He thought perhaps he too might be highly strung, especially given how things had turned out for his father.

Mila, he guessed, had been counting to some unspecified number in her head. He was reminded of her patience with the dog. Now she said, gently:

"Will you help us do it, Pep?"

Was he really about to cry? Passions flushed his acne-scarred cheeks and brimmed behind his eyes.

"Of course I'll bloody help you! Why do you think my dad agreed to it? Who do you think put him in the Orange Hotel?"

"You mean apart from the courts?"

"Dr van Gelder! He took the witness stand and lied through his teeth. Denied all knowledge of dad's van Gogh being a copy – when he was in on the bloody swindle!"

"Why would he do that?" Bradley asked.

"I don't know. Because he was an NSB'er."

"What's that?"

The bitter wince became a vicious sneer.

"Our home-grown Nazis. The only well-fed swine in the Netherlands. Only now suddenly it stands for *Niet So Bedoeld* – We Didn't Mean It!"

Bradley caught Mila looking at him again. He nodded. If the museum's Deputy Director was hiding such a secret, he would be open to all manner of propositions.

"Can you prove that?" he said.

But Pep, of course, began wringing his hands.

"No. And it's probably not true. More likely it was because

he'd been tricked before into authenticating some of Dad's reproductions. Maybe he was even the one who ratted him out. But it was his testimony – or lack of it – that completely punctured our defence. Van Meegeren gets a slap on the wrist. De Klerk gets immunity. Dad gets twenty years."

Mila was studying him. Almost smiling. Almost.

"And your mum leaves?"

Pep shook his head.

"That was earlier. But of course she 'didn't mean it' either."

"I'm sorry."

"Don't be. We don't need her."

"Just each other."

She stubbed out her cigarette and flashed Bradley a look.

"We can do without the goods on Dr van Gelder. We'll put together a different plan. But we will need some provisions, because it's going to be a long day. And you, Pep, you're going to play a part in it. Are you up to that?"

The eyes raised. The face twitched. Still full of contradictory impulses and emotions, it seemed, but with the despair replaced by something else now, perhaps.

"Yes… Madam?"

"You can call me Miss Slavík," she said.

*　　*　　*

It was one of the water folk who had first reported it.

By the time the patrol officer had commandeered a rowboat and gone to investigate, the sun had dipped behind the buildings and the area between the barges under the Malie Bridge was deep in shadow. Still, it was obvious that the reports were not false alarms. A clothed body bobbed amid the old ropes and other flotsam. Adult male, face-down. A drunk from last night, probably. It was not uncommon, with the streetlamps being so fickle and there being no railings along the quay.

He was distracted by a thud and clatter of machinery from the south end of the canal, where it bent around the island and went under the temporary trestle crossing they had erected there. The workmen levelling the bombed-out cannon foundry would be downing tools for the evening, eager to sink a few bocks. Or more than a few. Perhaps one of them would be taking the plunge and sinking himself as well.

Pulling hard with one oar to swivel alongside, the patrol officer grimaced in disgust. There were rats on the body, on the torso and the back of the head, where something like ground beef protruded. He swung the oar at them and they swam off, their tails snaking like the coils of oily rope.

A drunk, or a vagrant. Likely filthy even before he'd gone in and drowned. And now the rats. What had they done to him?

He considered calling it a day, finding the nearest police telephone and summoning the coroner's people, letting them deal with it, if they hadn't yet knocked off like the workmen. But there were onlookers on the bridge now, and if there was anything suspicious about the death he'd get in trouble for not reporting it to the detectives.

He used the oar blade to anchor himself to the body and then grabbed hold and turned it over. As it rolled, slowly, heavily, he tensed first in horror and then in shock.

The sick-fish face had two holes it, one below the eye and one in the temple, each oozing a slick, greyish fluid and ringed by whitish, water-swollen flesh. When the sodden coat slid open, it revealed something odd strapped around the torso.

An empty shoulder holster.

CHAPTER SEVEN

Something had been found, explained the man from the Department of Public Works and Water Management, twitching his mean little moustache and sliding the bridge of his thick spectacles back up his prominent nose. At his side, the heavyset Municipal Police Patrol Officer nodded gravely. And furthermore, the local jobsworth added, strangling his vowels, it was a matter of Public Safety. An urgent matter.

Martin van Gelder had been on his feet behind his desk since his secretary, ineffectually fluttering their authorising paperwork, had shown them in. Now he turned his back on the pair, fitting his considerable bulk into the dormer window space to gaze out over the Hofvijver, beyond the octagonal tower of the Binnenhof, to its little island. Why had no one notable painted this view, he mused. Probably because they'd have ended up making a post-Romantic symbolist mess of it like that awful Böcklin.

"I have done as you requested and ordered the museum closed without delay, at no little inconvenience to ourselves and the general public. I think I am entitled to insist on knowing why."

"Of course, Doctor, er…"

Someone really ought to teach these petty officials to speak properly before sending them out to address civilised people, van Gelder thought. He wondered what this one had been doing during the occupation – along with his stony-faced police companion – and decided they had probably been rooting out and rounding up Hebrews. Not that there was anything wrong in that, of course; particularly if one brought in the right person

77

to 'catalogue' their art collections…

"Spit it out, man!" He spat himself, on the window pane and the island. "*What* has been found?"

He could practically hear the jobsworth glance up at the patrol officer for approval.

"Er… a bomb, Doctor. An unexploded British bomb from the Bezuidenhout tragedy. A big one. 1,000 kilogrammes."

"I see…"

In place of the island in the Vijverberg, an enticing image popped into van Gelder's head of the famous *View of Delft,* merging with van Poel's apocalyptic aftermath of the 'Thunderclap', when that city had been laid waste by its own gunpowder store. A van Gogh, I could get, he thought. Two. Or even a few Mondriaans. Elevate this place from all those over-varnished Royal Cabinet paintings, which have had their blasted day! Structural damage… the need – and the funds! – to modernise. A bold curator, placed in sole charge by the Trustees, as in the days of that arsehole Bredius, the hem of whose garment we are still not worthy to touch. That would be enough to put the nasty rumours to rest.

He shuffled around to face his visitors with an accommodating smile.

"You were quite correct to request the evacuation. A dislodged cornice… The lunchtime crowd… it doesn't bear thinking about. Is the bomb really that near?"

"Near enough. On – or rather under – the Korte Voorhout."

"Then surely you must also evacuate the other museums, and the ministries!"

"Our teams have that in hand."

"Of course."

"But this is just a precaution, Doctor. You need not fear for your collection."

"*My* collection," he scoffed, before adding, grandly: "I think you mean the State's."

Oh well, he could still hope…

At which point, presaged by the inevitable creak of

floorboards, they were interrupted by a knock at the door. Van Gelder knew, from the faintness of it, who it was.

"Come in, Bartholomeus."

Another, even feebler knock.

"Yes, yes, yes, come in!" He threw his visitors a deprecatory smirk.

With a protest from the old, warped door, an equally worn out figure entered. It was the attendant from Room 13, in the opposite rear corner and on the floor below. He was a man of well past retirement age who had the advantages of being far too deaf to respond to the public's presumptuous questions and, even more agreeably, extremely cheap. In fact, van Gelder wasn't sure that he or anyone else paid Bartholomeus at all.

"What is it? Is everybody out?"

"The… the public, sir?"

"Well obviously the public! We aren't about to leave the museum unattended!"

The old man frowned. It was as well that the staff in the more important rooms and at the front were rather more switched on, or at least in the land of the living.

"Mr Deputy Director… Most of our visitors have already left. There is a party from the art school that is still gathering up its things on the ground floor. They were in the Golden Room…"

"Of course, well I'm sure that's good enough…"

"…but there is a problem."

"A problem?"

"Trouble, sir. In Room 13."

"Your room, Bartholomeus."

"Yes, sir. A visitor refuses to leave. He sent me to tell you this."

"He sent you out of your own room? Leaving him alone in there?"

"Well he's not going anywhere. That's the whole problem."

"That's the whole problem…" Van Gelder found he had clapped his hand to his forehead in disbelief and exasperation, like someone in a bad theatre piece. He turned to his guests, unable to think of anything to say.

Thankfully the hitherto silent policeman sprang into action.

"I'll go check it out."

"Thank you. Down the staff stairs here, left, across the landing and then left again at the far end."

"I'd best be getting back myself, sir," Bartholomeus said.

But the municipal jobsworth had other ideas.

"First a few questions for both of you, regarding the, er… standard procedures for evacuation." With a remorseful cringe, he pulled a notebook from the breast pocket of his overalls. "It is a formality, for the report, if you don't mind…"

Van Gelder was about to dismiss both such trivialities and Bartholomeus himself when quite by chance, as the fellow glanced up from his notebook, he caught the official's eyes above the thick spectacles. His animal instincts were shaken by the inflamed contempt he saw momentarily exposed there.

"Um… I suppose not," he managed to say.

"…only, it's probably a good idea for some people to keep in with the authorities, isn't it? Rather than to leave any more unanswered questions…"

What? What kind of challenge was this? Or was it even a challenge at all? While van Gelder's higher brain functions were still processing what he had or had not experienced, the ageless, sunless face of the man from the Department of Public Works and Water Management returned to the model of bland bureaucratic conformity.

Van Gelder swallowed – nothing – for no reason.

"Ask us what you like."

But even as he found the correct page in his notebook, located his pencil, licked its tip and repositioned his spectacles again, the jobsworth cocked his head.

"Is that shouting?"

It was, from somewhere at the other side of the house. And there was certainly no missing the thud that echoed up through the walls, or the thunder of heavy footsteps on the wonky floorboards.

By the time he, the jobsworth and a flustered Bartholomeus had scuttled down the narrow stairs and forced themselves through the private door, which was half-blocked by a fallen plinth, van Gelder was aware of a greater commotion – not here on the first floor but on the ground. Forceful male voices were yelling out repetitive or conflicting orders, the front doors banging shut and the iron bolts sliding home. Instinctively, he sent Bartholomeus down the main staircase to speak to his fellow guards and hurried with the jobsworth across the landing to the room in the far corner.

The policeman was in the middle of Room 13, on his knees. He was holding his head, which was hatless and bleeding but at least in better shape than that of Johan Maurits, Count of Nassau-Siegen, which lay in several marble pieces on the floor. It was not a big room and took only a rapid observation to establish that all the artworks were still present, with the exception of one untidy space where Frans Hals' *Laughing Boys* had hung.

"He hit me," the policeman groaned, almost unintelligibly.

Van Gelder watched open-mouthed as the jobsworth went over to the alcove. The side table upon which the bust of the former owner had stood by the window was now positioned directly beneath the shockingly empty display space. He seemed to be about to move it, perhaps to get closer to the damaged wall with its torn paper and chipped plaster, when the policeman called out, in a thick, woozy voice: "No! Evidence!"

Holding a red-stained handkerchief to his head, the latter got to his feet and gestured towards the little round table, which still had the tablecloth over it, albeit disarranged. Van Gelder saw what he had been pointing at. A dirty boot-print.

And suddenly he realised what it was: a filthy stain not just on the damask but on his career. Whatever the outcome now, he had failed in the foremost task of a proper museum director and curator, to protect his pieces. And this was not just any piece. The *Laughing Boys* was a new bequest. Before it had come into the possession of that ghastly de Klerk – and the Nazis, of course

– it had not been here in the Mauritshuis but in a private collection, owners now declared deceased. He himself had authenticated it from written records and preserved the chain of provenance. And now it might be lost!

Coming to his senses, he left the room without a word. By the time he reached the landing halfway down the stairs the sick feeling in his stomach was doubled – tripled! The front doors were open again, a throng of people coming and going through them…

Bartholomeus found him as soon as he descended.

"Sir, the thief got out before they slammed the doors. The art students were all leaving with their easels and canvases and there was some confusion…"

Van Gelder pushed past everyone, running out and down into the forecourt, where only the van from the Department of Public Works and Water Management sat waiting on the cobbles. He realised that most of the uncommon activity involved his museum guards and attendants – even his secretary – stopping and searching the long-coated, uncooperative art school students who had been making their studies of the Golden Age Masters. Beyond them, surprisingly, were the customary clumps of sightseers.

"He won't get far, sir." Bartholomeus had caught up with him. "Running around with a big panel painting. There's people everywhere."

"Yes. But I thought…"

But there wasn't time to think it. There wasn't time for anything. Or anything productive he could do. Feeling as though he were the one who had been bludgeoned about the head – or that, somehow, that damned bomb had gone off – he watched in astonishment as the man from the Department of Public Works and Water Management and the Municipal Police Patrol Officer, the latter now with a bandage showing under his cap, carried the little table out of the museum and down the steps to their van.

"Evidence," the policeman grunted again.

"He says time is of the essence and it's quicker to take it to the station this way than to wait for the forensic detectives," the jobsworth offered anxiously. "I'll have to go with him. It's my department's vehicle and if I let him requisition it, well, you can imagine the forms we'd all be filling in…"

But this was awful! He wanted to say *And now my little table too?* But he knew how ridiculous that would sound. Why wasn't there time to think of a better response?

"Don't worry, I've done you a receipt." The man thrust a page from his notebook into van Gelder's hand. "Unorthodox, I grant you, but it's official."

"Thank you…"

"Oh, don't thank us, sir. Terrible business! I hope you catch him."

"Yes, yes," Van Gelder forced a thin smile. "So do I!"

*   *   *

The figure running with the unwieldy circular object, which was draped in a drab brown cloth of some kind, was seen by several Dutch tourists, as well as visitors of many nations going to and from the Binnenhof parliamentary complex in preparation for the State Opening on Prince's Day. As it ran towards the Korte Voorhout, it passed a picket line of actors and production staff who were protesting against a change of management at the Koninklijke Schouwburg. Most witnesses, when questioned later, described only a thin man with a beard and dark glasses, wearing a baggy suit and homburg hat. Several of the performers from the ousted theatre company were able to enrich this description fulsomely, but unfortunately none of them could agree on any of the details.

The timely outflux of the art students from the Mauritshuis, and their unhelpful way of entwining their own cumbersome burdens as they assembled in the forecourt to retrieve and load their bicycles, had given the fugitive a head start. But had Dr van Gelder been able to follow the figure's flight as he wished he could – watching from on high as it weaved among the other

83

figures on the chalky surface of the Korte Voorhout towards the construction site like a protagonist in one of Hendrick Avercamp's winter landscapes – he would have been frustrated. Reaching the junction where the Cannon Foundry had stood, the figure was swept up in a sudden tornado of dust and steam as a mechanical crane of some kind performed a pre-arranged act of demolition.

On the other side of the clouds, walking casually across to the Nieuwe Uitleg, Mila made sure that the four-piece wire armature, which she had been carrying linked in a circle to give the impression of a solid disc, was now tucked away inside the sleeves of the brown raincoat she had just slipped over her shoulders. Her hat, beard and sunglasses, bundled with a handy half-brick, were already at the bottom of the canal. And the broad suit trousers? They were quite the fashion for the modern urban woman.

Pausing on the quayside opposite Number 16, she lit a cigarette and watched unobtrusively for pursuers.

When the knocking and hissing of the steam engine subsided, she became aware of police sirens passing on the Korte Voorhout. Once she thought she heard a police whistle. But here on the Nieuwe Uitleg there was no unusual activity.

A small smile had begun to creep across her face when, suddenly, she rolled her eyes in frustration at herself and delved into one of her deep coat pockets.

The paper bag with her sandwiches. Sam had told her to start looking after herself and she had almost forgotten again.

As she bit into the second of them, she spotted a policeman heading along the quayside towards the bench she had chosen for her picnic – although it would have taken Mr Brouček, the drunken time traveller in Leoš Janáček's opera, to identify him as such, since he had already discarded his uniform, fake bandage and body padding.

"Look," she said. "I'm eating it!"

Coming alongside, Sam Bradley grinned.

"Can I have a bite?"

She pretended to shove him away.

"Get your own!"

But she tore the fish paste sandwich in two.

"Lovely," he said with his mouth full. "I was worried that blow to the head might have damaged my sense of taste – I've known that to happen."

"But then you remembered you'd just had an accident with some of Pep's red paint… How is he anyway? He must have held up his end wonderfully."

"Yeah he did – especially covering for me when I fluffed my couple of lines in Dutch. He's doing swell. I left him repainting his van at his workshop."

"And the *Laughing Boys*?" It was too much, too soon, to refer to 'Pavel'.

"Completely unharmed by doubling as a second tabletop, although it wasn't easy to carry the two together under the tablecloth. Now it's safely tucked away for examination when Pep thinks the coast is clear. Incidentally, he has invited us for dinner the day after tomorrow, along with some of his art school friends who ran interference."

"Food again! You're spoiling me. I wonder if van Gelder has worked it out yet."

"I wouldn't have thought so. If all intellectuals are like him, I'm gonna stop feeling so sore about dropping out of high school."

Mila laughed.

"He probably won't twig until he speaks to someone in authority and discovers they know nothing about the bomb or anything. Possibly not even then."

"That would suit me. I know he's a talented forger in his own right but Pep's disguises were beginning to slip. They might not fool a determined police artist."

"Only a great art expert, eh?"

"I reckon he won't be that for much longer."

"Let's hope not. It's going to be very interesting to see what all the fallout from this will be."

Companionably – hoping it wouldn't be too forward, or misinterpreted – she leaned her shoulder against his. She felt, or thought she felt, Sam reciprocate.

Along the quayside, another couple were also seated side-by-side. Their presence made Mila begin to feel uncomfortable, in several different ways.

"Well then, we had best get on with things," she said brightly, to hide her regret at bringing the moment of quietness to a close. "It would seem that I don't need the old MERCURY network after all. I think we're doing pretty well with the new one!"

CHAPTER EIGHT

The Resident handed him a tumbler of Scotch, without rocks, and said gruffly: "Get that down you."

Ever compliant, the Broker did as he was bidden, but not before casting a sceptical look over a poorly arranged and furnished hotel room made dingier by the heavy red plush curtains which had been pulled more or less shut against the afternoon glare.

"Take a pew," the Resident commanded, his unshakeable manner undermined somewhat by the hint of a stammer. The few sticks of aged furniture did not look very trustworthy. The Broker chose the armchair. The Resident settled on the iron bedstead, which sank under him. "I'd offer you water with that, but the only thing coming out of the bathroom tap is *centipedes*."

The Broker didn't know what to make of such information and so said nothing. The Resident was obviously half-cocked and, from his well-crumpled appearance, permanently so nowadays; but did he also frequent the local opium dens?

"Don't look so scandalised, man, you're not on your honeymoon! It's a hole up, not a secure location. For when anything's better than being out in the bazaars."

"Is this one of those times?"

The Resident flapped a hand.

"Too many eager eyes in Stamboul. Plus I stash my booze here. And it has its charms…" He pulled up one sleeve of his wrinkled lightweight suit to revolve a large gold wristwatch into bleary eyeshot. "Mid-afternoon, any minute now…"

Nothing, except the ticking of his watch and his rather heavy, nasal breathing. The persistent cries of seagulls. A ship's horn sounded beyond the curtains – was that it?

Then there came the distinctive lilting wail of the call to prayer. It was in Turkish, of course, as it had been since Kemal Atatürk had banned the use of Arabic. The Resident levered himself off the bed and drew back the curtains. The tall windows were open. The Broker went to join him, leaning out over the iron balustrade.

A paroxysm of reflected light and noise. To their left churned the choppy Bosphorus. Ahead and stretching around to the right gleamed the stiller waters of the Golden Horn, brush-stroked with white horses. Scattered below lay the roofs of Pera and beyond, across the bridge, the minarets and domed mosques of old Constantinople. The Resident drew an appreciative breath and then chuckled, gesturing towards the hazy mosques.

"I was here with a fellow the other day – no, not like that, you dirty devil – who said he thought they looked like big, firm breasts. Not an Orientalist, I'm afraid, nor a poet."

"The profession is changing."

"Isn't it just? Wanted kippers for breakfast. I told him to order yoghurt and green figs." The Resident produced a pack of French cigarettes and lit one, shaking out the match with a disdainful flick and tossing it over the balustrade.

His next words came amid a dense fog of smoke that rivalled the steamers across the Horn.

"And how is our inscrutable friend in Vienna? Set you any other interesting projects?"

"Only as before, to stick close to the targets and their pursuers. I believe the expression was 'like bathhouse birch-leaves'."

"Well, of course. He wants to know who's in play. So do we."

"We know who is in play. Abakumov and Beria, as usual, or at least their myrmidons. Abakumov has the Ministry of State Security evolving into as disruptive a force as his beloved SMERSh ever was – and now through his protégé Kruglov he has manoeuvred Beria out of direct control of Internal Affairs as well. He has MGB and MVD combined. Plus the resources of the GRU, under this new foreign intelligence directorate, the 'Committee of Information'. So Beria and Malenkov, as technically their superiors, are busy setting up a rival bloc of troublemakers to thwart their efforts and cause disruption of their own."

"It isn't the badge you wear so much as who you report to."

"And whether there's an R in the month – or is that shellfish?"

"Ha! You're very well informed for someone who hasn't walked the Arbat in a while."

"I would hardly be able to do my job otherwise."

The Resident hummed thoughtfully, moving back from the windows to mash out the greasy mess he had made of his cigarette in a well-filled ashtray. He took the bottle and topped up their drinks, or rather his guest's; his required a complete refill, to the brim.

"Mmm. Disruption, that's the point of it. Ostensible objective: destabilise Western influence, in Europe, Asia, in the Middle East of course, even Africa. Real objective?"

The Broker hesitated and fought the urge to scan the darkened corners of the room. Friends in Moscow or not, this was dangerous territory, in any number of ways.

"Further the Revolution?"

"Balls. The real objective is to impress Stalin and stay alive long enough to still be standing when the old bastard drops. And what impresses Stalin?"

"People who compete for his favour."

"Simpler. People to shoot. Plays to his paranoia, or his murderous fucking tendencies, I don't know. Give him a plot and he's happy as Larry."

The Broker studied the Englishman's world-weary features – the sarcastic curl of the lip, the heavy bags under the drink-glazed, seen-it-all-before eyes.

"So if the two camps are watching MERCURY, they are really watching each other?"

"And the Omitted has you watching both. It would be rather

interesting to know what it is that they all think they're going to catch the others doing. Or, given the personalities involved, what they intend to *claim* they caught the others doing."

There it was, delivered in that offhand, *gentlemanly* way. The appraisal. The admonishment. Must try harder.

The Broker shuddered.

"I do have something for you, sir," he said.

*　　*　　*

The Marsdiep was a far cry from the grand straits of the Bosphorus, yet with an early squall off the North Sea, the tide-race between the sandbanks into the Waddenzee could be heavy going. Sheltering under the *Zeemeeuw*'s half-cabin, Mila looked close to fainting again.

For Bradley, his face tilted to the rain and salt, the stomach-churning pitching of the T.E.S.O. ferry was all too reminiscent of the run-in to Omaha Beach in the Higgins boats. That was enough to send him someplace else, PDQ.

So instead of seabirds and seals – instead of airbursts and bodies – he focused his tunnel vision on a hidden alley in The Hague's Zeeheldenkwartier, and an apparently derelict mews house that was tucked away at the end of it: the de Hoogs' studio.

She had been happier that evening, just under a fortnight ago. There had been a definite spring in her step as they'd made their way on foot across the centre of town to Pep's dinner party. In an uncharacteristically devil-may-care mood, casting off the anonymous staff outfit she favoured at Nieuwe Uitleg 16, she had even dug out a dress for the occasion, a full-length gown with a figure-hugging shape that might once, they joked, have been Mata Hari's.

He had accepted her eagerness, of course. It was her sense of fun that took him by surprise. She had even insisted on bringing a bottle of White Curaçao, which he carried in his spare hand.

"Hurry up, Sergeant Bradley! We mustn't keep our art students waiting – not after their impeccable timing the other day." Far from politely holding his arm, crooked self-consciously for the purpose, she had taken it for real, propelling him along. By the time they'd located the entrance to the alley, her heels had slipped on the cobbles more than once, her hips had knocked against his, and Bradley had begun to suspect that No.16's wine cellar had already yielded up more than that one bottle of fancy liqueur.

But it hadn't all been nerves, or recklessness. Her spirited performance had charmed the wary Pep and his students, who were with a sole exception awkward young men, most of them clearly, painfully, in love with their one female colleague, a rather frosty Delilah by the name of Anouk. Generously prompting their host to regale them with tales of his audacity in the Mauritshuis, while never once stealing anyone's thunder by making anything of her own part in the scheme – and even tricking a tongue-tied American into joining in – Mila had guided them expertly through a convivial meal and precisely the sufficient quantity of digestifs to put everyone at their ease. Herself included.

Finally, under a lamp in Pep's cluttered workshop, a select few had gathered around the painting of her son.

The little ship crashed into a wave and lurched around it. With a further twist in the pit of his stomach, Bradley was dragged back to their present predicament. He looked for Mila. There were no high spirits now. She was more like another Anouk.

The memories of that evening in Pep's workshop, layered like paint with painstaking explanations and incomplete revelations, were too muddled by the drink and the persistent waves. Bradley recalled instead how they had reported the salient facts afterwards to Jones and Sloane, via a postcard to South London.

Dear Auntie Jenny,

This place! We're glad to see the back of it! It's the kind of thing you'd find next door to King's Cross (and that "ain't" what I hoped for my old Dutch trip!)

We'll be back on our tour next Thursday and in touch after that. Did you solve today's crossword? One across had us puzzled but I'm sure you found it plain sailing! Sal and Sarah

The image on the reverse of the postcard was a sepia reproduction of *The Coast near Den Helder* by Ludolf Backhuysen. When Mila had composed the message, with amused suggestions from Roger, constant interruptions from Susie and scant help from a Philistine like himself, Bradley recalled how the map had indeed made it seem an easy crossing from the naval port of Den Helder to the first island in the West Frisian chain, named Texel (though pronounced *Tessel*, all Philistines were duly informed). So much for that!

As for the rest, Mila swore blind that Jenny was a natural at deciphering such puzzles: from the property alongside King's Cross station on the *Monopoly* board – the Angel, Islington – to the confirmation of that name in the lyrics of the old music hall song, *My Old Dutch*, describing how 'Sal' or 'Sarah', the singer's beloved mate, "ain't a angel". Roger had been particularly chuffed with that one.

The painter of the *Laughing Boys*, it now seemed certain, was an Amsterdam forger who went by the professional name of 'Engel'. Following the resistance bombing of the public records office, which had delayed the Nazi pursuit of Dutch Jews and led to the execution of his friends in the art world, he had gone to ground, Pep said. On Texel.

He must have painted Mila's son there.

Bradley stole another concerned look at her. Deep in thought. Or trying not to be sick. Her good mood hadn't lasted much beyond the dinner party, although he rather thought her drinking must have done. It was plain to see that she was barely eating again.

No stranger himself to judicious juicing, he thought perhaps he understood a little of her anguish and her need to stave it off. She had been on this pursuit for so long, and at every turn, it seemed, there arose something to beat her back – as surely as this weather was preventing the ferry from making a simple crossing. To have one's excitement and anticipation rebuffed, so many times, could only leave one fearful of each new clue: doubting the raised pulse of expectation, dreading the sensation of hope.

It wasn't pessimism, like his. She still had hope. But it was getting harder and harder to endure it.

He ought to go inside, ask her how she was bearing up. There was certainly nothing to be gained by speculating whether they'd find this 'Angel', whether he might furnish them with another clue, or whether, however unlikely, Pavel would still be there on the island. Yet he could sit with her, put his arm around her. She didn't have to endure it alone.

But he thought again of that comparison he had made, of Mila and Anouk. And of his own version of hope and dread.

He could not be one of those art students.

At length the wind and tide shifted, or the plucky Deutz engine prevailed. They came into the harbour at 't Horntje. The other end of the island was only 20 kilometres away and so, as elsewhere throughout the Netherlands, rented bicycles were recommended. Bradley, however, had painful memories of those too. As they negotiated for an alternative, his thoughts turned instead to his arrival on the Cowal peninsula. Although the only motor transport turned out to be an exhausted Mercedes truck hauling blocks of stone, he was relieved to find its driver a lot less *blootered* than Darroch had been, despite the late hour, and speaking more comprehensible English.

"You'll see the damage up at the north end," he told them as he swerved round a herd of sheep. "It was so bad we haven't got around to fixing it all up."

"The damage?" Mila said.

The driver was one of those. Although she was seated between the two men, he craned his head to address Bradley instead.

"You don't know? *Tessel* is the scene of the last battle in Europe! Long after Hitler was gone and the rest of the *Moffen* had surrendered."

"They held out here?"

"They had their own war to fight! There was a garrison here. Georgians, with German officers. They rose up, killed their officers. We helped them. But you – the Allies – did not come. The Nazis sent reinforcements, and they held the coastal batteries. Everything was blasted. Everything burned. We hid as many of the Georgians as we could, but they came from house to house."

Bradley looked out of the window at flat fields and distant windmills casting long shadows. Not a place to hide out. He wondered why the Angel had chosen it.

"Then, weeks after the real war is ended, the Canadians come to disarm our Germans. Out come a few remaining Georgians, all wounded. And now the fun begins."

"What do you mean, 'fun'?"

Perhaps it was her accent. This time he answered her.

"Soviet Secret Police, in army uniform… what did they call themselves? 'SMERSh'. Our Georgians had been in a German legion. They are in Siberia now."

Mila caught Bradley's eye and shook her head in wonder. She mouthed it.

"SMERSh were here."

Gradually, the terrain changed. Pasture and hedgerows gave way to dunes and grasses. They passed rows of burned cottages and shattered concrete structures: remnants of the Atlantic Wall and the bunkers inhabited – later fought over – by its garrison. This much was evidenced by the structure on the furthermost dune, towards which the sandy road was winding. A tall, once-elegant lighthouse, still painted red but spotted liberally with shell-holes. The Georgians' last redoubt, the driver said.

"And this is it – Eierland, north of Cocksdorp?" Bradley looked at Mila. There were people to be seen: local craftsmen around the ruined cottages, with carts and donkeys, rebuilding roofs; sunburned labourers in threadbare clothing, POWs perhaps. But it didn't look as though anyone lived here.

"Hugo Kleyn?" Mila gave the forger's assumed name.

The driver switched off and hauled on the parking brake.

"The painter? He's here, or he should be. Lodged in Cocksdorp but picked up one of these ruins for a song – said it was a perfect studio."

"Which one?" She was rising in her seat to peer through the

dusty windshield.

"There. Now that's our business done. And you owe me five guilders."

That was double what he had quoted and, as far as Bradley could tell, an exorbitant price, but she had seized her purse before he could begin to remonstrate.

Though she held the note tightly, both men could see it was a 'tenner'.

"Did he ever have visitors? Was he ever seen with a young boy?"

The man reached out. Mila let go.

"I've no idea," he scoffed. "We keep ourselves to ourselves here."

Bradley heard her defeated sigh, but he registered the economical swipe of her other hand, flattened, at the edge of his perception and he reined in his reaction. They climbed down from the cab without another word, while the driver went to busy himself with his load. Had she not given Bradley the signal, the guy would have been busy picking up his teeth.

He had to take her arm again as they approached their second derelict-looking studio in as many weeks. It was a long, low barn that appeared to have been converted into a dwelling, before the battle had converted it back to a ramshackle shell. The repaired roof, a precarious-looking arrangement, was a crazy patchwork of doors and windows reclaimed from the other houses, which no doubt granted the Angel the celestial light he sought.

"You knock," Mila said, in the voice of a girl scout selling her first cookie.

Bradley swore inwardly. There was something wrong here and he had been about to pull the Tokarev from his waistband. But with Mila's anxiety stemming surely from the hope – *okay, pipe-dream* – that Pavel might be here, he could hardly blunder in brandishing a weapon.

Instead he rapped on the door with his bare knuckles, then tried the latch.

Locked.

Mila peered through a window, but it wasn't just cracked and dusty, it was whitewashed on the inside.

Before they went around to the rear, instinct made Bradley check on the work parties further along the settlement's single street. They were leading their donkey carts and prisoners away, their day's work done. In a cloud of smoke and dust, golden in the late sun beneath the cloud, the Mercedes-Benz went with them.

He turned back to her, casually raising two fingers to scratch his cheek in an only slightly odd gesture. As an honorary member of the MERCURY network, he had learned their old wartime signal. V-for-*Výstraha*.

Warning. Danger imminent.

There was a back yard filled with salvage, some of it looking very old. Essential resources, if you were a forger. The large stable door here was also barred or bolted and the slit window, though unglazed, was too narrow even for Mila. All it gave them was a view of a bare hallway.

Catching light from above was a puddle of something dark on the stones.

Bradley looked for a strip of metal to jemmy the door, but it was snugly fitted anyhow and quite immobile. He considered going back to the front and breaking the window but couldn't be sure that all the locals had departed. Then he saw Mila's urgent gesture – kicking off her heels, play-acting a leg-up.

He linked his hands to hoist her onto the roof, momentarily astonished by her lightness and agility, even in her skirt and coat. A loose section of corrugated tin rattled. An old four-pane window frame slid down the roof and Bradley caught it before it shattered in the yard.

When he looked up, she had vanished.

By the time he heard the bolts on the back door, the pistol was in his hand. No need for caution now, or not that kind of caution. The look on her face as she let him in said as much.

The hallway opened out into the well-lit studio space. Easels, canvases and loose stretchers were scattered everywhere, a few probably as a result of the girl's drop from the roof, the rest in a typical creative jumble. There was an unmade bed beneath the painted-over window at the front and an arch that must have led into a washroom of some kind. She would have checked that.

The Angel, if that was who it was, lay face-down on the stone floor, in a puddle of tacky purple-black blood. They turned him over carefully, but two shots in the back of the head, with the victim already prone, did not leave the face looking much like the newspaper photographs.

"He has paint ingrained in his fingernails and his hands smell of turpentine," Mila said. "Could be an assistant, of course, but I'd say it's him."

Her examination, though surely unpleasant, had been made easier by virtue of the fact that his wrists were bound behind his back with picture wire.

"Last night?" Her expression was unreadable.

"Most likely. He's pretty cold and stiff."

"They didn't even bother to fake an accident or suicide."

Bradley looked around.

"Or a break-in, either. He let them in. And they didn't rough him up. They weren't here to find out anything."

"Just to execute him." Mila said.

"Was it retribution? I know he supposedly worked with the resistance, but maybe he played both sides… dropped a dime on those art world buddies of his, in return for a fresh start in this place?"

She shook her head. Bradley could feel the pent-up fury and despair that slowed her words to a deliberate crawl.

"There was no feeling here, no passion. It was not personal. When you execute a traitor, you look them in the eye. But the back of the head? We know who does this."

Bradley took a moment to recover his concentration. *When you execute a traitor*, he was thinking. The voice of experience.

He rubbed the stubble on his chin.

"De Klerk and his Nazis, covering their tracks?"

She opened her fingers and showed him something she had

found under the body. A dull brass cartridge case. She tipped it into his hand. With its bottleneck shape, resembling a miniaturised rifle round, it might easily have come from a German 'Broomhandle' Mauser. But the Russian head stamp code made it Tokarev. Just like the ammo in the pistols they were carrying.

"The Soviets," he said at last.

Her mouth and jaw had set in a grim, knowing smirk – almost an unconscious mockery of the Angel's rigor mortis, and about as far now from the *Laughing Boys* as you could get.

She nodded.

"SMERSh were here again."

CHAPTER NINE

Sam Bradley had told her to take the bed while he kept watch. An old soldier, he had soon uncovered a Chesterfield armchair to make his vigil more comfortable. How had he known that it was buried there under the canvases? Mila's tense features twisted into a grudging smile. One of the unfinished paintings propped against the wall was a portrait of a local man, affectedly languid, smoking in the well-worn studio chair.

She could rest her eyes, her fears. Sam would never doze off.

But neither, of course, could she.

It wasn't just the presence of a day-old corpse, left where he had died with only a dust sheet to keep the flies off him. True, they were in sore need of a better idea than alerting the local police, having already made themselves likely suspects, to say nothing of robbing the royal gallery. But they had both slept in worse circumstances when required, and with the arrival of autumn the thick stone of the converted barn had kept the Angel relatively fresh.

It wasn't even the proximity of SMERSh, or that department's latest incarnations. Whoever had killed the forger, for whatever purpose, would surely have had ample opportunity to eliminate or capture her and Sam – here, upon their arrival, or earlier in The Hague – and had not done so. Nor, she suspected, had that attempt in Scotland been all that it had seemed. But there was no value in fretting about it. She didn't have the information to draw any conclusions.

It was this place. It was Pavel. Possibly in that very chair. Wouldn't one urge an over-active child to sit down, calm down, keep still…? How had the Angel got him to laugh so naturally?

She would never be able to ask him now.

Nor find out where de Klerk – or others – had taken him.

They could not light lamps. Moonlight flooded through the improvised skylights. Sam had seen the forlorn exhalation of smoke.

"You gotta sleep, Mila. Whatever happened has happened. Quit beating yourself up about it."

His opinion of her was higher than she deserved. She had not been considering that, but now she did.

"Did we get him killed, by coming looking for him?"

"Like those guys in Germany, last year?"

"Like those guys in Germany."

"We never found out if we were leading the killers to them or someone else was leading us, the whole lousy time. So in a way, maybe, this is like that."

And then she did close her eyes, tight. But only to wince.

"They were Nazis, evil men, murderers. This is different."

"The Angel ain't a angel, remember? Not if he was in cahoots with de Klerk."

"I suppose not. For many people, being a hero of the resistance and being a collaborator are – what is it you say? – two sides of the same coin."

"That's what we say."

She took a drag, expelling another moonlit gust to match the thin clouds passing overhead.

"Resisting, collaborating. Like fear and courage, they come and go."

She heard him breathing, pondering.

"Like hope and despair."

Her heart skipped a beat. She had no business commanding such loyalty in him. Yet she understood, on some level, that he needed to give it. It was what else he needed that eluded her.

"Yes, exactly like that."

And then, for a long time, they said nothing. The only sound was the surf beyond the dunes and, fainter still, the clanking halyards of small vessels. Mila finished her cigarette and tried to sleep.

She let out a sigh.

"If we led them here, they came on an earlier boat. So it was the postcard we sent to Jenny."

"Or Pep." Sam didn't sound very convinced.

"How would this help him? He needs to find a way to return the *Laughing Boys* and reveal that it was a fake. That's how he discredits Dr van Gelder's testimony and begins the process of freeing his father. Now we have no lead from the Angel – and a Russian hit to cover up, most likely – we can't give him the go-ahead to begin that process."

"Which also means we can't get de Klerk's SAFEHAVEN deal scrapped, to flush him out that way…"

"So it's back to what you'd call the usual suspects," she said.

"Jones. Sloane. Playing their usual games."

"Or Roger Hemsby, I suppose. We don't know his story."

A dismissive snort.

"You heard him yucking over your postcard. Roger never had the smarts to come up with that Mata Hari gag. And a safe house just around the corner from the museum, right by a bomb site, to give us ideas? It must've been Jones, from the get-go."

"You think Richard confided in him?"

"Or in Roger, who reported to Jones. Who reported to Sloane. They already knew the painting was the key – whatever their game is."

"They just needed someone off-books to steal it," Mila blinked, astonished, but not really. She could picture the look on Sam's face.

"A couple of real chumps. They were ahead of us all along."

"So they manipulate us into tracking down the Angel – and then what? They get suddenly careless with the information?"

"It's got me beat. Plus how any of this matters to the Reds. Are they trying to put *us* in the frame?"

Largely because of their present surroundings, it took her a moment to understand what he was saying. When she did, she wished she could repeat that coy line about the strange language he spoke; but there was more than gloom and dusty moonlight separating them now.

"I don't see why."

"Nor me. They could've reported us by now anyhow, and I reckon our truck driver could be persuaded to put us here before the murder, if that's what they want."

"Mmm…" She wasn't really listening. An idea had started forming far back in her mind, in one of those treacherous places she was reluctant to revisit, where loyalty counted for nothing.

Richard, set upon in the Haagse Bos.

The furniture lorry in Scotland, soon after Sam had told her everything that Sloane and Jones had revealed about de Klerk and SAFEHAVEN – so soon, in fact, as to be downright suspicious.

The body recovered from the canal at the Nieuwe Uitleg. Local gossip and rumour, but it fitted now.

The Angel of Texel, coldly executed, *made an example of…*

What Sloane had told Sam…

What had Sloane told Sam? What word had he used?

Untouchable. De Klerk was untouchable.

What if…?

It must have been the rhythmic intensity of her breathing, or perhaps her stillness. She didn't know how long had elapsed but Sam had waited patiently. She could sense him waiting now, with growing anticipation.

"There could be an explanation," she said at last. "It raises a dozen other questions, but it does explain everything."

"Go on."

"What if de Klerk wasn't just untouchable because of SAFEHAVEN – what if he's under Soviet protection too?"

Now it was Sam's turn to look at all the angles. That he took less time than she had done was a blessing, she reflected. For all the hurt that he kept bottled up, for all the guardedness and inhibition, he did not have those treacherous places to re-enter.

"Then why not us?" he said when he had followed all her

thoughts as far as he was able. "Why bother throwing us off the scent when they could just blow us away?"

"That's one of those other questions. Perhaps they don't want to alert Sloane and Jones to the fact that there *is* something to investigate..."

"You said it was SMERSh, but we both know that got broken up. Pendleton reckoned it might be the different remnants competing against each other..." She could make out his silhouette in the moonlight, rubbing its temples – then the whole head waving back and forth in incredulity. "Jumping Jesus! If one faction's bumping off anybody who gets too close to de Klerk – and the other ain't – and we're still breathing... mightn't that mean that we're also under Soviet protection?"

*   *   *

The early October sunrise took an eternity to arrive but by seven, unrested, they had consumed their last rations and were searching the studio. The No.1 priority was confirmation of the corpse's identity. The next, also by way of confirmation, to find any signs of Pavel's sometime presence here. Then it would be the big ones. Evidence of a link with de Klerk or Anselm Kuhlmann, escaped Nazi and presumed owner, though not rightful, of the authentic *Laughing Boys*. Clues that might point their way towards either. Indications of which other parties had joined the game.

The first turned out to be easy enough. Like Schim, the Angel had dabbled in self-portraiture, but where Schim's, likening himself to van Gogh, had embodied a kind of self-pitying pride, the Angel's leaned disturbingly toward self-disgust. One was signed 'H. Kleyn' and modelled, so Mila said, on the work of an artist she knew called Egon Schiele. The broken-doll pose revealed a small tattoo of a flower on the inside of his left wrist, no doubt self-administered and judiciously concealed beneath a wristwatch if required. The dead man bore the same token.

The second, remarkably, proved scarcely more problematic, though it would have a proportionately greater effect on Mila's mood. Only twenty minutes into their search, Bradley heard her give such a gasp of alarm that he feared she'd somehow spotted the local police or a team of Russian assassins coming down the path. He found her standing motionless above an overflowing steamer trunk, clutching something soft and white in clawed hands. Before he could compose his question, she had plunged her face into it and he saw that it was a stringy needle-lace collar from the olden days. He had seen it before of course, loosely fastened around the necks of the ersatz *Laughing Boys*.

"Oh dear," she said in a strange voice, when he had gone over to touch her shoulder. "Now I've got my tears on it. But Sam, I can *smell* him!"

Her eyes were bright and moist, and he noticed again how this caused individual lashes to glue together and form little starbursts. When she wrinkled a red-tinged snub nose, he returned her tentative smile. Who was he to doubt a mother's memory of her child's distinctive scent – or even that such a scent could linger sufficiently to be detected now amid the pervasive odour of paint, spirits and the thing beneath the dust-sheet by the hallway?

"Pep called it right," he grunted.

Her face crumpled again. Amid the flushed summer freckles, the white scar gleamed.

"He was here!"

Bradley was poised on the ball of one foot. He knew the proper thing was to embrace the girl. He understood that much about the need for comfort, which was sometimes more like needing someone to grab you as you teetered over an abyss. Instead, once again, he took a step back.

Members of the MERCURY network would never take such liberties. Vojtěch and Marta would not. Dušan and Emil would not. Marek would not. 'Uncle' Ludvík would not.

Miro had not. Stas had not. Josef Voda had not. Karel Sec had not. And they had given their lives for her.

Perhaps, in a way, that was the proper outcome.

At length Mila folded the lace carefully and placed it in her coat pocket. The first two clues having revealed themselves so readily, they resumed their search, hopeful of stumbling immediately on pointers to de Klerk and Kuhlmann. But after more than three hours, having gone through every scrap of paper and upended the already chaotic studio, they were each growing nervous. If the Angel or the Russians had left them anything, it was too well hidden. And time was not on their side.

Bradley steeled himself and frisked the corpse again, which left him in a bad enough mood to voice what needed to be said.

"We're gonna have to go. Get off the island. Before someone comes for him or the driver blabs..."

Mila bit her lip.

"There has to be something. We can't leave empty-handed."

"Or get caught red-handed," Bradley said, tapping the Russian pistol in his waistband. "Not with these."

And then he drew it for real and was aware of Mila drawing hers. A fist hammered at the front door. A shadow appeared at the whitewashed window.

Whether local police or Russian assassins, they were here.

*   *   *

Pressed against the solid back door, Mila trained her pistol on the place where something – an arm or a close-shaven *muzhik* head perhaps – might just appear through the slit window alongside it. As she did so she registered, in the corner of her vision, the Angel's shrouded form slide fully back into the studio and out of sight. Where Sam went to ground afterwards would be his own business, but she knew that he'd be covering the front door and window, and the hole in the roof, from in there.

It would surely all be resolved in a moment. Unless acting on a specific tip-off, the police were unlikely to force entry; the Angel had only been missing a day and there was nothing except that black, lumpy smear to raise their suspicions – hardly an alarm bell, on the floor of an artist's studio. But if they did smell a rat for whatever reason and broke the door down, she and Bradley would have to talk their way out of it: an enterprise that would no doubt involve Roger Hemsby at a minimum, as well as what he'd term a 'frightful stink' back in Whitehall and maybe even an official clamp-down on their mission. There was no way around that; they could hardly add assault of a law enforcement officer to grand larceny.

If it was the Soviet counterintelligence team – whichever bureaucratic star chamber they represented and whatever the validity of her and Sam's latest theory – any notional protection had evidently been revoked. They would have to fight or die.

But what came through the slit window turned her grim resolve into a reluctant giggle. A white handkerchief on a stick of driftwood was accompanied by a quotation from Yeats, delivered delightedly in a ragged-edged English public school drawl.

"'And what rough beast, its hour come round at last,
Slouches towards Bethlehem to be born?'"

It was 'Pat' Pendleton, announcing his Second Coming.

She kept the gun lifted, but responded in kind.

"'Surely some revelation is at hand...'"

"Let's bloody hope so, Miss Slavík, for both our sakes."

"Are you on your own?"

"Well… 'all about reel shadows of the indignant desert birds' – seagulls actually, and I think one's shat on me – but I'm unaccompanied."

"Then you'd better come in. Give me a second."

Sam Bradley had followed the exchange and was at the front door, one hand on the latch. She nodded. Putting her gun away, she made a fuss of unbolting the rear door and saw Sam slip quietly out of the front.

Pendleton had dressed the part. His shabby fisherman's attire suited the unruly hair and the dark stubble better than his Scottish outfit had done. But fishermen's eyes were bleached and boundless as the horizon. This Sambian amber held dark secrets.

She shook herself free from that lure and contrived a smile to match his harmless grin. As she looked down, she caught the blur of Sam Bradley moving into the back yard, pistol in hand. She stepped back and slightly to the side.

"Hello, Pat. How's your arm?"

"Fine, thanks. Are you inviting me in or keeping out of Sergeant Bradley's line of fire?"

Behind him, half-lowering the Tokarev, Sam muttered a curse.

"No flies on Mr Pendleton here."

"Pat, please," the Englishman turned to acknowledge him, before brushing at the shoulder of his jacket. "But as I said, I think I've a bit of bird shit on me. May I come in and have a stab at washing it off?"

"There's a pump in the yard, over there," Sam said.

"So there is. Well, may I come in anyway?" He flapped open one side of the many-patched wool jacket. "I have brought a bottle."

"Anything else in there?" Sam asked.

Mila held Pendleton's gaze.

"He has a commando knife on his right hip and a .32 Webley self-loading under his left shoulder."

"That's my girl!"

Pendleton stumbled as Sam pushed him into the hallway.

"There's a jalopy parked up the street," he said. "That yours?"

"Mmm. Mil Six's actually."

"So you're admitting it now," Mila said.

He was staring at the blood-stain.

"Think we're going to have to come clean with each other…" Appearing distracted for the first time, the superior smirk wiped from his face, Pendleton pushed past her into the studio. He knelt by the body and raised a corner of the sheet.

"'The blood-dimmed tide is loosed, and everywhere the ceremony of innocence is drowned.'" A dark cloud crossed the already swarthy features. "I suppose you found him like this last night. No sign of the sods who did for him?"

"None." Mila waited until he had replaced the sheet and stood up again; there was no hiding the smouldering anger in his eyes – the Becherovka bitters were bitter indeed and held a hint of the Angel's self-observed self-loathing. "Was he one of yours?"

"In a manner of speaking."

"And that's you coming clean?" Sam scoffed.

Seizing something from his pocket, Pendleton shrugged out of his coat and tossed it onto the chair. Beneath, over a grimy undershirt, he wore a shoulder holster. In his hand was a half-bottle of Jenever.

"Dutch courage…" he pulled a sheepish face and then took a slug, wincing. "You ask if the Angel here was an asset of ours and my answer is no, except as an experiment. He was an innocent, and I fed him to the beasts."

Mila accepted the bottle.

"How did you do that, Pat?"

"A better question might be why. We live in mixed-up times, Miss Slavík. In our world – *my* world – things have very definitely fallen apart and the centre cannot hold. The falcon cannot hear the falconer. Or he finds he's been working for a completely different falconer all along…"

Grimacing, she passed the bottle to Sam. They were still standing over the corpse, but that didn't seem to matter now.

"*Mere anarchy is loosed upon the world,*" she quoted.

Pendleton nodded appreciatively.

"That's the idea, you see. Sow mistrust. Paralyse everything. The Jerries did it to us here in Holland during the war – and out in the Balkans, my old stamping ground. Now the Sovs are doing the same."

"You're talking about doubling agents," Sam said.

"Give the boy another coconut! And tripling them and God knows what. We need to find out which falcons are working for the wrong falconer, and if they even know it. And vice versa of course. But how do you do that, when they're all out there, 'turning and turning in the widening gyre'…?"

"You conduct an experiment?" Mila said.

"You conduct an experiment. You feed certain key people discrete bits of information and you keep your beady eye on where it goes and what happens next. Among the more radiographically-minded in our profession, it's termed a 'barium meal'. The poor Angel here was the second helping, I'm afraid."

"And what was the first?" Sam demanded.

"You were," Pendleton said. "Both of you."

Mila kept her eye on Sam.

"That's why you were there on the spot in Scotland," she said to Pat. "Equipped with surprisingly accurate intel and your .32 Webley self-loading."

"That toy!" Sam exploded. "He thinks it's a game. And he could have got us killed."

"I'm the one who got bloody shot! And I took them out!"

"One of them. *She* took the other – and saved your ass doing it!"

"All right, Sam." Mila threw him a stern look which she knew would put him in his place, if only because it was a place he desperately, inexplicably, coveted. "I assume you arranged for someone to leak the Angel's location to the Soviets. Why? Because he was our next port of call?"

"Yah. That's what they want, you see – to keep you from tracking down de Klerk."

"We'd surmised as much. So you intercepted our postcard to Miss Simmonds? Please don't say 'in a manner of speaking' again or I shall let Sergeant Bradley shoot you."

"Then I won't say that. Nor – given my shameful poetic outbursts a moment ago – that we're all on the same side. Although we are."

"And that side is…?"

"The falcons who are still loyal to their original falconers. The falconers who still look out for their original falcons."

"And these are not defined by the organisations they represent but as individuals…"

"On both sides of the pond."

Sloane and Jones, she thought. Again.

"The problem being," she said. "That these individuals are defined by you."

"I can see how it looks like that."

"So you're going to have to work harder to win our trust, Pat. Such as by telling us who you leaked the intel to."

"I can't do that. None of the names in the chain would mean anything to you in any case. But I can tell you the likely recipient."

"Beria?"

"Good guess. No, Abakumov, actually. He has more or less taken control of all internal and foreign intelligence."

"The former head of SMERSh," Sam said. "We thought as much."

"You clever devils!" Pendleton's smirk was back.

"So Beria…" Sam began, giving her her cue.

"…is the one keeping us alive. I wonder why, mmm, Pat?"

"OK, OK… We don't know for certain, but it looks like Beria and Secretary Malenkov are trying to expose whatever it is that Abakumov is up to with de Klerk and his nefarious cohort…"

"Anselm Kuhlmann," Mila said. Pendleton's eyes widened.

"Busy bees! No wonder Abakumov's people were trying to shut you down. And no wonder Beria's want you buzz-buzz-buzzing around a while longer!"

"But you don't know where and what it is, his business with de Klerk and Kuhlmann. Or you wouldn't tell us if you knew?"

"I actually might… If I knew, and if I had authority."

With the teasing mood restored, there was something disrespectful about their pacing vigil around the martyred Angel. Mila took the remains of the Jenever and crossed to the piles of unframed canvases on their stretchers.

"Here's what doesn't make sense to me," she said. "You were prepared to sacrifice *him* – OK, that I get – but if you *actually* want to find out what they're up to, you burned your own lead. Or did you?"

Picking up on her cue this time, Sam resumed the role of the heavy, as last played in the cramped cell at the Orange Hotel. Snatching the gun from its shoulder holster, he gave Pendleton a hefty shove and sent him staggering into the Chesterfield. From the grace with which the latter accepted this, she suspected that he too was playing a part, but that didn't matter now either.

"When did you arrive here, Pendleton?" Sam said with loaded breeziness.

"On Texel?"

"No, here. This place," Mila said.

"I followed you – in fact I fell behind. Problems with the 'jalopy', Bradley. Otherwise I'd have been here yesterday to watch over you, like in Scotland. And incidentally, I'm very far from being the only one following you, you know…"

She could think about that later. For now Mila had other fish to fry – or other fishermen.

"Nice try. But let's narrow it down to two alternative scenarios. One, you came here in time to speak to the Angel and find out what he knew. Two, you arrived after he'd been killed but you got in – the same way as us – and you found the clue we've been looking for."

Pendleton shook his head.

"Neither of those scenarios accounts for why I'd be happy to sacrifice him in the first place. He might not have told me anything, or I might not have found a clue."

"No, but you did get it, didn't you? And I didn't say you were happy to sacrifice him. I saw the look on your face when you pulled back the sheet. So you hadn't seen him dead. You visited him before Abakumov's people came."

Pendleton said nothing for a moment. Then he looked at Sam.

"She's really very good indeed, isn't she? A great loss to the Service… Yah, all right, I met the poor bugger just before they got to him. Not the most depressing experience of my life but certainly not one I intend to dine out on. He didn't tell me anything. Too afraid of de Klerk, more fool him."

"Then why can't you help looking like… what does he look like, Sam?"

"Like the cat that ate the canary."

It's a strange language…

"Like the cat that ate the canary," she said. "You found something, didn't you?"

"It isn't much."

"Show us!"

Pat bristled.

"If you keep pointing that TT-33 at me, Bradley, I'll show you a new place to put it." He gave his best disarming smile, which was also, Mila reflected, very good indeed. "The Angel and I shared a bottle of wine. I thought it might calm his nerves. It didn't, as I said, but it improved my mood. I started taking an interest in his paintings."

"We've seen them," Sam said. "The portraits."

"I meant the landscapes," Pat waved a hand. At intervals around the walls hung charcoal sketches and watercolours depicting flat fields, rolling dunes and empty wave-tossed shores.

"Texel," Mila said idly. "Pep said all forgers are closeted crowd-pleasers."

"You're not looking," Pat said in the voice, once again, of her old instructors.

She looked. Hedgerows. Horses. Fishing boats drawn up on the sands.

A pointed hill. Almost conical. No such feature existed on the island.

"And here…" Pat rose and from underneath a set of drawers dragged out a warped portfolio tied up with string. Inside were dozens of sketches, all of them of the strange conical hill. "I found these while he was throwing up outside."

"It doesn't look anything like the Netherlands."

"No. But I'll tell you what it does look exactly like…" He leant into the washroom and brought out an empty wine bottle. A drawing of the hill was on the label.

"This is the bottle we polished off. My guess is he received a case in grateful payment for illustrating it. It must have been one of his few legal commissions."

"A commission from whom?"

"Well, who do we know he worked for…? And this wine, which as you can see purports to be a Cabernet Sauvignon, hails not from Bordeaux but from Cape Province in the Union of South Africa."

"A South African wine?"

"Going to be a big thing, apparently. French production rather fell behind in recent years. See below the name of the estate, 'Boschkop', where a few lines of the drawing resume? It's a signature, of sorts, but not the Angel's, of course. A cheeky proprietary nickname, perhaps? I'm told they're not uncommon among the recent immigrant winegrowers there. *Dutchie.*"

"Schim told us that was de Klerk's handle in the States." Bradley said.

"He probably picked up some good import/export contacts there."

Mila was frowning.

"It's a bit of a stretch."

"It would be, I grant you. Except believe it or not Mil Six has an even better intelligence registry section than the hat counter at Arding & Hobbs. And I've just discovered that de Klerk makes regular trips to South Africa. Even managed to do so during the war. Someone involved in SAFEHAVEN kept that gen from seeing the light of day."

"No wonder your jalopy broke down," she said. "Those Mark III wireless sets can drain the battery in next to no time."

"So I'm told."

"Is that where he has disappeared to? Is that where he's taken my son?"

"We don't know. If he has, then this time he travelled under a different name. But our Nazi-hunting colleagues say there's a distinct possibility that Kuhlmann skipped to South Africa too. What with the locals down there speaking a version of Dutch and German, it might have its appeal for anyone wishing to blend in. Not to mention the fact that half of them will actively side with anyone against the Brits – ask the ship's captains who got torpedoed as soon as they snuck out of port. Or perhaps the silly sod just misspelled 'South America' on his emigration forms…"

"And where exactly is this Boschkop estate?"

"That's the thing, the hill's not called Boschkop and it doesn't look like that. That's very much an artist's impression. The vineyard is actually on the back of a much bigger pointy hill, small mountain really, name of Chapman's Peak, right down below

Cape Town on the Cape peninsula. Mil Six has more than its fair share of oenophiles, as you can imagine, and they're not even convinced that anyone could grow the black grape on those slopes. It's possible the whole shebang's a front. However, there's definitely a mansion on the site, well off the beaten track. Kind of place one might hide oneself away and hang one's stolen pictures – but then you'd know all about that."

She peered into the amber. The flicker of humour had returned. But what else lurked in there?

"It seems you do too."

"I told you, Miss Slavík, we're all on the same side. Some of us."

She laughed – infected by that flicker – but nastily.

"That's you in a nutshell isn't it? All of you."

Pendleton ran a hand through his hair.

"*Touché*. But unbeknownst to you we've been tidying up after the pair of you ever since Scotland. The last thing anyone needs is you and Bradley getting your collars felt."

"You can't monitor who's on our tail if the authorities are too…"

Another glance of respect. A shrug.

"Why make things hard for ourselves?"

"So if you keep the authorities off our backs long enough for us to make another trip – to South Africa, say – are we going to be another of your barium meals?"

He swivelled to face Sam Bradley, then back to her. Studying them. Gauging them. No, more like giving them a last once-over, as one might check a weapon one had already reassembled and reloaded for the next sortie.

"If you'll pardon the analogy, Miss Slavík, we were thinking more of an aggressive purgative this time."

CHAPTER TEN

This time he was gratified to find the other party had arrived early at the blighted coffee house on the Ringstrasse. The fellow had even set up the board for their return match.

The Omitted shrugged off the waiter's hands as they attempted to guide his shaky progress between the tables. In the kind of German that caused the locals to soil themselves in memory of their interminable interrogations at the war's end, he said quietly:

"Touch me again, idiot, and I'll break both your shitty knees with this stick."

The Broker rose and unfussily pushed back the chair, his brief smile of invitation judged to perfection.

The Omitted, who preferred the unsettling effects of noncompliance, remained standing.

Could this one even be unsettled, though? There was increased confidence in his manner, compared with last time and the time before that. Such a transformation might partly be explained by his growing familiarity with his contact's mask and hands – or rather his lessening horror. But not entirely.

A curious appellation, 'Broker'. Presumably he'd chosen it himself, as had Stalin with his laughably inappropriate 'Koba'. (An irresistible image popped into the Omitted's mind of that great defender of the poor struggling through Kazbegi's novel with lips and moustache moving, *while missing the whole fucking point of it.*) Not everyone, after all, had their anonyms thrust upon them by virtue of the enforced erasure of their identity. And in this case, of course, it suited the man it represented, far better than

Stalin's vain evocation of a literary folk hero ever did. The habitual middle-man, working for all parties and none – the ultimate agent.

"Would you prefer a different table?" the smarmy bastard suggested at last, evidently unruffled. "Or perhaps you'd rather face the other way…"

"How would you know which way I'm facing?"

Tiring abruptly of his underwhelming dramatics, the Omitted collapsed into the waiting chair like a sheared off marionette. With a clatter, he set his cane against the partition and then attempted to reposition a chess piece he had disturbed.

The Broker cleared his throat. The cheeky sod was invoking the touch-move rule. Increased confidence didn't even come close!

By chance, it was the white Queen's Knight he had replaced; therefore, he must now play the unfashionable Baltic opening.

"Very well. Knight to Queen's Bishop three… well go on, you horseradish, make my move for me!"

Smoothly, the Broker did as bidden. There being no clock, he kept his hand hovering over the board and countered with the obliquely mirrored move of his King's Knight.

The Omitted leaned closer.

"Interesting response."

"I thought I'd open things up a little. Maybe have a look at this colour complex theory of yours."

"No agitation without exposure…" To give himself time to think, his next utterance was not a move, nor another pompous quotation from Lenin, but an apparently casual remark. "How was Istanbul?"

"Byzantine."

It was all the Omitted could do not to laugh out loud. The balls on this one!

"You ought to be more careful," he said, holding his gaze until the man's eyes lowered to the slit beneath the mask. "I used to have a lip like yours."

They played the next few moves in silence, save the curt

descriptive instructions. Their game had developed into the Italian Four Knights, transposing into some variation of a Petrov gambit. A draw looked likely. Neither player was giving the board his full concentration.

"The Resident asked after you," the Broker said.

I'm sure he did.

"Yes?"

"He was curious about the nature of the Dutch connection. With your own state organs and their representatives, I mean."

"It's certainly a puzzle. What did you tell him?"

"What we agreed."

"Good. And the British and Americans?"

"The same. Of course, they are conducting their own investigations..."

"Of course. But they're still unaware of my – *our* – involvement?"

The Broker nodded. Then his expression darkened. For a moment the Omitted thought he might be brooding over the game, but that would have been uncharacteristically artless. This Romanov eagle had enough faces for both of them.

"There's something else. Someone new watching the MERCURY team."

"You mean apart from our two opposing factions?"

"*Da.*" The man's natural impatience was showing through. When all was said and done, it required a healthy (or unhealthy) dose of arrogance to pull off a job like his, and that, the Omitted knew only too well, had a habit of expressing itself in restless annoyance, with everyone. "Yes. Apart from your people, who want her dead, and your other people, who kept her alive, and us – *you* – kicking the whole game off in the first place by getting me to downgrade the kill order to an incompetent snatch... A new faction, or at least it's only recently we've spotted them. Just before Texel, in fact."

"That sounds rather slack."

"When you're watching for watchers, one watcher looks much like any other. To the average watcher."

"I haven't retained you to provide average watchers."

"You haven't retained me at all."

"Point conceded. So who might these new ones be?"

"That's the funny thing, they appear to be common gangsters."

If what passed for skin, stretched tight across what remained of his facial muscles, had not been *crawling*, all the time – and if the end result of that had not been permanently hidden, for everyone's sakes – the Omitted might well have joined his opponent in pulling faces.

Since his return – his incomplete return – from his enforced absence, he had acquainted himself with the MERCURY woman's activities during the intervening period, which in addition to the brazen insult to Comrade Abakumov's MGB had included a run-in with London's criminal fraternity. He had even hoped that in employing Glasgow gangsters instead of Party assets to carry out the initial operation against MERCURY, he would spark some escalation that might help to reveal Abakumov's schemes, among others', including those of the British and Americans. Now it looked as though that strategy was about to bear fruit, if only because the more rats that joined the chase, the easier it became to pick off one or two.

Moreover, should the whispers of a link between that criminal fraternity and what the Broker had termed the 'Dutch connection' prove to have substance, this might present an opportunity to reveal any such affiliations. Unless, of course, the whispers themselves had emanated from the Broker and his slippery associate in the Istanbul bazaars… because as anyone who had haunted sufficient darkened alleyways could tell you, that was the thing about whispers: it was very hard to pin down what direction they had come from.

Another concern was the timing. If the gangsters had been on her tail from the outset and had only just now betrayed themselves to the watchers, might that not mean they were ready to step out of the shadows? If so, that was a complication. Did they not understand the touch-move rule? This was supposed to be the agitation phase, not the time for exposure.

"*Häferlkaffee. Zwei.*" He addressed the lurking waiter, before returning his attention to the game. "Now then… what are you playing at?"

*   *   *

With the arrival of summer, the flame trees of Southern Rhodesia had burst into an inferno of orange and red. Out here in the sprawling farm country near Sinoia however, the blood-tinged cloud to the east was not blossom but dust; and it was bearing down on them rapidly.

Perched on the folded roof of the 'Sixty Two' convertible, with their dusty shoes on the leather swathe of the rear seat and their pre-emptive sundowners in hand, Jimmy Lonsdale and Dominic Franzetti exchanged a look.

"One a yours, Dom?"

The dapper Italian-American studied the way the approaching vehicle, distorted in the heat haze, was bouncing over the terrain and twisted his lips dismissively.

"All-a mine have this now," he patted the leather-trimmed bulkhead of his enormous Cadillac. "Independent coil spring, 'ydraulics…"

Lonsdale nodded and turned to the third man, a stocky figure in over-tight short-sleeved safari shirt and shorts. 'Willi' Nohl, who had been propped against the open driver's door like a garden gnome, set down his gin and tonic, smeared the strands of greasy black hair across his shiny pate and went around to the open trunk, reappearing a moment later with a long gun. This was equipped with a telescopic sight but was no hunting piece. That was not the nature of Nohl's business. With a foldaway bipod, an enormous muzzle brake and a large magazine hanging off to one side that made it look more like a machine gun, it was a Nazi paratrooper rifle. And a sales sample, of course.

Beefy arms held its considerable weight motionless as he put his eye to the scope. In the German accent that he insisted was Swiss, Nohl said:

"It is your man. Parsons. And he has not seen the *donga*."

Jimmy Lonsdale winced. The terrain here was barren-looking, dotted with small, flat-topped trees and clumpy grass that appeared to offer scant sustenance for the occasional skeletal cow or wandering antelope. To the west, towards Sinoia, there were extensive tobacco plantations, worked by imported coolies, as well as by the local Mashona tribespeople. Maybe this poorer land was given over to sustain the Mashona, or there was some sort of crop rotation system in operation. He was a city boy and uninterested in people's vegetable patches. But it didn't take a local to grasp that even up here on the plateau between the Zambesi and the Limpopo, the rivers only flowed during the rainy season, which was only just beginning, and the rest of the year they were dried-up beds, hardly distinguishable from the plains. Parsons, barely in control of Lonsdale's speeding Humber Hawk, was heading straight for one of these: a nameless offshoot of the Doondo that marked the edge of the farm.

Before anyone could react, before the expensive-sounding thud reached their eardrums, car and man stopped dead and vanished in a fresh eruption of dust.

Stowing their drinks, they slid back into their seats, Franzetti behind the wheel. What Lonsdale did know, because Franzetti had told them both, multiple times, was that the Cadillac had the same engine as the M-24 tank, and those things were *fast...* Within a minute they were at the *donga*, where a shaken Parsons was extracting himself from the Humber and brushing himself down.

Lonsdale couldn't bear to look at the front of his car. He spotted the Nazi rifle on the front seat of Franzetti's and snatched it up.

"You got a deaf wish, Vic?"

"I fink I'm alright, guv. Just shaken up a bit."

How did one cock this thing? Like a machine gun. The noise didn't half get Parson's attention. He turned pale.

"I 'ad to find you quick, guv. I been in Salisbury, on the blower to the blokes back 'ome. I dashed back to the 'ouse, but you wasn't there."

What had Nohl called it? Selective fire. Lonsdale tilted the gun and turned the lever to D for *Dauerfeuer.*

"It's the MERCURY bird, guv, and 'er… American. We picked them up again. But guv, we must've missed *them* investigating *us* or something…"

Reluctantly, he flicked on the safety and propped the gun on his shoulder. This did indeed sound important enough to warrant a madcap chase across the highveld. Not to mention being a little bit tasty for the ears of Nohl and Franzetti. But there was sweet FA he could do about that now.

"Well spit it out, Vic."

"They was in 'olland, guv, like we thought – but now they're on the move again."

"Going where?"

"That's just it. It looks like they're coming 'ere!"

Handing the gun to Nohl, Lonsdale clambered off the car and down into the ditch. Parsons had his widow out again and was dabbing at a bleeding nose. It was all widows and claret with the both of them, these days. Weakness. At least the wanker had clocked the need to lower his Rolls at last.

"Sorry guv," he continued in a murmur, his widow masking his lips. "We've 'ad word they're booked on the next 'Flying Dutchman' out of Schiphol, Amsterdam, landing at Tunis, Kano, Léopoldville and Jo'annesburg! I mean… 'part from the first part, that's the way I come 'ere – then the Central flight via Bulawayo to Salisbury."

"Booked when, Vic? When do they depart?"

"This coming Wednesday, and what is it now, Monday?"

"And a day per leg, yeah?"

"That's what they normally do. Weather permitting. They can do the Central flight in one day though, if they got a connection booked, which we ain't found out yet, or I s'pose they could charter something…"

"So if they get to Jo'burg Sunday, they could be here a week today."

121

Parsons half-gestured apologetically towards the mangled Humber.

"That's why I was 'urrying, guv..." With the bloodied rag pinching at his swollen nose again, his words were pathetically distorted, like some snotty street-kid's. Jimmy pulled out his own widow.

"'ere, for God's sake, put that on it."

Parsons took the embroidered handkerchief gratefully and blew into it instead. Jimmy rolled his eyes.

"But what we gonna do, guv?"

"I know what you're gonna do, Vic. You're gonna sort yourself out and then you're gonna sort out my motor too and meet me back at Franzetti's gaff."

"'ow'm I gonna do that?"

"'ow do I know? Get some o' the darkies to tow you out with their oxen. That ain't my problem, Vic. Thanks to you I got another one to fix, ain't I?"

"An' 'ow you gonna do that?"

Clambering back up the side of the *donga*, cursing his shortness of breath and dreading the coming wet season, Jimmy Lonsdale did not bother replying. Parsons was another bloody mosquito or tsetse fly, most of the time, and he wiped his mind of him to concentrate on the things that really mattered now. Two things, both of which came with their own element of dread. The first was the clear acceptance that despite his precautions he had no option now but to let Franzetti and Nohl in on this and, worse, to ask for their help. The second was more vague and even harder to admit, but it was there alright. A chill, deep inside, like the malaria. A harbinger, possibly, of something just as deadly.

She had come for his brother. And now she was coming for him.

Willi Nohl stood by the Cadillac where he had left him. He raised an eyebrow.

"Trouble?"

"It's nothing. I'll take care of it." Lonsdale caught Franzetti's eye in the huge rear view mirror. "I'll tell you about it back at your ranch house."

Franzetti nodded. *Good.*

Willi was more of a showman, of course. He had been keeping an eye on three kudu which had emerged tentatively from the cover of the thorn trees a few hundred yards away: two adults, the bull with his full, spiralling horns, and a juvenile, grazing. In one fluid, startling movement, Nohl lifted the paratrooper rifle and flattened the group with a burst of automatic fire. A leg kicked several times as the dust settled and the sound of the shots echoed across the savanna. Then nothing.

"We will help you out," he said.

*   *   *

The ranch, located near the Rowdy Boys drift on the Hunyani, was owned by one of Sinoia's Italian families, but Franzetti had quickly replicated Lonsdale's cuckoo routine with 'Dickie' Daylesford. Sinoia had been founded by an Italian, Lieutenant Guidotti, who had invited other wealthy Italians from the Cape to join the settlement, and these had been followed recently by poorer folk who'd been captured in Italian Somaliland and held at the Gatooma internment camp for the duration. But they were all of them civilised, or thought themselves so, as Daylesford had – no match for a man like Dominic Franzetti.

He had come out with the rest of Lucky's capos to explore opportunities for gambling franchises in Southern Rhodesia (South Africa, it was rumoured, being on the cusp of swinging the other way under the influence of the Calvinist nationalists). Putting a little distance between oneself and the wives and sweethearts was a regular recreational necessity, they'd explained to Jimmy, even if here it also necessitated developing an appetite for the dark shanks. But when Lucky had returned to house arrest in Naples, and the other Genovese family delegates to America, Franzetti had stayed on. Jimmy wasn't sure to what extent he represented his own, as opposed to the Genoveses' interests, nor did he really understand what had happened at their previous get-together in Havana, which a few months ago appeared to have resulted in the tragic demise of one of their beloved associates. However, it was clear that Franzetti was eager to explore opportunities beyond the establishment of a casino and the acquisition of a gambling licence. That was why Jimmy had introduced him to another business acquaintance, Willi Nohl, and why they had been out on the edge of the property today, examining sales samples.

Now he was going to have to wade deeper into this nest of vipers.

"This is my kinda country," Franzetti was saying as the staff served the evening meal, a braised venison curry. "Chartered as a private enterprise by your Queen Victoria, and ruled by a private company!"

"A white man's paradise," Nohl agreed, raising his glass.

"A businessman's paradise."

"'course it's a British colony now," Lonsdale shrugged. "We gotta be seen to follow the rules…"

"Who gives a *fig* about them, eh?" Franzetti made an abrupt gesture with his thumb protruding between his fingers. "Jimmy, my friend, you sit at my table, your problems are my problems – that's the only rule that matters."

"That's awful decent of you, Dom…"

Lonsdale tried a piece of meat. The curry was nearly strong enough to mask the gaminess, but not quite. The flavour, he knew, was an acquired taste. Some called it richer or wilder, but to him it was the taste of vigorous life ripped violently to shit: the taste of sudden death.

Then Franzetti leaned over and speared a piece from his plate.

"All I ask is I get a little share. Just a bite. Just a bite." He was smiling broadly while he chewed, the sauce running down the side of his lips. "Now, your problem… it ain't the normal woman trouble?"

"It ain't." With one eye on the shamefaced Parsons – daring him to contradict the decidedly potted version of the story he was telling – Jimmy outlined the basics for Franzetti, Nohl and the third danger-man, Franzetti's silent counsellor, who went by the apparently ill-suited name of 'Sparky' Scintilia. Suspecting that no one of Italian ancestry would understand his inaction in the wake of his brother's death, he left out all reference to Gerry, instead emphasising Bradley's murderous activities in Sicily and suggesting that the woman had played a part in them.

"But my friend… you speak of Don Ciccio, in Castelmola? His first-born son, cut down like a dog – why did you not tell us this before? After the Don's decline, his brother in America swore revenge. He has been looking for this man."

"Well now he's found him."

"And this woman? She wants her own revenge?"

"We were involved in breaking up her organisation. She's angling to break up ours."

"Another loose end! Well, now we gonna snip it off."

"You get it that I ain't got the manpower here…"

Franzetti raised a hand and shook his head. He swapped a look with the lugubrious Scintilia.

"Nothing's gonna happen here. We gonna intercept them *en route*, that's the way."

Out of the blue, Nohl chimed in with one word.

"Léopoldville."

Scintilia permitted himself an appreciative wince.

Franzetti laughed.

"You know the place? *Bene!* We also have connections in the Belgian Congo." He was looking at the 'Swiss' with renewed interest. "Tell me, sir – I'm sensing that your market extends beyond Southern Africa?"

Nohl regarded Lonsdale, who gave a hesitant nod.

"That is correct."

"In which case, I imagine that your customers include our kosher brethren, who I believe are by far the biggest buyers in the market at present?"

It was Lonsdale who took over answering.

"They got something going, yeah."

"They do indeed!" Franzetti flashed another look at his *consigliere* and received another miserable pout. "I tell you something, between friends. Your recent house guest, Lucky, used to have a *cumpari* who was also *ebreo*, a Jew, yes? We call him Bugsy, but never to his face. You heard of him."

It was not a question. Nor did it require an answer, not in their world, where the organisation that Siegel, Lansky and Luciano had founded had become the prototype and paradigm for all collaborative underworld undertakings: Murder, Incorporated.

Franzetti pushed aside his plate and took his time over lighting a fat cigar.

"Bugsy is a good friend of mine also. And when he sees what's happening to the 'righteous' in Palestine – by which he means his people being set upon by the A-rabs, not the other times when it's the other way round – he asks me to help put swords in their hands, by which he don't mean swords. Which I am happy to do, via Norfolk shipyard and by air via Sicily."

"I have heard something about this," Nohl said.

"You betcha. Now I ain't saying it's why Bugs got his brains blasted onto his couch and his eye onto the rug, but I am saying this kinda put a crimp on the whole operation. Which is a pity, 'cause there's fellas would wish to see it continue. One thing we like even less than rats in our business is Commie rats, and they're a-sniffing round those A-rabs like flies, same as in Cuba."

Lonsdale caught Nohl's eye. When he put his mind to it, it wasn't hard to signal *No, or else*. Especially if you'd just experienced another chill at the thought of certain people finding out who was bankrolling the Zionist transaction.

"That sounds like something we might be able to help you with," he said.

Franzetti clapped his hands, summoning a manservant with a bottle of Marsala.

"Well hell, then let's solve your li'l problem. I reckon Willi here knows plenty about air movements in and out of Léo, am I right? So what's this 'Flying Dutchman'?"

"It is the regular K.L.M. flight. They use a four-engine DC-4."

"Which will be a backwards conversion from one of our C-54 Skymasters. Trust me, I know 'bout this stuff. I bet there's

American ground crew out there at Ndolo to keep them R-2000s turnin'. And any American who's taken that gig in that shit-hole has either a powerful reason not to go home or a powerful need for dough. Makes them my kinda people."

It was Vic Parsons, who Jimmy had assumed was too bruised and exhausted to do anything but eat and drink, who got it out first.

"Beggin' your pardon but you ain't seriously talkin' about crashin' a plane?"

From the way Franzetti chose to stare at him, not Parsons, Lonsdale knew he'd be expecting punishment to be exacted for the impertinence. Poor old Vic! Then the Italian's face split into a broad, white-toothed grin.

"Course not! What do you people take me for? But we oughta be able to have the plane grounded with an engine fault – have the passengers disembarked and put up someplace. Willi here knows people. So do I. And I know the going rate to get the *Force Publique* on our side. They'll make sure for us."

"Sure of what?" Jimmy asked with a shiver.

"Sure that Bradley and the MERCURY woman never leave the Congo alive."

INTERLUDE

From the bone place behind the big barn he can see the *Puffpuff* sometimes. A shiny flash, and the spaced-out smoke – poof – poof – poof – so quick, but so far away.

The spooky sound it makes in summer time when the wind is from the south.

Then it is past.

Sometimes he sees a dust devil, wandering like an *Alki* all over the desert between the dry yellow grass.

But today it is a car coming.

He takes the skull of the baby baboon and removes it from the front of the long train of sheep bones. Now it is not a locomotive, calling, calling, like when you first hear the air raid sirens in the dark. Now it is a…

Squinting through the wobbly air. Still too far away to make it out.

Auto Union streamliner, he thinks. As he makes the motor noise with his lips, the skull carves through the hot sand and skids wide into a cooler bank of ash.

Bernd Rosemeyer at the Nürburgring. He has seen a picture of him in a book.

Ach! though – in all the drama, the ash has come over the sides of his tackies and he will have the gritty powder between his toes. Painstakingly, he unlaces the rubber-soled shoes and brushes off his feet. Now his feet are safe but the palms of his hands are as black as a *kaffir*'s.

Except that is how his *Vati* talks and his *Vati* is stupid and not his *Vati* at all. If he used his eyes and he played and he worked with the boys on the farm… If he joined in with the thrill and the craziness of jumping on the ostriches and pinning them down – four, five boys a bird – until you can pull the old money bag over their heads and their necks to quieten them… If instead of bossing around the builders or sitting with his pictures he went out into the desert to trap hares with Klaas, who is from the donkey cart people and the bushmen before them – and the first people of all people before them… he would see that no matter how copper-brown and wrinkly his face is, the palms of his hands are pale and bright.

The boy goes back to his collection of spine-bones and skulls. On a whim he throws one of the sheep bones hard against the back of the barn. He expects it to shatter, but it does not. Perhaps it is a fossil, an unopenable remembrance of another time.

I wish, he thinks…

I wish I had something alive, unlike these bones, unlike those pictures. I wish I had a *Wauwau*. Like Klaas and Hintsa. Like that man by the funny canal with *Oom* Maxi, before we had to come here on the big ship. That *Wauwau* was friendly. I was afraid but it wanted to be my friend.

Ach! again. They say that here too, especially Meneer Van Rensburg. *Ag, ag, ag.* And *Eina!*, Ow!, it hurts.

Something sharp under his bare foot. Probably just a stone, not a nail, not a piece of broken glass or china, nor all your toys and dolls shattered, nor a blackened twist of bomb, not here. But it has brought him around enough to notice that the car is closer, and turning onto the track up to the farm.

It's only a dusty blue Oldsmobile. But any car is rare enough.

Sneak up to the corner of the barn, still barefoot on the hot stones, *Eina! Eina!*

I can be that *Wauwau*… Down on hands and knees where no one will look, sniffing, peeking round the corner.

Meneer Van Rensburg's men are at the door to the homestead, with their guns. The Oldsmobile pulls up to the stoep and two more men get out. They are the same as Meneer Van Rensburg's men, even though they keep their pistols hidden. Men in everyday clothes who look like they'd prefer to be in their uniforms. Now *Vati* is coming out, with the lady who is definitely not his *Mutti*. They smile and raise their hands to greet the visitor who is climbing slowly out of the car.

Their smiles are lies. Their bright, clean palms are lies.

He hears their nervous laughter and lip-reads the joke between them – also a lie, although he remembers it from when he was little.

"Lernt schnell Russisch!"

They are joking about the letters on the old air-raid shelters: LSR for *LuftSchutzRaum*. Which the grown-ups used to say meant 'Learn Russian Quickly', especially when they were slurring and swearing and wandering like dust devils too.

Why they find it funny now – and not funny, also – he doesn't understand.

He doesn't understand any of these people.

I wish I *was* a *Wauwau* – I'd run over there with a big snarl and rip their shitty throats out!

And I wish… I wish I had…

Stepping back over the thoughts and the half-thoughts, even as he steps back over the sharp-edged, sun-cracked stones to the safety of the sand and the bone place…

Eina!, Ow!, it hurts.

PART TWO

AFRICA

CHAPTER ELEVEN

Forty-four passengers. One steward. One stewardess. Four flight crew, including a spare wireless operator to maintain round-the-clock contact. The crew were all Dutch, the passengers a mixed bag. With Europe half-broken – and thoroughly broke – all manner of people were leaving to make new lives, in Australia, the Americas and in Africa.

There were Dutch and Afrikaners bound for the Transvaal, as well as British who were connecting for Southern Rhodesia or Durban; more British were staying on the flight for the Cape. There were Belgians set to disembark at Léopoldville to commence postings there, and Congolese *Évolués* returning home to practise what the Belgians had preached. Several on the manifest appeared to be young couples seeking a fresh start, such as the pair in Seats 5 and 6 above the leading edge of the port wing. Occupying all four seats of a row in the mid-section, there was even a dark-haired, German-speaking family with two teen-aged daughters who, it was rumoured among the other passengers, had survived the war in hiding as 'U-Boats' and were now *en route* for Brazil, but they kept themselves to themselves, as well might the habitually submerged. And speaking of habits, there was 'Mother Superior', the stern-faced Norbertine canoness travelling alone in Seat 42 by the passenger door and the way through to the galley and the men's and ladies' lounges.

Any one or more of them, with the possible exception of the two teen-agers and the middle-aged nun, might be Soviet informers or agents.

But Bradley didn't think so. Neither did Mila. In the departure tent at Schiphol – and then during the *Schiedam*'s extended refuelling stop in North Africa which, combined with favourable winds, had removed all need to set down in Nigeria – they had subtly observed and interrogated their fellow passengers, coming to the conclusion that it was more likely the Russians had radioed ahead to draft their local assets into the surveillance. In which case, those waiting at Kano would have been disappointed, but in Léopoldville, they'd be on their toes.

Lowering his gaze from the insubstantial alps that stretched out beyond the two droning props, he marvelled at the small head asleep on his good shoulder. *The young couple…* He had parted and slicked his hair in his best approximation of an aspiring junior executive and now sported a pair of round eyeglasses to go with the fountain pen that protruded from the pocket of his short-sleeved collared shirt. Mila's disguise, of course, was on a whole different level.

As the DC-4 bumped lightly on a denser layer of atmosphere, the girl shifted her head and murmured. She had slept on and off since their breakfast of ham and eggs, skipping the soup, roast chicken and tomato juice that the stewardess had served for lunch. A touch of airsickness, she had said. Bradley made sure she was still covered by her blanket and fished for his cigarettes.

When his lips drew one from the pack, a hand appeared in the corner of his vision. A flick, and a blurry flame followed.

The man in Seat 7. They had already exchanged pleasantries in Amsterdam, in Tunisia, and across the aisle, but little else. He was travelling alone and, it seemed, had long ago exhausted all conversation with the passenger beside the porthole to his right, the young Indian lawyer on his way back to Durban whose nose was forever in his books. This guy, in his showy striped suit, was harder to read. Practically all Bradley had gotten out of him was that he had an engagement in the gold-rich city of Johannesburg – something to do with insurance.

When you focused on it, it was one of those faces. Not prematurely old, like Roger's, but similarly hard to pin down. His easy smiles moved in well-worn grooves, almost mechanical in their repetitive precision, but there was no warmth in the lean, tanned cheeks, nor the eyes.

Even his accent was slippery, with a neutral (if unnatural) English pronunciation that flirted one moment with the strong Rs and vowels of a fellow American, the next sounded almost east-European ('Tcho-burg', 'Een-surance'). Mila had agreed that if there was a Soviet agent aboard, he was both the only plausible candidate and the most preposterous.

As yet, Bradley hadn't managed to catch sight of his passport. But then, thanks to 'Pat' and 'Mil Six', he was hardly a shining example of the trustworthiness of such documents himself. And as even the most innocent international traveller discovered, sweating in line for passport control, at certain times, in a certain light, every name and photo looked downright phony.

"Oughtn't to be much longer now. In Léo by teatime."

Bradley exhaled into the ventilation grille above the parcel racks and flicked him a nod of thanks for the light.

"You know the route. Do you fly it regular?"

That seemed to amuse him.

"I'm something of a go-between, you might say."

Bradley checked the clock on the forward bulkhead, which was coming up to three in the afternoon, local time. Léo by 'teatime'…? It was one of those typical Limey non-specifics, like 'well enough off' or 'mustn't grumble', and might mean they'd be on the ground in half an hour or two. He wondered how the fellow was so apparently confident of their position. From what little he could see from his aisle seat, the occasional gaps between the clouds showed unbroken jungle.

"…of course, when they weren't raiding the Shinkolobwe mine for its uranium deposits, your people took it upon themselves to extend Ndolo during the war," the man was saying now. "To ferry bombers to the Middle East and China – so there's no need to worry about a 'bush landing'."

"I wasn't."

He leant back to appraise Bradley with those cool, unsmiling eyes.

"No, I expect not." Then the smile slid smoothly into place, like the wing-flaps opening. "That's a funny story, as it happens. The engineering force your army shipped in was an all-Negro unit. Scared the crap out of the Belgians, who thought the Congolese might see them as liberators. Had to make them bloody unwelcome, bloody quick. Ha!"

"Are they that afraid the natives will rise up?"

"Well, there are always troublemakers. Mind, you need some nerve to go up against the *Force Publique*. They're the local police and military rolled together. Rule with a rod of iron, so to speak – or a *chicote* rather, which is their favoured tool. It's a whip made of rhinoceros-hide. I don't know who's more savage: the askaris or their white officers… There you are, what did I tell you?"

It took a moment for Bradley to catch on. The engine note had changed as the 'Flying Dutchman' began its descent. Within minutes the red cabin light came on.

"Honey…" he said softly, tapping the girl's foot under the blanket and extinguishing his cigarette.

"Mmm…" She stretched, looking momentarily embarrassed to find that she had been resting on him. He helped her to stow her blanket overhead and return the hydraulic seats to the upright position. Then, at the steward's urging, they fastened their seatbelts.

In the general hubbub, and the excitement of the ETA sweepstake, he leant towards her and lowered his voice again. "Remember what we agreed…"

Her head moved against his.

"…if anything happens, we play along with it."

As the airplane went into its circuit, they saw the great shining loop of the Congo River, where Brazzaville, the capital of French Equatorial Africa and lately of De Gaulle's Free France, faced the Belgian development of Léopoldville, Kinshasa and Kalina. Suddenly they were looking down on parks and golf clubs, wide paved streets bordered with palm trees and smart white buildings of several storeys that charmingly combined curved art deco corners with colonial balconies.

Before they knew it, the DC-4 was thundering in to touch down on the concrete wilderness that was Ndolo airport and the base of the Belgian SABENA airline. The captain came on the intercom to welcome them to the Congo and to issue the customary warnings about heat and mosquitos. When the airplane made its turn onto the taxiway, they spotted the long rank of armed troops waiting for them. They were very dark skinned and dressed much like any other Allied troops in tropical drill, with khaki shirts, shorts and puttees, except that for headgear they wore tall red fezzes with khaki neck curtains. They all carried Belgian Mausers, bayonets fixed.

"Hell's bells, something's up," said the man in Seat 7, leaning across them both for a better view. "That's no guard of honour – that's the *Force Publique*."

* * *

"These ones?"

Because the door was at the rear of the aircraft, the passengers from the front were among the last to disembark. Captain Janssens had watched them all, taking a perverse pleasure in observing their reactions, one by one, to the wall of heat and humidity that greeted them at the top of the boarding stairs.

At his side, dabbing face and neck with a sodden handkerchief, the Londoner grunted.

"Yeah, that's them."

He would not have noticed it without being forewarned, but Janssens thought there was something odd about the way the man and woman descended the steps. The man stood aside to let the woman go first, then after two steps he overtook her, offering her a helping hand the rest of the way, as a dutiful husband should.

They were American newlyweds, thriftily combining their honeymoon with his provisional posting to a transnational corporation in Cape Town. The man looked healthy – probably played tennis or baseball or whatever it was these American expatriates indulged in – but there was a softness about him too, in his diffident hunch, that awkward limp on the steps, and those spectacles, which prevented him from immediately donning movie-star sunglasses like many of the others, his wife included.

She, by contrast, looked decidedly glamorous. There was no hiding that. Shapely, with the cascading red hair of a young Rita Hayworth – it was only that she seemed to be trying a little too hard for the tell-tale cheapness of her hat, purse and shoes. Janssens found himself picturing her moving her way up through better quality labels, and through the executive ranks of her husband's company...

He shook his head to clear it of the alluring images. It was all a lie. As Monsieur Parsons had laid out for him, these were dangerous people, in disguise.

The Londoner had an unpleasant softness about him too. Janssens would have liked to open him up with a single lash of a *chicote*, or have one of his askaris do it. But that would have been most unwise, and not only for the loss of the bonus he'd been promised. Monsieur Parsons had his own back-up with him, and there was nothing remotely soft about them. Italian-Americans, two of them were: a sour-faced gentleman named Scintilia and his companion, a nameless brute who appeared less likely to be mistaken for any kind of gentleman than one of the lowland gorillas in the east. The third character he knew from previous arrangements at Ndolo: the so-called Swiss trader, himself resembling some balding lesser ape, Willi Nohl.

"But you don't want them separated yet?"

"Not for the time being, if you please, Captain." It was Scintilia who replied. Janssens realised that Parsons had only been required to make the identification. The hangdog Italian-American was in charge. "For now, it is only important that all these passengers are – 'ow you say? – *quarantined*. Due to rumours of a mutiny at Coquilhatville, and the need to ensure that no more communist agitators come in. Later, naturally, it may prove necessary to question one or two of them..."

It was almost enough to feel unperturbed by the unauthorised nature of the undertaking. Parsons and the Americans, representing the two main Allied nations, spoke as though they really did have the best interests of the Belgian Congo uppermost in their minds. And as for Nohl, why, he would hardly be able to maintain that unmarked warehouse of his behind the SABENA hangars without some kind of official blessing, would he? It was surely enough. Almost.

"I can arrange for buses to take them to the American barracks, about a kilometre from here. For various reasons, the Americans never moved in and there are plenty of unused dormitories – a logical solution, which saves the passengers in transit from having to go through customs and passport controls."

"That sounds perfect, for their own safety and comfort. Alas, it appears the 'Flying Dutchman' has developed an engine fault that may take some time to fix."

Janssens couldn't help looking. The four props had only just stopped turning and there were as yet no maintenance or refuelling crews in attendance. Only the baggage handlers and his own *Compagnie Marche* of the *Force Publique*, of course.

"I understand," he said.

*   *   *

The rain came late in the afternoon and seemed like it would never stop. By the time they drove under the sign for 'Camp Presnell', the light had almost gone and the dirt roads had turned to a quagmire.

Bradley tried to recall what he had managed to make out through the streaming windows of the bus: it would be important later, possibly vital. A long, broad street going downhill and losing its battle with the local undergrowth. Wooden frame barrack huts built on stilts and rocks either side, faced with plywood and rattan screens and appearing both unfinished and in steep decline: the unpainted wood waterlogged, the tin roofs already rotted and repaired on several huts with palm thatch. An open-sided mess hall and a similar infirmary and ablution block. Sturdier-looking administrative buildings. If there was a

141

perimeter it was hidden by the curtains of rain and the surrounding bush.

What else? Dim electric lights by the steps up to each hut. At the foot of the incline, in what might once have been a parade ground, a park of rusting Chevy trucks, their tyres long gone.

And everywhere, the *Force Publique*. With the onset of the rain they had stowed their boots and puttees and gone barefoot. Some were in further stages of undress, suggesting that they were billeted here. All carried a rifle or a stiff, tapering whip.

He checked with the girl but she had seen even less from her position in the bus.

Now they were all gathered in one of the better preserved dormitories, which the authorities had endeavoured to make more welcoming. With the extensively draped mosquito nets and the warm glow of the kerosene lamps – and of course the rain, sheeting down outside – there was almost a campfire ambience. As they swapped stories and tucked into the cold cuts, local fruit and liquor provided by the airline, Bradley wouldn't have been surprised to hear them break into song.

He looked at her with concern. Like him, she knew there was something sinister ('fishy', she'd probably say) about the enforced lay-over. Mila would have noted too the strange tone to the *Force Publique* captain's announcements, which even in ponderous English sounded lazily insincere. There was no need yet to compare notes. What was needed was to find out who was behind this and what they intended to do next.

Had it been arranged by the Russians? Were Abakumov's agents about to strike – perhaps with Beria's protectors left behind in the Netherlands?

Or had their journey south already alerted de Klerk and his Nazis? If Captain Janssens had been in his home country during its occupation, maybe he had collaborated with the Germans, maybe in the Flemish Legion of the Waffen SS. Might that explain his volunteering for a colonial posting now – and perhaps an openness to blackmail?

Shifting his idle gaze from the girl, he met the eye of the man from Seat 7, which as ever gave nothing away. Still, the smile slid automatically into place as they raised their glasses to each other in a silent toast.

Then came a courteous knock at the plywood door. It was Captain Janssens, with two of his troops. He had some questions, he said. A mere formality. Would the first two passengers accompany him, those who had occupied Seats 1 and 2 – ah, but they had been Congolese nationals who had already been permitted to go home. Apologies – and of course it had been the steward and the spare crew member who had taken off and landed in Seats 3 and 4… my God, what a mix-up!

Well then, would the couple from Seats 5 and 6 make themselves known, please? Monsieur and Madame Crawford, yes of course...

Momentarily, Bradley registered the fierce narrowing of Mila's eyes. *Not yet.*

He stood up and extended a helping hand for his 'wife'.

"This way… it is not far."

Janssens opened an umbrella, but 'Mrs Crawford' lifted her raincoat over her head instead. They hurried to the other side of the street, where a covered veranda ran to the admin block.

Bradley checked his wristwatch. Twenty-three hundred. He listened for the sounds of the bush but heard only the rain on the roofs and a generator someplace. Still no clue to what they'd encounter at the perimeter, assuming the front gate was always guarded. He almost checked the back of his waistband for the Tokarev too, but he wore no jacket to cover it there and anyway they'd brought only one pistol, which Mila had hidden.

They went through stout doors into a decaying corridor plastered with peeling notices, then an office with just a small window, barred. *Force Publique* troops were everywhere outside, but only the two who had accompanied Captain Janssens entered the office with them. There would hardly have been room for any more. Not with the four civilians waiting in there for them, one of whom required the space for at least two men.

A ceiling fan turned ineffectually, stirring air that already seemed more composed of sweat and cigar smoke than oxygen. Bradley, acting feeble hearted, felt a genuine stab of fear in his chest – not for himself, but for the girl.

"Listen," he said, his voice quavering. "I want to talk to the U.S. Consul – he'll clear this up."

Three of the four civilians returned to their seats and ashtrays on the other side of the table. The fourth, the big guy in shirtsleeves and suspenders who was still wearing a straw porkpie hat a couple of sizes too small for him, shuffled behind them to lurk by the window.

Of the remaining three, one was another ox, albeit shorter, rounder and balder. He was got up in some kind of white hunter costume. The other – prematurely aged – was a wreck, mopping at himself with his handkerchief and cradling a crumpled seersucker jacket like a bedraggled pet.

But it was the one in the middle, the Bela Lugosi type in the well-tailored suit, who answered in an American accent he knew only too well.

"Not for nuthin', but clear up what exactly, Sergeant Bradley?"

The captain slammed the door shut behind him and Bradley flinched. The two askaris pushed him and the girl down into the waiting chairs.

CHAPTER TWELVE

"So how come youse got tickets through to Cape Town?"

"Because we're going to Cape Town."

"When was you gonna switch to the flight to Salisbury?"

"We weren't. We aren't. Where's that at?"

Bradley considered throwing in a line about the cathedral town in southern England, and nearly did. But Hal Crawford wouldn't have known about it. As far as Bradley had it figured, old Hal was a 4-F pencil pusher on his first trip overseas and had certainly never bust his knees on the crimp-strewn pavement of the French village on Salisbury Plain.

Nor was 'Sparky', as the others called him, the kind of guy you'd want to crack wise with at the best of times, which this was not.

Nor did any of it make any sense. The Jersey accent had gotten him worried that these were wise guys from back home. The fellow by the window might be more monster than mobster, but he too looked the part. It began to seem that Sicily had finally caught up with him, and the only small comfort there was that maybe, just maybe, he'd be able to keep the girl out of it. But this greasy-looking, German-sounding white hunter, 'Villi' or something... and all this bull about Southern Rhodesia?

'Villi' was up next, rocking back in his chair to clasp together beefy arms that had more hair on them than his dome – and wicking up a piercing gaze between the knitted nut-brown brow and the spiky black moustache.

"Sergeant Bradley..."

"Who's that?"

"…we know you have no business in the Cape. We know you are going to Johannesburg to catch the Central flight to Bulawayo and Salisbury."

"Then you know a hell of a lot more than me."

"Our question is what you were going to do there. Who were you to meet?"

"Buddy I don't even know where that is. You obviously have me mistaken for someone else…"

And so on. And on. Giving nothing away. Growing no wiser. All that mattered was to keep up the increasingly brazen pretence that he was 'Mr Crawford' – and to keep 'Mrs Crawford' from speaking altogether. Acting dumbfounded was no stretch for either of them, but an American accent of any kind might be, for her. The only hope was that these guys would let something slip that would give them an opportunity to improvise. Because at the moment their captors held all the cards, and they had nothing.

They might not yet be restrained, true, but it was unnecessary. The three guys at the table looked like they were all of them packing something. 'Villi' wore a full-blown holstered sidearm, and the monster-mobster hid something big under his folded jacket. But even that was irrelevant, because behind them were the two askaris, and the Belgian captain with his rhinoceros whip and 13-round Hi-Power pistol.

He stole a look at the girl. She was acting nervous of course, and perhaps not acting. But no sign of anything else. And no signal.

Then it came. The first clue.

Not wanting to be left out, the prematurely-aged guy finally opened his bazoo. As well as being British, as Bradley had predicted and the rotten teeth confirmed, he was a Londoner.

"We ain't mistaken you for no-one, China. We been on your Aris since Jockland!"

Bradley had heard talk like that before. He didn't need Jenny Simmonds to tell him that it wasn't just working class London dialect, it was East End Cockney.

China plate for mate, much like (but not quite like) 'my old Dutch'. Aris for Aristotle, which for some reason meant 'arse'.

That gave a whole new perspective to their situation.

He remembered that day at the airstrip on the Sennelager ranges, when he had first encountered the senior Lonsdale brother, Jimmy. Had this foul-smelling streak of sweat been there too? Or at the sea fort? He didn't think so. But he was one of them.

So. London gangsters. Jersey wise guys. A German *Jäger* type. When all they'd been expecting was the latest incarnations of SMERSh!

What the hell had they stumbled into?

"I haven't the first goddam idea what you're talking about," he told them all.

Bela Lugosi cocked an eyebrow, flashed a look. Bradley had no time to react before the two askaris had seized him from behind, twisting one arm each to pitch him painfully forward, face against the table. He felt his collar go, heard his shirt back tear in half. Then nothing except the sluggish pulse of the overhead fan and the breathless air of anticipation.

A whistle as the Belgian captain brought his *chicote* down. The girl's involuntary shriek and the impact arriving as one… just an ill-defined blow at first, like when you touched a live wire and it felt like a kick in the ass, or the Aris…

Then the pain.

The second lash brought something else. Moisture – not just in the fine spray of sweat or blood in the air but as a consciousness of liquid flowing freely, both outside and inside. And with it the fear, of permanent injury and incapacitation.

The third he greeted with an animal howl, fighting against the hands that pinioned him. The thought occurred that the captain must not have a clean swing, with his askaris so close, and that perhaps the cuts were not as bad as they seemed. Perhaps he could take this…

Then he realised that everything had changed. It was no longer the two askaris holding him down but rather the German and the monster. The askaris had taken hold of the girl instead, bending her onto the table. As they did, her flowing red locks came loose, revealing the close-fitting actor's hair net tightly pinned beneath.

Through salt and fury he saw Janssens rip her blouse and brassiere open. Two sets of eyes were on his – the girl's, wide with terror, and Janssens', challenging.

He had bitten his lip. He tasted blood as he grunted out the words.

"OK, OK… I'm Sam Bradley."

The Cockney's voice, somewhere close.

"And she's the MERCURY bird – Mila Suková."

"No, no… she's just a stooge I picked up, to throw you off the scent…"

"You *fink* we're *fick* or some*fink*?" Closer now – he could feel the spit, as he had felt his master's, that day on the airstrip. "Fucking *do* 'er!"

Bradley put all his strength into one, desperate heave, but it was only his shoulder that gave. The shock of possibly dislocating it again – which would surely be the end of this – seemed to numb all the other pain and brought him abruptly to his senses.

"No! You're right, of course it's her!"

Bela Lugosi now:

"And you was going to Salisbury, because of your beef with the Lonsdales."

"That's it."

"To do Jimmy harm? To kill him?"

"Sure. You got it."

And the monster, presumably, right above him, with a surprisingly high, breathless voice…

"Like youse *moidered* Don Ciccio's boy in the Old Country."

And there it was. The verdict and death sentence. The last hope gone.

"Yeah."

The vice-grips released and they were manhandled back into an upright position in their chairs, but with each of them hunched forward, in shame or self-consciousness, in fear and resignation. Bradley tried and failed to catch the girl's eye. Instead he found himself looking at Bela Lugosi's. Sparky. Presumably it was an ironic nickname, based on his long-faced demeanour.

But now, he was smiling, sort of.

"I guess that's enough for tonight. We can give Mr and Mrs Crawford some privacy, can't we, Captain Janssens? A room of their own? They'll want to freshen themselves up, I reckon… can we have their baggage brought to them?"

*   *   *

When the *Force Publique* – which was always really a *Force Privée* – had taken the captives away, Willi Nohl could contain himself no longer.

"You're not going to kill them?"

Franzetti's man, Scintilia, shrugged.

"No I ain't. The war's over. You can't just execute people, even in Africa. These are civilians. They were seen to arrive at Ndolo. One day, folks are going to come here, asking questions."

Scintilia's sidekick, the one known only as Rocky, chimed in.

"So we makes sure there's answers to them questions..."

Scintilia nodded patiently.

"We make sure there's answers... There was a mix-up. They were interrogated. Maybe they were trouble-makers and they guessed they'd been rumbled. Or they were what they said they were – but foolish. They were put up for the night and they slipped out. Who knows? Maybe they thought they'd make it into town, or back to the airport? But this is a dangerous, unfamiliar country and there are crocodiles in the Congo, right, Willi? I'd say it's possible that they'll never be seen again."

"But we 'ave to be sure. Mr Lonsdale…"

"Will sleep soundly at night, Mr Parsons. You have my word." Making sure he had tidied everything from the table before buttoning his coat, Scintilia turned back to Nohl. "I said I wasn't going to kill them and I ain't. You are, with your fancy paratrooper gun – and Rocky here, with his Room Broom…"

At that, the heavy pulled out his arm from under the jacket he had draped over it. To an armourer like Nohl, the thing in his hand was as much a monstrosity as its owner: a modified Colt 1911 handgun with a ludicrously extended magazine and the foregrip and muzzle device from a Thompson submachine gun. It was rumoured that Lebman had made these fully automatic pistols for Dillinger, 'Pretty Boy' Floyd and 'Babyface' Nelson. Evidently he had made one for 'Rocky' too.

"We know who they are," Scintilia said. "So we know they're gonna try to break out tonight. The room we've put them in has a window that won't hold them up for long. All you gotta do is be there waiting."

*   *   *

With the drumming of the rain on the tin roof, it was probably unnecessary to speak in such a low voice, but you never knew who was listening.

"So it's Jimmy Lonsdale," he muttered.

They had their backs to one another, stripping off their ruined clothes, unpacking new ones. They didn't know how long they'd have before the *Force Publique* or their interrogators came bursting into this storeroom at the rear of the administrative block.

"I never met him."

"No..." Bradley was struggling to find the words.

"And now he's somewhere in Rhodesia, near Salisbury."

"So it seems. He must have fled there after we bust open his smuggling operation."

Even in a whisper, he could hear the exasperation in her voice, on top of everything else:

"So this is all just a misunderstanding? We happened to come south and he assumed we were on our way to get him?"

"I know it's crazy, but I guess he had people watching us. They put two and two together and came up with five."

"And what about these Americans?"

"That's something else, something to do with when I was stationed on Sicily. I was detailed to protect an officer, a diplomat, from the Mafia. They sent men to get him. One of them was the son of a local don who must have had connections in the States."

"The Mafia," she said. "And now they're working with the Lonsdale gang?"

"That looks to be the size of it."

"And the German, if that's what he is?"

"No idea. But I don't reckon he's connected to de Klerk and Kuhlmann. Like you say, I think this is all a coincidence. Damn…"

He was trying to slip on a fresh shirt, and failing. She came up behind him. He heard her suck her teeth in a sympathetic wince.

"Don't do that. We have to dress it first. How is it feeling?"

He recalled her expression as they tore her clothes apart and forced her down to await the whip. How was he feeling? Sick to his stomach. Sick to his soul.

"It's OK. And my shoulder's just stiff – it didn't pop all the way out this time."

He felt her cool hand on the back of his neck.

"We have some sterilised gauze and some sticking plaster. Not enough, but I can put it where the lacerations are going to rub against your shirt. It shan't take long."

"Listen… I feel real bad about what happened."

"Hush. Just hold still."

He held still and put his brain to better work, studying their environment. By the light of the single unshaded bulb, he could see that the storeroom was depressingly empty and constructed not of plywood but of solidly jointed timbers. Without a crowbar it would take an age to pry anything loose.

The door was solid too and well-fitting. Had this been an armoury? There was no integral lock but they had heard it bolted twice from the outside and there would either be padlocks on the bolts or an askari standing guard. Most likely both.

And there was the window. Like the one in the scene of their interrogation, it was shallow and barred. But the bars weren't sunk into the sill, they were screwed on from the inside. Simple flat-head screws, rusty, sure, but the wood was weathered too.

He heard her tear the tape. When their belongings had been returned, they had not included anything sharp. No scissors, no penknife, not even his safety razor. But all you needed for a screw-head was the pull from a zip fastener – or the clip off a junior executive's fountain pen.

"Easy, tiger!" Kneeling behind him, she had to pull him back into the crouch. "Nearly finished… there you go."

He had selected the navy shirt this time, the one for carefully losing his golf game to his superiors, perhaps. Only when he had shuffled into it and buttoned it did he turn to face her.

She had on a dark sweater and skirt. No… as she stepped back… what were those things called? Culottes. And flat slippers. She had kept on the hair net.

They pulled faces at one another, the intended, outward emotions as uncertain as those hidden behind them.

He retrieved his fountain pen and signalled her over to the window.

*   *   *

Boots light on the creaking boards, Captain Janssens made his way around the veranda to the door of the storeroom. Beyond the waterfalls that streamed brightly from every roof surface in the glow of the veranda lamps, this unoccupied area of the camp was in darkness.

The airless humidity had him licking his lips, not with anticipation of the ugly business to follow, exactly, but more with the excitement of a simple fantasy he was indulging, a fantasy that had started forming in the back of his mind – or wherever else such fantasies had their beginnings – at the moment he had seen the American woman's torso laid bare.

Janssens stopped and touched the braided handle of his *chicote* where it was hooked onto his belt. If he drew it, the stiff, swordlike strip of twisted hide, he knew that its point would still be tacky with her husband's blood.

But of course he wasn't really her husband and they were not what they claimed. That was why, if one were careful, they could become mere pieces in a game, *playthings*.

The reality was that his job now was to dismiss the guard on the storeroom door and – without even shooting the bolts – to stir the two imprisoned trouble-makers into action. Bang on the door. Shout through it that their time was nearly up. Play it by ear. Listen for the window bars coming off, or for people squeezing through. Keep his head down when they did.

The fantasy? That would be another way to provoke them. With the man subdued… choked out or, better, made to watch…

Reluctantly he released his grip on the whip and approached the door, returning the salute.

"Off you go, Corporal. Get some rest."

Removing his cap, he pressed his ear against the door.

* * *

Hunkered down behind the steps that led up to the next hut in the row, Willi Nohl peered through the 4-power telescopic sight of his FG 42 *Modell II*. Although the lights on the veranda and the rest of the admin block were dim and mostly shielded by the bulk of the sturdy wooden building and the scattering effect of the rain, the light through the window of the storeroom itself spilled out sufficiently to illuminate the sodden ground immediately beneath it.

He had seen the pairs of hands remove the bars – first one bar, then a second, a third, a fourth, a fifth – which only made the narrow window shine even brighter. Now, as he watched the first figure hoist itself up and clamber through the gap, he made sure the paratrooper rifle was set to continuous fire and let his finger hover over the trigger.

It was the man, still surprisingly nimble after his flogging. He could bring him down in an instant, just as he had brought down the family group of kudu. But the thing was to get the woman too, otherwise it would become messy. He only hoped that Rocky, secreted somewhere in the shadows further along the wall in case one or both of them managed to make a bolt for the darkness, would also stick to the plan.

Verdammt nochmal! It was just as he'd feared. Even as the silhouette of the American, having checked that the coast was clear, turned back to assist the woman in her escape, there came a wheezy cry and that ugly brute stepped through a veil of rain into the light, brandishing his ugly gun.

"This is from Don Ciccio, you sonofabitch!"

Nohl had raised his head from the sight to see what was happening. Before he could reacquire his target and beat the brute to the kill, there was a double flash and a double crack that had not come from the gangster gun.

He raised his head again, only to see Rocky hit the puddles with a considerable splash. When he looked back for the American, he was gone.

Nohl was a deer hunter. He was used to losing his target and quickly finding it again. He had the patience of Job and the purposeful reactions of a cheetah. So why were his sights swinging this way and that like an amateur's? Why was he shifting his position, with no possible outcome other than to give himself away?

It was his heart, which was drumming like the rain. It was the tension in his fingers, which had turned instinctively to defensive claws – the worse possible tools for a marksman.

It was this, he realised, in what was to be one of his last ever thoughts: until now, his prey had never shot back.

A piercing female voice through the pattering rain and his gasping breaths and his heartbeat…

"Sam – the captain, by the door on the veranda – I've got this one!"

When the hidden figure moved, casting its shadow against the sheet of rain and flashing brightly like before – just once, this time – he recognised the black, flowing robes of the Angel of Death.

Then his heart beat no more.

*　　*　　*

Bradley rounded the corner of the building and vaulted up onto the veranda in one. He realised later that he must have been invisible until his feet penetrated the drapes of water and felled the Belgian captain.

What the hell had the guy been doing while the ambush played out? Unfastening the bolts, drawing his pistol, it seemed – and completing neither task.

But now they both came up on their hands and knees on the rain-slicked veranda, and the captain's holster flap was unfastened, the pistol tantalisingly half-drawn. Bradley seized the fountain pen from his junior-executive pocket. The top was already removed, having done its service as a screwdriver.

With a roar, he put the nib to work as a blade.

And eventually… a hand on his shoulder, tender, tentative, like the girl's had been when dressing his wounds; but this one more forceful, more commanding…

Mila. He looked up at her. She was still wearing the Norbertine nun's vestments that had been her disguise since leaving Amsterdam, albeit with the white habit now stained dark by the rain and the black veil pulled back to reveal her look of concern. In her shooting hand, she held their remaining Tokarev pistol; in the other, a stick-up artist's Room Broom that must have come from the monster.

She handed this to him as he finally let go of the pen.

"I don't know what's happened but I know it must be bad," she said. "Where's Jenny?"

Bradley shook his head to clear his eyes of rain and sweat and blood.

"In there – she's safe. Just… God, Mila!"

Her eyes went down, fleetingly, reluctantly, to the thing at his feet. She nodded.

"We thought we were being clever with this masquerade but we've been stupid. We're still in big trouble. There are *Force Publique* everywhere. And whoever those were…" She cocked her head around the corner. Bradley didn't have to ask.

"It's the *Lonsdales*," he told her, widening his eyes to mime disbelief, as if to say *How could we have planned for that?* "Plus the stateside mob, working with them."

She regarded him without expression. He could tell that she was suppressing all emotions, to be postponed for later. Chief among them, surely, was the sense of guilt for what they had put poor Jenny Simmonds through.

Then her words had taken on substance in the obscure Congo night. Shadows flitted across the coruscating puddles. Dark shapes crept along the veranda, behind the rail. A bayonet glinted. Low murmurs were taken up, curt commands hissed.

Mila hissed one of her own.

"Inside, now!"

CHAPTER THIRTEEN

They were gunshots, unmistakably, even smothered by the racket of the rain. When they had rung out, she had dropped instinctively below the level of the window and had not raised her head again. Although it had taken time for her scrambled senses to decipher the first shout, the one that had preceded the shots, she had clearly made out Mr Bradley's entreaty to *keep down, stay there!* And she had. Even when she had heard Miss Slavík's instruction to Mr Bradley, and then the third and final shot… Even when the desperate noises had come from outside the door – the thuds and gasps of grappling men, and the shrill, awful denial of the Belgian captain: *Non! Non! Non!*

Jenny caught a glimpse of the captain's body as Mr Bradley and Miss Slavík flung themselves through the door and slammed it shut again. Those cries had not emanated from someone with more than a few seconds of life left to struggle in. Was he dead?

Were they?

Still crouching, she watched as Miss Slavík tore off her veil and used it unscrew the lightbulb. Now the only light came from the glittering curtain of rain across the window. As her eyes adjusted to it, she saw Mr Bradley's shadow take up position, both hands full.

"We're going right out again, the way I went, Jenny. Before we're trapped in here…"

"I'll lay down some covering fire," Miss Slavík was saying as she reloaded and raised her pistol. "In case they're watching the window."

But Mr Bradley only shook his head. He hefted bulky objects.

"No. I will, with these. Because you *know* they are already."

Miss Slavík stood close to him for a moment, then beckoned Jenny to her feet.

"You won't be able to hit anything like that," she told him.

And he laughed. He actually laughed.

"I don't want to hit *any*thing..." He thrust both guns through the window. Jenny saw that at the end of one extended arm he held the Belgian captain's sidearm, at the end of the other a kind of machine pistol with a wooden front grip to steady it, which Mr Bradley would not have a spare hand to hold.

"...I want to hit *every*thing!"

Before she knew it, Jenny was being lifted up and through the gap next to the two guns. Miss Slavík had thrown off her cumbersome habit and wore only a sheer camisole slip that was surely not standard wear in the Norbertine order. With the heavy ageing make-up now running down her face and throat, she looked more like a drowned cat than a fighter, but there was astonishing vigour in her.

"When you hit the ground, wait for me," she said as Jenny managed to swing up a leg to avoid falling out face-first. "And cover your ears."

She would have done so anyway. The noise was a brutal assault, coming as it did amid a searing blast of flashes and sparks and a hail of what she supposed were cartridge cases. It could only have lasted seconds but it seemed to go on forever. Then she felt Miss Slavík prise away one of her hands and she allowed her to drag her into the shadows further along the avenue of huts, her ears ringing fit to burst.

"Mr Bradley?" she asked, although she had no way of knowing whether she had spoken silently or bellowed it out, as she was tempted.

Close up, just enough light seeped between the darkened shapes of the huts for her to see Miss Slavík give her a warm smile.

"Just behind us," she mouthed. "And I think you've earned the right to call him 'Sam' or 'Bradley' – and me, Mila."

As they ran at a crouch from darkest shadow to darkest shadow, all the while moving steadily uphill against the meandering streams of muddy rainwater, Jenny realised that they were making for the front gate. Had they forgotten that there would be armed guards there? Of course they hadn't. That was why Miss Slavík – Mila – held her Russian pistol at the ready, and why Bradley was doing the same with the captain's pistol as he brought up the rear.

At the next pause, he took the time to examine it, setting it down with a rueful shake of his head.

"Guess I fired all thirteen before I climbed out. Plus twenty or more from the other thing, pretty much all at once… My guess is they've *still* got their heads down!"

But surely the jungle would be the safer option, she wanted to say, glancing between a pair of huts at the encroaching blackness and disorder. She didn't say it for at least two reasons.

In the first place, she trusted Mila and Bradley to handle situations like this. It was they, after all, who had cooked up the ingenious identity switch that left Mila free to 'screen, guard and cover', as Bradley put it – and had invited lowly little Corporal Jenny Simmonds to play a key part in the deception. And they had done this in anticipation of just such a danger, even if they hadn't predicted the particular circumstances or the actual foe.

In the second place, she did not want to let them down, to be more of a burden to them than she was already or in any other way to divert them into taking the wrong action, tactically speaking. And why was that? Because she loved it, danger and all! Because speaking, thinking and acting tactically, which had dreamed of doing all the time she had served Colonel Smith as his driver, knocked selling hats into a flippin' cocked hat!

Halting at the next junction, awaiting Mila's signal, she felt Bradley come up behind her and give her a double tap on the shoulder. As she swivelled with a grin, she realised how simple yet clever that was, when a single tap might have been *anything*.

He had seen her peering down the alleyways.

"I'd give us good odds in the bush against anyone else coming after us," he whispered. "But these guys? Forgetaboutit! Better to see if there's a way out onto the road."

Catching up with Mila in the next block of deep shadow, Jenny had to clap her hand over her mouth to avoid crying out in fright. Pinned beneath Mila's hands and knees was a very large and not completely unconscious *Force Publique* soldier. Mila must have come upon him from behind, the sound of her approach thankfully muted by the rain, and… what? She received the answer to that as Mila hit him over the head again with her Russian pistol.

Fierce cycs sought out Jenny's in the uppermost layer of shadow, which was not quite as inkily solid.

"I'm not going to kill him, but these askaris are too happy obeying orders."

She offered the man's rifle to Bradley. Jenny saw the crouching silhouette tap its own shoulder, perhaps with an unseen, apologetic grimace. Mila nodded and detached the bayonet instead.

As she passed the ferocious thing back to him, Jenny caught herself wondering what he had used on Captain Janssens, before pushing the thought from her mind.

*　　*　　*

At the far corner of the last hut in the row – actually the first in line from the gate, on this side of the main street – Mila went prone behind the pile of foundation stones and carefully raised her head without extending it beyond the shadows.

There was no sign of life in the small, palm-thatched guardroom beside the gate. The gate itself was just a square, wooden arch which on its opposite face, she recalled, bore a faded American Stars & Stripes and a few remaining letters of the name CAMP PRESNELL. There appeared to be no pole or chain barring the road itself.

Cold, uncertain and aching from her recent struggle with the stunned askari, she was relieved when Sam crawled into position beside her. Together they watched the guard hut, waiting for the silhouette of a restless occupant to cross its open window.

Meanwhile, from further down in the camp, there came shouts, muffled by the rain.

"What about vehicles?" She felt Sam's urgent breath on her ear. "The last airline coach?"

She understood the temptation – not only to crash unstoppably through the gateway, but also to put themselves swiftly a fair distance down the road, either into Léopoldville or back to the airport – but she gave a grudging, negative murmur.

"It left. When I snuck out, there was nothing outside the dormitory."

"Then let's just…"

They both heard it at the same time. Not a coach, nor a worn-out diesel truck from the park down there but a car, its engine racing and transmission whining as it skittered and spun wheels up the main dirt road towards the entrance.

There was no time to think it through. No time, even, to berate herself for not taking the rifle and giving Sam the pistol. As she turned to him, she saw him reach for Jenny's hand and nod.

"Let's do it."

Together they ran along the side of the hut into the main street. The shock of emerging into the brightness there – the brightness of porch lamps, the brightness of headlamps, the sweeping brightness of the rain – was compounded by the growing awareness in the corners of her vision of armed figures moving: out from the cover of the huts at the bottom of the street; out from the guard hut at the top.

She stepped into the blazing beams of the headlamps and stood motionless, one arm extended, aiming the pistol at the windscreen of the oncoming car.

It came to a lurching halt. In that instant, Sam was at the driver's door, wrenching it open, bayonet drawn back ready to strike.

The car growled and burbled. Now the engine wasn't roaring, she could hear the angry shouting drawing closer through the rain. Yet time, it seemed, had slowed down, almost stopped.

The saloon was bigger than she had first thought. The close-set side-by-side headlamps were actually mounted behind a swept-back front grille, between substantial wings. A flashlight, swinging back and forth somewhere behind the car, revealed a single occupant. Ample room for the three of them and little resistance to overcome.

Sure enough, Sam's bayonet arm beckoned Jenny out of the darkness. Keeping the pistol levelled, Mila hurried over.

At the wheel sat Sam's neighbour from the plane, the passenger in Seat 7. If he recognised 'Mother Superior' without clothes, make-up or modesty, he hid the surprise.

"Get in, quick!"

It was French, his car – a Peugeot, she thought – with those infuriating suicide doors. She and Jenny managed to squeeze into the cramped rear bench while Sam took the front passenger seat. As the man from Seat 7 jammed it into gear again and gunned the engine, she tapped Sam's shoulder and handed him the pistol.

One kneeling, one standing, two *Force Publique* gate guards had taken positions beneath the arch and were bringing up their rifles. Sighting through the windscreen with his arm out of the window, Sam probably had no intention of hitting them either, but the eight shots he fired must have put them off their aim at least. As the car bore down on them and clattered through the open gateway, she saw them fling themselves aside.

Turning to peer through the small, rain-smeared rear window, Mila thought she saw the flashes of several rifle shots from the figures assembled there. And turning back she thought she saw something else: the flash of relish in Jenny's wide-open eyes.

She found her hand and gave it a squeeze.

"Well done. We're safe for the moment now."

The man from Seat 7 let out a humourless chuckle.

"'For the moment' is right! Those fellows looked mighty miffed with us, and except for the European city, it's their town."

Mighty miffed! Who spoke like that? Mila studied the back of his head.

162

"So get us to the European city."

He turned around to look at her. Only a glance, too rapid to judge the expression, but alarming enough in a car that was speeding through what looked like dense jungle.

"Are you under the impression this is a rescue attempt, Miss Slavík? You just got in my way!"

With affected casualness, Sam handed the pistol back to her across his shoulder. Mila blinked. He'd have known, as she did, that their driver must be well aware it was now empty. This fresh encounter with him – and the fact he knew her *nom de guerre* – confirmed their prior suspicions that the man from Seat 7 was someone well versed in exactly how many rounds a Tokarev held. What was surprising was that Sam assumed she had a spare magazine about her person.

Hadn't he seen what she was wearing?

She gave a humourless chuckle of her own. Perhaps he just wanted her ready to pistol-whip their driver as she had done with the askari, in case this non-rescue took a turn for the worse.

"Then where are we going, may I ask?"

The man snorted and did indeed take a turn, but only into what looked like a sleeping suburban street.

"Good question! I need to make a telephone call."

Another turn brought them onto a broader boulevard that was lined with palm trees. There were even street-lamps here. Their driver pulled into the kerbside between two other cars. Mila squinted through the side window at the two-storey building. White columns and balconies. *Hotel de Belgique. Bar. Restaurant. Friture.*

"I shan't be long…"

"I'm coming with you," Sam said.

"As you wish."

Once the two men had gone inside, Mila climbed into the front and began searching the cubbyholes for anything useful. All she found was American cigarettes. Camels. She lit two and handed one to Jenny.

"Let's get out. We can wait along the street, under that tree,

---

163

just in case."

The rain was lighter now, if yet to stop. Mila saw the girl look her up and down.

"I've a blouse and bra on under this," she said, endeavouring to pull off her sweater without extinguishing her cigarette. "Can't 'ave you catching your death – or gettin' arrested!"

Mila felt a surge of affection. She had seen Sam's face on the veranda, when she'd remarked that whatever had happened to them must have been bad – and she'd recognised in Jenny's those feverish sparks of thrill and rashness that had sprung from the experience. So she still felt guilty for having brought the girl into this, of course she did, as she knew that Sam would. Yet there was no doubt that they had chosen well.

It was as they were strolling away from the car, with the rain abruptly ceasing, that they heard the sounds from the trunk.

Thud – thud – thud – and an indistinct voice calling in desperation.

Mila leant back in and found the release mechanism. As they levered up the long, low lid of the trunk, which was hinged at the rear, it became obvious that despite appearances the Peugeot was in fact a cabriolet. The trunk space was big enough to accommodate the complicated folding steel roof and the mechanism that went with it, or would have been, had it not contained two men, gagged and bound at wrists and ankles.

"They're the other ones from when they was asking us questions!" Jenny said. "Only 'e don't look too clever, that one…"

Mila drew hard on her cigarette to flare the tip. It illuminated the flushed, sweaty face of the man who was struggling: a man in a buttoned-up chalkstripe suit, with the jacket wrenched down over his arms. The other face would be pale and grey in any light. Mila touched his chest and pulled away bloody fingers.

"Here, look…" Jenny pulled her back a couple of steps behind the huge trunk lid and pointed at the bodywork below the hinges. Whatever colour the car was, it was light enough to show the bullet hole.

"He was a Cockney," the girl said without emotion. "One of Lonsdale's, I s'pose."

"Well, he's 'brown bread' now," Mila said.

Jenny widened her eyes.

"Blimey, we'll make a Londoner of you yet!"

"And the other one? American mob?"

"That's what Mr… that's what Bradley said. They wanted revenge on him for something, but they also wanted to know why we – you, I mean – were coming to mess up their business, in Rhodesia."

"I wonder what gave them that idea. But this man, this *Mafioso*, he also wanted to know that?"

For the first time, the girl stumbled, biting her lip.

"He wanted to know all right!"

Mila pulled her into an awkward hug. She could feel her trembling.

What a shambles! For the first time the enormity of their predicament began to register. It was the enormity of Africa, and of being lost in it, so far from any friends. Suddenly she saw herself and Jenny for what they were in this moment: two weak, abandoned women, hunted by the local gendarmerie and any number of others… half-naked, half-drowned, standing helpless in a place they did not know, beside a car they could not start, with only a pistol they could not fire and a body they could not explain.

And you, she said silently, meeting the frantic eyes of the mafioso.

Who the hell are you – and are you more trouble yet or our only trump card?

Whichever it was, she had to find out. Fetching the empty pistol, she thumbed the release to let the magazine slip down just enough not to lock the slide open and reveal that it was unloaded. Then she racked it noisily to cock it.

The man's eyes were already wide, but now they fixed on her. Keeping the gun at his head, she worked the gag out of his mouth.

"One chance," she said.

He looked at her, looked at Jenny, looked back at her, nodded.

"Youse is MERCURY."

The hammer was already back. There was nothing she could do to make the gun more threatening. She tapped him hard on the eyebrow with the muzzle.

"This is not about who we are."

She saw him struggle to rein in his shock and anger, but at last he succeeded.

"Lemme sit up at least." Seeing her nod, he wormed around to free himself from the other man and shuffled both legs over the side of the trunk. It was still an uncomfortable position, since his hands were bound behind him and he was trapped in the V-shape where streamlined bodywork met the angle of the raised lid, but a wave of the pistol made it plain he'd be permitted to extract himself no further.

"My name's Gerardo Scintilia. They calls me Sparky. I'm a legal advisor to Dominic Franzetti, who works for the Genovese family in New York. And sure, I know we ain't on the same side, Signora, but the man who kidnapped me is nobody's ally…"

"At least he hasn't whipped us," came Jenny's shaky voice behind her.

Mila spun around.

"He *whipped* you?"

"He whipped Mr Bradley, or his soldiers did. He was going to whip me. Mr Bradley stopped him."

"Signora… Signorina… please." Scintilia grimaced, as if sympathetic to their plight. "You're in a big trouble here. I can help youse. Just lemme speak to the *Force Publique*…"

"Their officer is dead."

"I heard. That's why Parsons and I was on the lam – before this hijacker took us and our ride. But there are other officers, if you got deep pockets, and we got deep pockets."

Mila stood up straight again and made a show of thumbing down the hammer to de-cock the empty pistol. Scintilia, lugubrious as he looked, wary as he was, began to permit himself a satisfied smile.

"*Bene…*" he said.

She put her spare hand on the cleverly weighted trunk lid, which stood proud like a spinnaker sail behind the car, then closed it as far as it would go on his lower legs.

By the time the two men returned from the *Hotel de Belgique* – and even though the bawls had slackened off to tormented grunts – dogs were barking and lights going on at windows up and down the street.

Sam, watching for danger, did not spare her a glance, but she noticed now the way he turned without twisting, to keep the damp shirt from dragging on his back.

The man from Seat 7 was carrying his suit jacket casually: a wider, flashier stripe than even Sparky's. He regarded the ill-fitting trunk lid, which was for the most part closed again.

"What in God's name have you done?"

She lit another couple of the American cigarettes for herself and Jenny, before flashing him a scornful look.

"Started your next job for you, I should imagine. I presume you grabbed these two to make them talk? Well, the one who's still alive is coming round to the idea."

Now the rain had stopped, insects were circling the street-lamps and hordes more chirping in the darkness. The man from Seat 7 had to flap a huge, persistent moth away from his face. There would be other nuisances to harass them soon.

His features slid into a newfound look of respect.

"I got through on the telephone. I have an address we can go to. A safe house."

"The Party faithful," Mila sneered.

"I think you'll be glad of them, under the circumstances. Or I can leave you here, if you prefer. You'll soon have plenty of company – the Africans are permitted back into the European city at daybreak."

She looked at Sam, who shrugged helplessly.

"So who are you?" she demanded of the stranger.

"Not a friend. But not an enemy. Something in the middle."

———

167

"A go-between, he called it," Sam chipped in.

"Working for Beria?"

"We all function under the auspices of the Curator of the Organs of State Security – but no, I do not report to Comrade Beria."

"Abakumov?"

"Again, no. Especially no."

"And you have no name?"

"Nor does the… entity I report to. But I can say this: he is known to you. And he has taken an interest in your survival, which is more than you ever did for his."

Another smile. Another insect. Another light going on. Or was that now a hint of lightness in the east?

Mila checked Sam's and Jenny's faces before nodding.

"All right then. We're in your hands. Or your mysterious sponsor's."

The man from Seat 7 turned back as he opened the car door.

"He has no hands either," he said.

CHAPTER FOURTEEN

The tram to Beyazıt was packed to bursting by the time it left Taksim Square. Perhaps that was why the Resident's instincts had let him down; or perhaps it was the effects of the afternoon he had spent with the Greek diplomat's wife in Şişli.

Still, even by the dingy interior lamps he ought to have spotted the priggish features of that little ponce Dmitriy long before he was able to sidle up to him in the aisle and take his arm.

"My friend! How are you? And how goes the delightful Madame Zalokostas?"

Swaying from the grab-handle, the Resident looked down at the MGB officer in his not-quite-right civilian get-up and composed the sort of smirk a proper Russian would appreciate.

"Like a fucking train, Dmitriy."

"And have you enjoyed any more visits to your grubby little hotel room in Pera? From our mutual acquaintance, perhaps – with news of *his* acquaintance, the one we must not mention?"

"Now that would be telling, Dmitriy."

With an arcing flash and a clatter as the pantograph crossed a junction, the ageing tram faltered momentarily, causing the smaller man to shuffle forward and place a hand on his chest. The Resident had to refrain from checking his jacket pockets afterwards. Casting a quick eye over the other passengers in the car, he identified three goons who were occupying themselves in whatever nonsense with newspapers and guide-books they'd picked up at the Special Purpose School last year. Tragically, he even knew their names. Kostya, Sasha and Seryozha. But every year's intake would have a Kostya, Sasha and Seryozha. Their true talents lay in other areas. In the *mokroye delo* or 'wet-work'.

Another pat on the chest.

"Why do you persist in calling me Dmitriy?"

"Because, in my mind, you're 'False Dmitriy'– it's that or 'Boris Good-Enough'."

"Now you're teasing me..."

The Resident pursed his lips and whistled a few bars of the Fountain Duet from the Mussorgsky opera.

"Borya," he said, blowing a kiss. "You'd have to buy me dinner first!"

Not quite understanding, but trying gamely to play along, Major Boris Mikhailovich Lebedev gave a knowing chuckle and pretended to gaze intently at the evening panorama as they rattled through the switches onto the Galata Bridge.

"I know exactly who buys you dinner, all over Istanbul, my friend. Incidentally, I must thank you for the latest consignment of Albanian counter-revolutionaries, who, alas, expired shortly after returning to their native soil."

"I've no idea what you're talking about," the Resident scoffed, looking Lebedev up and down with unmasked contempt. "For such an unhealthy fellow, you have quite a tan, Dmitriy. Been down south? The Congo, perhaps?"

"Oh, considerably further!"

"Fancy that. So you hadn't anything to do with mucking up anyone's plans in Léopoldville, for example?"

"Why would it be in our interest for the MERCURY pair to reach their supposed destination?"

"Why would it be in anyone's?" the Resident said. "Even the poor woman herself…"

Lebedev's hand was back on his upper arm, giving it a little squeeze.

"It might be dangerous to play both sides in this matter, I think?"

"I've a licence to disbadge whenever the fancy takes me, as well you know. And you're hardly averse to trailing your own coat, Borya."

"Trailing, yes. But you seem to be flourishing yours like a *muleta*. Is that correct English, *flourishing*?"

The Resident tightened his fist on the strap, using his muscles to shake off the weak grasp.

"I know what they teach you people on Day One at Chelebityevo, but sometimes the job *is* a wolf and *will* run off into the forest if one does not act pre-emptively. Or did you miss Day Two of Foreign Intelligence training? Is that why your tutor wrote on your report, 'Boris Not Good Enough'?"

With that, he pushed brusquely through to the exit, putting as many outraged passengers as he could between himself, Lebedev and his men, as quickly as possible. If he was to shake them off for real, there would be further tricks to play that had not been taught at Chelebityevo, nor in London for that matter.

This wasn't his stop, but he had a rendezvous at the caravanserai of the Mahmut Pasha complex – not only to pass on Madame Zalokostas' latest pillow-talk, post-haste, but to add to the growing list of wartime records requiring prompt destruction, 'to protect our allies'. He was reluctant to lead the so-called Committee of Information straight there, even if said committee did seem to keep up with his every move.

Or at least, even if they thought they did.

*   *   *

Far away, on the fringes of the sanitary zone and the banks of the Congo River, stood the house on stilts.

African in design, colonial in execution, at the same time unremarkable and unique, it was known to everyone yet somehow absent from maps and memories alike. Its owner, an eccentric, had a shady past. Such people were best left alone, or so ran the prevailing opinion fostered by all the other shady eccentrics of the Léopoldville *environs*. His wife, it was rumoured, was a *mulâtre* and together they had something to do with the print shop in the new LECO building on Avenue Banning: books for the mission schools, and the occasional religio-political pamphlet that appeared, like the house on the river, to lean both left and right and therefore to be charmingly harmless. But they weren't seen at any of the bars and clubs that constituted social life in Léo, and so nobody knew any more about them or looked any closer.

Certainly, there was no one to notice or remark upon the recent house-guests, for the owners kept no servants, took no deliveries and had no visitors. Until now.

The Congo nightfall brought a dusty wind off the shore and the sudden blackout of the summer rains. Soon the screens were battering in their frames and the palm thatch of the veranda whipping around the edges. Beneath, it seemed the river was leaping up to meet the monsoon. Peering out through the cataract, they all jumped as a distant fork of lightning pierced the livid clouds above Stanley Pool.

Not an evening to be out and about, Bradley thought. The new arrival was fortunate to have been ferried into the boathouse just before the onslaught, although they had seen nothing but a vague form swathed in oilskins as the boat slid past.

Seated in the dark with Mila and Jenny while their host struggled to light the lamps, Bradley wondered if the two women shared his apprehension and was sure they did. Whoever the visitor was and however true the tales that they had heard – of missing hands, of a missing *face*, of a heart of ice – there was little doubt that he had control of their fate now. More so since they had hidden out here for five days, awaiting his arrival.

They were not prisoners, of course. This had been impressed upon them by 'Monsieur Sept', as the man from Seat 7, amused by their nickname for him, had taken to styling himself. When he had brought them here and introduced them to Pierrot, the local communist cadre whose house it was, he'd repeated how it had never been his intention to rescue them from the *Force Publique* but that now, having communicated with his client, he would do his best to harbour them. Even so, they were capable individuals, as he had seen, and it would be perfectly possible for the three of them to walk away, hitch a ride into Léo, and from there to anywhere else in Belgian Congo. Or they might steal a boat and make for the French side... Except, alas, they had no passports, no papers of any kind. However far they got, it would not be far enough. This was not Europe, where one wretched soul was much like any other and a whole region, even a country, might be crossed in a matter of days.

Better to wait for the client, who would arrive any day now. How? Perhaps by boat. From the French bank? That too was quite possible. And why was he coming? Perhaps to meet them, in the flesh, if that was not an inappropriate way of putting it. But also to question their other house-guest, who most certainly was a prisoner here.

That was why, on the veranda now, Bradley found the hairs on his arms and the back of his neck standing up. It wasn't just the electrical storm.

Like Sparky Scintilia, they were at the mercy of a man who had none.

Pierrot had lit the lamps: sombre bourbon glimmers that cast more shadows than light. Bradley saw the moisture in their eyes and on their faces as they sought out his.

"We need to be clear what we want out of this," Mila said, her words almost lost in the rain.

As always, Bradley admired her confidence. Our necks, he would have suggested, but didn't.

"Which is?"

"Safe passage back to England for Jenny. Onward passage for us."

The other silhouette shifted in its armchair.

"Now 'ang on a tick! Don't I get a say in this?"

"No. You've done more than enough." Mila turned to him not just for confirmation but for a cruel edge to the kindness. They were a double act, after all.

He made himself sound callous. It wasn't hard to summon.

"We can't have our minds on the mission if we're worrying about you."

"Well thanks a bundle!"

Fanks. He hoped his half-smile was hidden in the gloom. But he had heard the hurt in her voice – felt it, like a dagger slipping in – and he hated himself for it.

Mila was right though. It was to him that Jenny had attached herself most forcefully, with a concern that was almost sisterly, if not maternal. That was the bond that needed breaking.

"We're going to need you to report back, too," he heard Mila say to her, and he hoped the girl was too shaken to recognise this for what it was. A crumb of comfort, crudely tossed.

A melodious voice from the darkness behind them, strongly accented yet as self-assured as Mila's, said:

"I wonder who you would be reporting to."

It was the flight instinct rather than any sense of politeness, he thought, that caused the three of them to rise so abruptly from their chairs. It was the sudden proximity of the strange voice and the strange silhouette from which it emanated.

And it was the face that came out of the shadows as the figure advanced another strangely inhuman step. Strangely inhuman did not even begin to describe the face, because it wasn't a face, or even an accurate representation of a face. It was a ghost of a face, a clouded memory of a face, imperfectly erased. A nightmare after-image on the waking world.

As a mask, it would have been unsettling. But without knowing how, Bradley understood that it was no mask. Or rather that the mask was all there was.

Then the creature behind it was speaking Russian, and not to them. Instructions to Pierrot and Monsieur Sept, it appeared. Bradley made out the word *plennyy*, or 'captive', and sure enough the other two men dragged a hunched, protesting shape onto the veranda.

Scintilia, or what was left of him.

"Good, good," the visitor said. "We can have a party."

Whoever he was, he liked a performance, that was obvious. Having made his silent entrance, he now moved awkwardly, noisily, with his cane. There was something familiar about that cane, but Bradley could not place it. He was too busy watching the man's artificial hands as he manoeuvred around the table and gestured for a chair to be pulled out for him.

At last they were all seated: Bradley, Mila and Jenny to one side, the visitor and Monsieur Sept to the other, with Pierrot holding – holding up – Scintilia at the end.

Pierrot's wife brought iced jugs of soda water and juice to complement the liquor bottles and glasses on the table (the local *cerise* and *citronnade* was recommended, the palm wine discouraged, but Bradley had opted for the Brasserie de Léopoldville's *Super* blonde). Although she was a formidable-looking woman with her hair scraped back in a plain, no-nonsense scarf, she did not allow herself to get too close to the visitor, nor to look at him before she retired. A little rude, perhaps, from a hostess, but then she knew how he had passed his time with Scintilia since his arrival.

As she left, another lightning strike, many forked and closer now, lit up the colourless mask. Before the thunder rumbled, Bradley heard Jenny gasp in fright.

When he spoke again, it was in a different-sounding dialect and at a different pace. As Mila started translating into English, Bradley realised he must be altering his Russian to be intelligible to a Czech.

"He's thanking us for waiting for him… which as an unperson he has no right to expect."

"An unperson?"

"He is known as the Omitted. His former identity has been… expunged from all records. It would be a crime to reconstitute it by any means."

It was a freak show, hearing her talk over him. Bradley could see his lower lip moving, and hear the stumbling Russian, but as he concentrated on Mila's words, it was as though the Omitted became a lifeless totem, mesmerically possessing her.

"Now… I am speaking to the American. Not to you, Mr Bradley, but to this criminal, this gangster… You, Mr Scintilia. Are you awake? You had something you wished to ask us."

Pierrot had been holding him by his collar. When he was released, Sparky slumped forward on the table, then slowly raised his head. Like the eyes, his mouth was swollen and the words came out slurred, but distinct enough.

"Where's Parsons? Whatcha done with him?"

Trussed up as he'd been, crammed in with his buddy's still-warm body in the trunk of the car, he must not have realised what had happened.

The Russian spoke. There was a funny look on Mila's face as she interpreted.

"He went to feed the crocodiles. You will be next, but not all at once. Stick out your tongue."

"Wha–?"

"Gerardo – Sparky – do as you are told. Stick out your tongue."

It was not until Pierrot reached around and clasped his jaw that he complied. Seeing the pain, and the blood, and the trembling, Bradley felt sick. It made no difference that this was what Scintilia had done to him. In fact it made it worse.

The Omitted switched back to his brisk, fluid Russian. When Pierrot drew his sheath knife, it was obvious what the instruction had been.

"Oh God," Jenny said. Mila threw her a furious glare and began translating again.

"Listen, Gerardo… During the war, that is what we called our captured Fascists. 'Tongues'. Because they would tell us everything. Are you going to take this one chance to make your tongue as valuable as they were? Or will it be the first of many delicacies the crocodiles can expect tonight?"

*   *   *

When it was over, Mila found the half-empty bottle of Filliers Gin and poured herself a glass that left very little room for tonic water. Downing it, she poured herself another.

So Scintilia had talked. Of course he had. He had been softened up. She had played her part in that. And the Omitted's trick of suggesting that Parsons was not already dead when he'd gone into the river was one she might have used herself in similar circumstances. It was even, surprisingly, merciful, in a way.

Why then did she feel so *polluted*? Why was she so compelled now to wash the Russian's words out of her mouth?

Lighting a cigarette, the flame shook. Bradley's hand on hers held the match steady. His arm stretched out of the darkness. She had to squint to see that he was sitting next to Jenny now, his other arm clasped around her while she sobbed.

Why? Because of what it was to see a man broken. To see another break him further, without remorse. And to have had to give voice to that.

Mila had made a pretty poor nun, but at that moment she thought she understood their vows of silence.

After Scintilia, no one was talking much anyhow. Pierrot had taken him away. Back to the cool store, he said. His wife was nowhere to be seen.

"And so?" the Omitted said at last, in English. "You are pleased?"

It was Sam who was first to respond.

"How could anyone be pleased by that?"

A laugh in the darkness. Somehow, it felt wrong that such an aberration had retained the capacity for laughter. It felt obscene.

"*Razvedka*, Mr Bradley. What you call intelligence work. In Russian, means doing whatever is necessary. Anything and everything."

She heard Sam curse under his breath.

"*Císař?*"

The Omitted's accent took on an even thicker edge.

"'*English not good, but...*' I wondered if you would remember."

"This," Sam said incredulously to her and Jenny. "Is the man who posed as a member of the MERCURY network in Prague and ended up leading me to you."

Mila rolled her eyes and broke her vows.

"He was also the SMERSh officer who instigated the whole BORODINO deception and was there at the end, on the landing field. Colonel Andreev, I presume?"

"Ha! Good, Slečna Slavík! But you are mistaken. That man

177

never existed."

"Lucky for him, because as I recall, he was hung out to dry by his superiors…"

"Excuse, please? Hung out to dry?"

She gave an approximation in Czech.

"Ah, yes. Well, that would have make him very angry. Very… *mstitel'ny*?"

"Vengeful," she said. "He would become their nemesis."

"Just so."

"And they would be Comrade Abakumov, who was then head of SMERSh, and Comrade Beria, who was rumoured to be behind the deception, before disavowing it."

"Disavow? No… I can work out. It is new orthodoxy in Soviet Union."

"But it wasn't you who leaked my location in Scotland."

"Was it not?"

Her head was spinning.

"Nor was it you who leaked the hiding place of the Angel…"

"If you say."

Then, like the rain easing, like a Mark III wireless set finding its station, it was clear again.

"But you leaked our plans to these gangsters – or a twisted version of them."

She heard Sam and Jenny react and was worried that Sam's reaction would be violent. She pressed on quickly.

"You gave them the idea that we were coming south to finish off Jimmy Lonsdale or to interfere with his business – because you wanted to bring them into the chase and flush out… what?"

"What we have heard, Miss Slavík."

"We've heard a lot of guff. About gambling in Southern Rhodesia and arms deals with the Zionists in Palestine. About someone called Bugsy, who's dead now. About this so-called Swiss, Willi Nohl…"

Somewhere in the shadows beside the Omitted, Monsieur Sept raised a glass into the light. A toast to her. She wanted to shoot him too.

"…and about some warehouse he kept at the airport, behind the SABENA hangar. What would that have to do with you?"

"What indeed? And what with you?"

"I've no idea. Except that we were dropped into this mess, by you."

A slight movement drew her eye. Sam had rocked back in his chair, his arms folded. She saw the two fingers of one hand form a V on his upper arm.

"You know who else… whose *nemesis*… I should be, Miss Slavík? You and Mr Bradley also hung me out to dry, and Miss Simmonds' employer…"

The mask leaned forward. As the puppet-hands raised to it, either side, she felt a sudden childish terror that he was going to take it off.

Then the apparition sank back into the shadows. Like a crocodile, she thought with a shudder.

But when the voice resumed, it was not the sly teasing of a predator. Although he chose a mixture of English and Czech to ensure that he was understood, for the first time his emotions showed through. An unperson he might be, but this was personal.

"I should have let them kill you, a hundred times. Instead, I kept you alive. You are pawns in everyone's game. You always have been. But sometimes, a pawn is all one needs. The stronger pieces can be so weak, without knowing it. And, if a pawn can make it safely to the other side… suddenly it is the most powerful piece on the board."

She too sat back, though it felt more like defeat than a triumph. Forcing herself upright again, she refilled her drink. On a whim, she poured another and slid it across the table.

A white hand came out of the shadows to meet it.

Chink.

The voice was now matter-of-fact. She had heard it, or voices like it, a hundred times; had used it herself. The briefing voice.

"Beria is arming the Jews, against the interests of the Revolution in the Middle East. Now I have put the pieces

179

together, I will have the evidence I need."

"And Abakumov?

"Trading with Nazis – enough to finish him. There is something called *Die weiße Spinne*. 'The White Spider'. You will get me more on that."

And there it was, without even stating it.

Licence renewed. Back on target.

Sam, for once, was still a step behind. He spread his hands in a helpless gesture.

"But Beria, Abakumov… they are whole departments, whole organisations. You're one man. How can you hope to bring either to justice?"

Downing the gin in one, it was Mila who supplied the answer.

"He doesn't need to bring them to justice. He just needs each of them to bring the other to Stalin."

CHAPTER FIFTEEN

"You like those boys, huh?"

The speaker was a well-muscled fellow in a short-sleeved shirt that seemed too small for him by design. It matched his overly trimmed beard and tight-slicked hair, as well as the taunting economy of his limited vocabulary.

M.H. de Klerk shrugged and wrested his eyes from the Hals as it was carried out of the room to be crated up and shipped to the new location. At the opening of the outside doors, there came an orchestral fusillade from the sun beetles and cicadas.

"I was just a custodian," he said.

"Yeah, but you like boys, right?"

"I'm married, Faf."

"Oh I know that, 'Maxie'. But I haven't seen her around for a while. Have you?" 'Faf' Joubert, Head of Security at Boschkop, gave a supremely confident smile that would not have looked out of place on a favoured sporting personality. Or a classical tyrant.

His pique duly punctured, de Klerk muttered something to the effect that he had not. He looked on as the Afrikaner supervised the removal of the next painting from the whitewashed plaster wall and could not help stepping forward anxiously when the men snagged its frame. They were more used to tugging at stakes and vines. Snakes too, in this one-time Eden.

"Now this one's *lekker*, Maxie. A man off to do an honest day's work under the hot sun."

"It's the artist himself – his first ever self-portrait and his only full-length example. Those tools he's taking to work in the fields are his canvas, easel and paints."

Joubert peered closer at the straw-hatted, red-stubbled figure before turning away in disgust.

"*Ag*, another *fokken moffie*," he said. "I'll go make sure the boys are loading these up properly – and I'll make sure *your* boys're tucked in there safe and sound."

He meant the original *Laughing Boys*, de Klerk realised as he deciphered the thick accent and the clunky 'Kitchen Dutch'. Another taunt. But just for a second, he'd imagined that Joubert was referring to his recent ward, Poldi, and he had bridled at the perceived threat. Even during the darkest days of the occupation in the Netherlands, even as he had surrendered what remained of his soul to a life of unforgiveable betrayals and mortal sin, he had detested the idea of holding people captive for the purpose of coercing others.

Not that Poldi was a hostage, except in the sense that all children were hostages and orphans most of all. The boy had simply been sent on into the hinterland with the first consignment of artefacts: another relic of a ravaged Europe. Yet M. H. de Klerk, an orphan himself and the eternal childless custodian, had assumed the burden of this child's welfare for long enough to know his loathing of his adoptive parents; his loathing and his fear. Taking his 'Uncle Maxie' away from him was another cruelty, to both of them.

The real hostage, of course, had gone ahead with the second consignment.

Once Joubert had left, de Klerk hurried to the racks and seized a bottle more or less at random. A red, smuggled out from the cooperative in Stellenbosch and re-labelled as one of *Dutchie*'s. It was more palatable than the few whites Boschkop actually produced. But for the moment the quality of the wine did not matter, only the quantity.

As the custodian here – if only nominally now the owner – he carried a corkscrew on his belt and soon had the bottle open. He would have liked to have used it on Faf Joubert's thick neck. The carotid artery should surely produce a lovely ruby tint with a deep body and a boisterous length... Instead, after a cursory check that no connoisseurs were present to witness his ingenious sampling method, he tilted the bottle to his lips and downed a good half of it in one.

His beloved Rebekka! For whom he had forsworn children, and that blackened soul of his. For whom he would lie, cheat, steal, betray and murder, if only to keep her safe…

The voice in his head that even the wine could not smother, every bit as taunting as Joubert's. *And did you keep her safe?*

Helemaal niet!

Downing the rest of the bottle, he bit back on the urge to vomit.

To have protected her from the Gestapo, for so long, in the Netherlands, and then to have spared them both through the SAFEHAVEN deal with the Americans… only to fall back into the clutches of his former co-conspirator, Kuhlmann! It was like a bad dream, except that it was even more inescapable than that, because it was Fate.

Fate had thrown him back together with the Nazi as he planned his own escape – had seen de Klerk's involvement escalate from helping smuggle paintings to arranging forgeries of those Kuhlmann refused to return, and then to taking young Poldi off the latter's hands while he called on his sinister network to evade arrest and flee south with his spoils.

Fate had brought him and the boy to that ditch in the Haagse Bos that day, and to the strange encounter with the Englishman and his dog which had precipitated their own departure for South Africa aboard the *Warwick Castle*.

And of course it was Fate that had seen him offer up his vineyard operation in the Cape as a safe haven of sorts while Kuhlmann established firm contact with the *Ossewabrandwag*, the nationalist Afrikaner underground, and then, incredibly, with the Soviets too.

It had been Fate, payback for all his activities during the war and earlier, in America – or Hubris – to imagine for a moment that those activities had made of him a convincing desperado and that Kuhlmann and the Boers would not simply take everything for themselves.

Including you, Rebekka, my sombre-eyed darling; including you.

Fate.

That was a pretty word for it.

Character, was the ugly truth. As in bad. As in lack of. As in the sort of character who could betray both his friends and himself: convincing himself and his poor wife that the only way to keep them safe was to keep in with the Nazis and to keep making money, kidding himself that the making of the money was just the means, when of course it was the only end. And when, finally, you looked into yourself and found that character staring back at you, then it was clear what your destiny had been all along.

Keep running this place, Maxie, Kuhlmann had told him. For show. For profit. For us. And we'll keep Rebekka safe in the hinterland. For you.

It was, the Nazi hinted, the kind of arrangement in which he had specialised during the war, first in the East and then in the Netherlands. De Klerk had never dared to ask Kuhlmann about that side of his work. It was enough to know that both the army's *Abwehr* intelligence service and Himmler's, the *Sicherheitsdienst* or SD, had done his bidding; to know that whenever required he could provide a V-man, a *Vertrauensmann* or 'trusted man', to infiltrate any group you liked; and to understand, without ever really acknowledging it, that you were one of his V-men yourself.

Coming briefly to his senses, he found that he had retired to his office and opened another bottle, this time of something stronger. He had made some attempt to light his pipe and given up. Likewise some business with the corkscrew and his wrist – call it the idle doodling of a V-man.

The photograph of Rebekka was face-down on his desk.

*   *   *

"Anselm Kuhlmann," Mila said when the waiter had brought the wine, a local Montagu *Steen* which, they were assured, went well with Knysna oysters. For his own part, Bradley would have been happier with a red, even a dubious one from their intended destination, but it was unlikely that the Blue Train's *sommelier* would stoop so low.

"What of him?" the guest at their table produced his customary methodical grin.

"We're quite refreshed now. It's time to tell us all you know."

Quite refreshed. Bradley marvelled at her restraint. She sounded like a lady who'd had a funny turn at luncheon and gone to lie down in her suite. As opposed to one who had walked in from Portuguese Mozambique through the lion-infested Kruger, where there was no border... As opposed to one who had then hitched from Komatipoort to Nelspruit, the fly-blown outpost a few miles outside of which their guest had 'accidentally' pulled the communication cord on the Netherlands–South African Railway Company train to Pretoria, allowing two filthy figures to sneak aboard... As opposed to one who had delved past the taken-down carbine in her rucksack to change into whatever bare minimum of civilised clothing would get her onto the royally-appointed Blue Train, where there was a selection of expensive outfits and an *ensuite* bathtub waiting to 'refresh' her for her onward journey to Cape Town...

Their guest, he saw, appreciated her style as well. As she sat up straight, the picture of tightly buttoned elegance, in the luxury restaurant car of the all-First-Class service, idly perusing the rugged terrain of the Magaliesberg mountains as though she had never so much as set foot on a trail herself, the slick sonofabitch raised his glass in tribute. Bradley recalled how the man had studied her with growing interest as she'd faced up to him in the puddles of Léopoldville, wearing Jenny's sodden sweater and not much else.

"Anselm Kuhlmann," she repeated now, drumming on the linen tablecloth with clean but broken nails.

Monsieur Sept set down his glass with a nod that clearly meant 'To business'.

"Worked with Arthur Seyss-Inquart in Vienna after the

Anschluss," he said. "Then in the General Government in what had been Poland, where he continued his mission of securing and repatriating 'Germanic' art. When Seyss-Inquart was promoted to *Reichskommissar* of the Netherlands, Kuhlmann again accompanied him, and this time the rooting-out of artworks extended to the wholesale rooting out of Jews. Being in the rare position of having both Hitler and Himmler's favour, it seems he became an unofficial conduit between the level-headed *Abwehr*, which badly needed the Nazi stamp of approval, and the SD, which like all SS branches was staffed by fantasists…"

"An unofficial conduit," Bradley remarked.

The unplaceable features cracked as the grin broadened. For just a moment, the unplaceable accent broadened too.

"The pow-er of the go-between! With so many overlapping and conflicting organisations, that was how the Nazis got anything done. It is also why he was never properly investigated or hunted down for his crimes. And all the while he was pursuing his private hobby of collecting Degenerate Art for himself."

Mila ignored the amused shrug, just as she was ignoring the oysters.

"Then what does Abakumov want with him? What can he possibly offer?"

"It's interesting you should put it like that. Because you are absolutely right, this is a horse-market. All over Europe, all over the *world*, former *Abwehr* and SD intelligence officers are trading information for freedom. One of them, Richard Gehlen, has offered up his contacts and his archives to something called The Org, presently spying on the Soviet Bloc for the Americans. The Soviets would dearly like to find their own equivalent."

"But you don't know if that's what's going on here."

The grin slid back to its neutral position. Monsieur Sept returned the cool look.

"If Abakumov is prepared to risk the charge of collusion with a former enemy who committed crimes in the East as well as the West, he must think he has something good."

Although they had barely touched their starters, they had

lingered too long and the main course had arrived. Bradley and Monsieur Sept ate perfunctorily, making small talk, mostly about the landscape of the Witwatersrand. Mila was silent and just sipped at her wine. Finally, almost wearily, she returned them to the subject.

"You think he has something. What is it?"

Monsieur Sept was careful to finish chewing before replying.

"We know that Kuhlmann was with Seyss-Inquart when the latter courted the Palestinian leader, Haj Amin al-Husseini – and when he persuaded Hitler that al-Husseini, with his Aryan complexion, could be a key player in the Middle East as an ally of the Reich. Our conception, since Beria is secretly supporting the Zionists, is that this is how Abakumov plans to neutralise him…"

"Your 'conception', meaning you don't know," Mila turned to Bradley in exaggerated frustration. He wasn't sure how to react.

Monsieur Sept sat stony-faced.

"That is your job to find out."

"Not good enough," she snapped.

"You are here because we put you here. I hardly think you're in a position to negotiate!"

Bradley had picked up on her cue by now, or at least imagined that he had. Stabbing the air across the table with his fork, mouth half-full, he sputtered:

"The Omitted sent *you*... His go-between."

"I hardly think we're in a position not to," Mila added.

"Really!" Monsieur Sept, normally an indefinable colour, grew suddenly darker in the face, perhaps with the effort of forcing himself to lower his voice. "Let me tell you – if Mr Lonsdale and his Sicilian friends haven't yet found out what happened in Léopoldville, we could easily help them with that. Not to mention the Belgians... The identities you are travelling under – paper-thin though they are – are Party covers and might accidentally be revealed to anyone tracking down agitators, yes? You would do well not to underestimate my patron's reach."

"Reach is fine and dandy," Bradley added messily, wiping with poorly feigned remorse at the tablecloth and Monsieur Sept's tie. "But he chose *us* to be his hands."

The shifty face went from disgust to amusement to acquiescence – perhaps. He rolled his eyes.

"Very well. The Arab connection is the most likely scenario. But there is another possibility."

"Go on."

"Like you, we wondered what in God's name someone with knowledge of Dutch wartime saboteurs could offer the Soviet Union. It's not the same as Gehlen, giving the Americans a ready-made network of assets behind the Iron Curtain."

"I suppose he might have contacts who could tell Abakumov what's going on in The Hague," Bradley ventured. "I mean with all the new international organisations being set up, and so on…"

"That's not enough," Mila interjected.

"No, Miss Slavík, it is not. But have you heard of 'Operation North Pole' – or the *Englandspiel*, as the Germans liked to call it? Of course not. No intelligence service publicises its abject failures if it can help it, not even to its own operatives."

"The England Game?"

"Indeed. Like many undisclosed intelligence failures, it was an unsung counterintelligence success – in this case on the part of the *Abwehr*, with support, perhaps facilitated by Kuhlmann, of the SD and the SiPo security police in The Hague. In short, it led to the complete penetration of all MI6 and SOE networks in the Netherlands. There was a talented *Abwehr* officer by the name of Giskes who managed to run the Allies' wireless operators back against them, to the extent that every piece of intelligence was useless, every agent and weapons drop met by a reception committee."

Bradley caught Mila's eye.

"Our friend from Scotland mentioned something about this."

It was as though he hadn't spoken.

"What happened in the end?" she wanted to know.

"There was no end! Not for two and a half years! Captured agents left out their security checks as they had been trained to do if transmitting under duress and were simply reminded by their home station to include them next time. One operator even dared to use the prefix and suffix CAU and GHT but no one noticed. The Royal Air Force special squadrons complained that their planes always reached the drop locations safely, yet were frequently shot down on their return flights – but to no avail. Eventually, however, there were changes of personnel in London and Herr Giskes decided to send a final radio message, thanking them for all their agents and assuring that anyone else sent from England could expect the same treatment. A brilliant man."

"And he might be working with Kuhlmann?"

"No. We think he is working with Gehlen now. But it is possible that Kuhlmann was instrumental in planning the operation and directing Giskes..."

"…or he's claiming that he was," Mila said.

A shrug of acknowledgement and respect for her cynicism.

"That is how *this* game is played."

"It's all pretty far-fetched," Bradley countered, clearing his throat. "Plus it hardly explains why they'd be sucking up to him anyhow. If it's his old network of informers and infiltrators they're after, how can he run them from exile in South Africa? If it's his talents – even if he's taking credit for someone else's – they'd just scoop him up and use him up in Moscow. Or somewhere worse. Believe me, I know how that goes."

"Oh well, that's that then," Mila said in a strangely aggressive monotone.

Monsieur Sept, ever the mediator, made a concessionary gesture.

"The Omitted also considers this explanation far-fetched. But possibilities, rumours, he knows better than to dismiss these…"

Another gesture – the English idiom eluding him.

"Out of hand?"

"You are a proper tease, Miss Slavík!" And with that misplaced pleasantry, Monsieur Sept stood to deliver a very un-Western bow. "Now I must leave you to enjoy the rest of your dinner. I am, after all, an old acquaintance you have recognised, not a travelling companion. Perhaps I will see you later in the Observation Car?"

"That would be the place for it," Mila shot back with an ironic smile that drew an equally insincere snicker as he departed. She waited until he had gone through the doors before asking Bradley what he thought.

He stared out of the window.

"I'd say he's blowing even more smoke than this engine."

"Funny, though, that Pat mentioned the England Game, if they're keeping it so quiet."

He tried to remember their encounter in the Angel's studio on Texel, playing back the words in his head.

"He said it had happened in the Balkans too."

"His 'old stamping ground'," Mila nodded.

The sun had dipped below the hills, its last rays glowing on the trailing loop of smoke as the locomotive laboured up a curving incline. They were now the only diners in the car, but still Bradley lowered his voice to an urgent whisper.

"What then? He's working with the Russians? Or this is another one of his 'barium meals'?"

Her face gave nothing away but he sensed the advancing movement of that cipher machine in her head, the cogs and wheels spinning, meshing, clicking into place and progressing and they sought to unravel the meaning. He had seen it before, but this time the routine appeared to fail, as though the initial settings had been entered incorrectly.

She threw him a brisk smile and all of a sudden began tucking into her food, being as ladylike only as her hunger permitted, which was not that much.

"I've no idea... It's all speculation, of course it is... Sometimes that's what your opponents want, to make you doubt everyone and everything... The 'England Game'."

"Sometimes it's what your allies want too," he muttered ruefully.

"Mmm…"

Bradley sat back and let her eat. Although he couldn't pin it down, something in her altered manner had irritated him. The way she dismissed Monsieur Sept – or both of them. After a while, without seeking permission, he lit a cigarette.

"So I guess we just play along?"

"We've tried that. Look where it has got us," she said.

"It's got us here, hasn't it? We've come so far, and he's given us our next contact, the reporter in Cape Town. We're within reach of our objective!"

"Or theirs. Whoever they are, the people behind the man we know as Colonel Andreev. And you heard what *his* man said about our papers. If we keep using them we'll always be at their mercy." She set down her cutlery, glancing over her shoulder for the waiter. "It's getting late. He did say the Observation Car, didn't he? It'll soon be deserted, I'd have thought. I believe it's at the back of the train."

Bradley frowned.

"You really think we need to see him again?"

Mila finished her wine with a downcast, glazed expression. For several seconds she said nothing, showed nothing, until Bradley began to feel self-conscious just looking at her. Finally, almost imperceptibly, her eyelashes flickered in his direction as she gave a miniscule shake of the head.

"I think we should see him off the train."

*   *   *

As the spreading veil of darkness extinguished the colours of the flame trees and the sweetgums, the large, rather shabby colonial house on the dirt farm road ten miles from Banket Junction was no hive of activity, nor the hub of any kind of active investigation.

Behind the screens of the unlit veranda, Jimmy Lonsdale sat shivering in the erratically padded peacock chair, alone but for the ever-present ghost of 'Dickie' Daylesford. There was no one else to talk to with Vic gone. The staff were natives, which didn't count, and his other men were all at the mines. He had already spoken again by telephone this evening with Dominic Franzetti in Sinoia, a conversation both all too familiar and, by virtue of the local party lines, frustratingly unspecific.

No further news from or of their friends in the Congo. Nothing much, in fact, since the vague accounts of a disturbance at a *Force Publique* camp outside Léopoldville, which seasoned Congo-watchers said was likely a euphemism for another bloody mutiny. No word from the 'wider family' on progressing the plans they'd talked about, nor on sending anyone else to help. That, apparently, was a 'Rocky' subject…

Jimmy sneered at the circumlocution. His eyes went to the embroidered widow that was resting on the arm of his chair. Really he was sneering at himself.

"I did get somebody to swing by our Swiss acquaintance's place of business while passing through from Brazil," Franzetti had reported, alluding to the warehouse at Ndolo. "Empty. With great big TO LET signs. I guess they just took off, like I said."

"The clients won't be too chuffed about that, Dom. Nor their flippin' backers!"

"I ain't too 'chuffed' about it neither, Jimmy. I tell ya, if your two have pulled a fast one…"

"Do me a lemon, pal. It's 'er, innit?"

"The MERCURY broad?"

"I said it before. It's 'er. And she'll be comin'."

"*I'll* be coming for you, if anything's happened to Sparky."

"An' I'm gettin' increasin'ly Listerine just listenin' to you."

"Listerine, what the hell you talking about?"

At which point, Jimmy had slammed the phone down, as one or the other of them usually did these days.

He sought out the ghost and thought he saw a half-smile of recognition.

"Anti-Septic, pal. Anti-bloody-Septic!"

Despite his better instincts, his fingers toyed with the corner of the handkerchief again. *JJL.* And the all-too-familiar stain of once free, flowing blood.

It was the widow he'd handed to Vic Parsons after the accident in the *donga*. And it had arrived, postmarked from the

Belgian Congo, in the morning mail.

*   *   *

There was something wrong with Sam, she could see that.

She knew she had hurt his feelings and she hated herself for it. But that straightforwardness which normally she found a source of strength and comfort could sometimes verge on piety. He would follow her down a blind alley and allow himself no room to manoeuvre, even as she changed her mind and saw another way out. That kind of thinking could end up leaving both of them trapped.

Or was that deeply unfair, as well as a terrible mixed metaphor?

She realised that what she was really rejecting – and scorning – was his acceptance of his role as somehow inferior to her in all matters, from scheming to improvising and taking action, which was plainly ridiculous. Yet for all that she rejected it, its effects were there to see, for her at any rate. To continue mixing metaphors, he was as blind as those alleys down which he followed her. Blind to what was, to her mind, a self-evident pattern: of journeys, facilitated by others, that delivered one into the clutches of the next enemy, as at Léopoldville. Blind to what had been, for her, a barely-concealed warning from Monsieur Sept: about the England Game, and reception committees…

Blind to her impulse to return to their cabin and its *ensuite* bathroom – to plant her face deep into an Egyptian cotton towel, wait for the next crossing and the next time the train blew its whistle, and scream and scream and scream…

But he was rejecting something too and it was driving another wedge between them. Less than two days ago, trekking together across the Kruger, watching for perching vultures because that was where there would be lions, navigating by the sun and the stars, she had felt pure contentment for the first time in as long as she could remember. Yet now, as he strode ahead along the carriage corridor towards the rear of the train, everything was wrong.

"Sam," she called, striking an uncertain note. He stopped, his hand on the rail, and lingered with his back to her before he turned.

"What is it, Mila?"

Reluctance, that was what it was, on both their parts. She tried to summon a goofy smile.

"Let's go forward to the Lounge Car instead. Have another drink. Bump some gums."

He kept a straight face, but it was twitching.

"Do what?"

"Bumping gums… is that not what people say? I mean join in the chit-chat."

"Sure, that's what people say." He came back towards her and lightly took her arm to turn her around. "And Monsieur Sept?"

"Can wait until tomorrow. Let's sleep on it."

He nodded. Gratefully, she thought.

"Let's do that."

*   *   *

The whistling, the piercing shriek – the sudden, creaking, echoing lurch – can only have come from that ghastly suspended moment when the coxswain threw the unwieldy landing craft into a kind of stall turn to avoid the incoming salvo. An eddy in his dreams had drawn him back into that snag in time where action and reaction had gotten mixed up for evermore. Before he knew it, he was crushed again between riveted steel, the weight of damp, burdened men – and the furious expectation of the imminent detonation…

*   *   *

When he felt her cold fingers on the back of his hand and across his salty lips, the first thing he heard was the absence of the pulse of the wheels on the joints and squats of the track. The second was the whoosh of the safety valves letting off excess steam.

The third? The urgency of her whisper in his ear.

As Bradley's senses returned and his eyes adjusted to the starlight that filtered through the half-open shutters on the window of their two-berth cabin, he saw that she was already dressed in a plain sweater and her Kruger shorts. She had not turned on any lights.

"We've stopped. What is it?"

Clearly they were in open country. There were no lights outside either, nor was there any indication of the hustle and bustle of a mainline station, at any hour. The next stop was supposed to be Kimberley, after breakfast.

"Get ready to move," she hissed.

"What's happened?" He was flinging on clothes, going through their bags, but he was aware of her hesitation. "Mila?"

"After you went to sleep, I remembered something I needed to ask Monsieur Sept. I thought he might still be waiting for us in the Observation Car."

"And was he?"

He saw her eyes flash in the starlight.

"Yes. But he was dead. His throat had been slit."

The barrage from his waking flashback was now composed of questions, each growing in menace as it was left unanswered. He tried to drown them out.

"You came straight back here?"

She shook her head.

"First I disposed of the evidence. Whether or not the assassins intend to frame us for his murder, we would be the first to be interrogated by the authorities. We were seen dining with him. And our papers are not to be trusted."

"You... saw him off the train?"

She caught Bradley's shoulders, shaking him.

"Never imagine he wouldn't have done the same for us. But obviously all I could do was to topple him into the darkness to one side of tracks. Perhaps we have been stopped because his body has been found."

He checked his wristwatch. It was a quarter past three.

"In the middle of the veld, in the middle of the night? Seems unlikely. No, I reckon you're right. This is the killers' doing. More than one?"

"He didn't appear to have had a chance to fight back. I spent a little time staking out our carriage, in case they had already got in or were coming for us next. But instead… this."

At that they heard the connecting door slide open at the end of the corridor and instantly they both had guns in their hands – Mila her Tokarev, Bradley the Winchester Model 1907 self-loading carbine, which he had just reassembled. There came the steps of an attendant thundering along the train, with a call to one of his colleagues that sounded like *You check the back!* In lower voices, they could hear other attendants urging concerned passengers to return to their cabins.

"Best guess," Bradley whispered. "They had already arranged for someone to meet the train here. It's not like anyone aboard could call ahead for reinforcements or the police. So their buddies are coming to take us off, maybe even before the crew and passengers work out what's going on."

Mila was at the window.

"They might be out there already."

He rubbed his unshaven chin.

"They might not. Think about it. They had to pull the emergency chain – how would they know when to do it? Someone must have signalled from the trackside with a lantern. More than one lantern, to be safe, I'd say. More than one guy."

"It needn't have been the same crew…"

"No, maybe it wasn't," he said. "But if you were setting out to ambush a train, wouldn't you wait for your stragglers to catch up again?"

"Even with the hydraulic brakes, it must have taken quarter of a mile to stop," Mila said. "But they'll have a vehicle, of course. And for all we know they have more than enough men, whoever they are."

"Yeah. But we still stand more chance in the dark than in a running battle through the train. Not to mention the other passengers."

"Agreed." She turned away from the window. "No chance of getting this open more than six inches, not quietly anyway. We'll have to use the corridor."

Bradley silently unlatched the door and was about to sneak it open an inch when he paused and frowned.

"Someone's coming…"

Thumping boots, running forward. More attendants – or the killers, hunting them down? He peeked out.

"Coast's clear," he said.

Covering one another, they crept to the end of the carriage and climbed down into the night.

CHAPTER SIXTEEN

He first saw her on Het Lange Strand. Jog-trotting the five miles home along the beach, as was his custom at the end of his working day, he had left the few bathers behind in Noordhoek and expected to encounter only the odd Cape Coloured fisherman with his lure rod and his *snoek* basket before he reached the promontory that blocked the view of the Long Beach at Kommetjie and the walled-off radio station on Wireless Road.

Yet there she had been, perched high on the red-rusted boilers of the *Kakapo*, a steamship which had run aground here at the turn of the century and was little more than a skeleton now.

She had a sketch pad with her and used it to shield her eyes from the sinking sun as she waved to him with her sun-hat. She wore khaki shorts, a mannish white shirt and well-worn *takkies*.

Probably a *koeksister*, he reflected ruefully.

"Howzit!" he called anyway, changing direction to loop towards the wreck through the white dunes.

"Good evening! Isn't it gorgeous?"

He nodded. It was. Turning to squint out across Hout Bay, he could see the sheer cliff of The Sentinel rearing in shadow above the harbour, while the bulk of the Karbonkelberg still caught the late sun behind it. Then, to the right, the Little Lion's Head and the massif that was basically the back of Table Mountain, before – most prominent of all – the great shark's tooth of Chapman's Peak, where he worked. Had they been at a higher elevation, which was impossible in this windswept valley but easily achieved up by the radar station on the Slangkop above Kommetjie, they might have glimpsed the South Easter setting out the evening's tablecloth across the top of the mountain and the city that lay beneath it.

Glorious indeed, he thought, checking that his bare arms looked suitably *gespier* in the golden December light.

"Sketching, huh? May I see?"

She was a *rooinek* of some less-than-certain kind and so he spoke in English. As he approached, she rotated the pad and showed him a thin pencil representation of the vista. It looked fairly accurate, but he had no idea if it had any merit beyond that.

"Where do you stay?" he asked.

"In Kommetjie," she gave a shy smile as she stumbled over the 'key' ending. "With my cousin Peggy."

"Is it? *Ag*, I think I know Peggy. The little two-storey house with the *broekie*-lace balconies, right down on Van Imhoff's, near the Kom."

"That's the one. Of course she and her father only have the ground floor…"

"Her father, *ja*. He's not doing so good now."

"No. Not since the war."

"Shame," he shook his head sympathetically. Then, almost as though a rip-tide in the warm evening breeze had started exerting itself on his lower half, he found himself stepping backwards through the rusted rib-cage of the wreck and the matching curls of sun-blackened kelp. "Well… I'll see you around, I'm sure."

It was the strangest thing. Had he simply lost his nerve, like some skinny schoolboy? Had she somehow produced that force herself, like when you got up close to a seriously electrified fence? Or was it some kind of danger signal, an animal instinct buried deep within his being? Whatever the cause, he was suddenly 'through the leaves', as his people said, with everything seeming far away and hidden. He hadn't even asked her name!

"I'm Annie, by the way," she sang out.

"Oh… I'm Faf," he called back. "Faf Joubert."

*   *   *

Despite its restrictive proportions, the upstairs bar of the Kommetjie Hotel would never have been mistaken for a carriage of the Blue Train. In place of burnished wood panelling freshly shipped out from England, here sharks' jaws and mottled photographs lined the discoloured walls. There were no windows. Casual visitors took their drinks onto the balcony that overlooked the dusty yellow bend on the road to Cape Point. Serious patrons arranged themselves along the bar, which grew dingier and smokier by the yard.

Near the far end, Bradley couldn't help thinking that the density of the cigarette and pipe smoke was no bad thing. Not only did it enable one to hide in the gloom, but it also helped to mask two distinctive odours blowing in from the balcony, the first being the local crayfish, which was all that anyone ordered here on a Saturday afternoon, the second the reek of the decaying kelp that habitually overwhelmed the tidal pool at the 'Kom'.

His companion appeared less certain, no doubt because she did not smoke or drink. She was a Christian Scientist – an American religion, she said, albeit one he knew nothing about.

"And how do you square that with the Party, Miss Henry?"

She fanned herself with her little pocketbook and took another sip of bitter lemon.

"Peggy, please. And I shall call you Sam."

"Sure." He had told her his real first name if not his last. Given the events of recent days, he was pretty sick of evasion.

"I'm no communist, Sam, you may be sure of that, only a member of the Springbok Legion, which like the Communist Party bars no one on the basis of race or gender. Our purpose is to represent the rights of all who served during the war, and to prevent those who did not from subverting the best interests of the Union and its peoples."

"And yet we were given your name – and the phone number of your place of business – by a go-between who worked with the communists..."

For all her serious-minded act, she looked amused by his suspiciousness.

"It's nothing sinister, Sam. My boss in the commercial art department of the advertising agency on Adderley Street is also an organiser for the Legion. He proposed me as a volunteer because he knows what *motivates* me most of all."

"Which is?"

"To be merciful, just, and pure," she said without a blink. "That is one of the tenets of our religion, my father's and mine. So I must be merciful towards the men who cracked Pop's head open when he was guarding the radar station on Slangkop – that's 'Snake Hill', above us here. But I must also be just in seeking to prevent others from committing similar crimes."

Bradley felt compelled to stub out his cigarette.

"How old are you, Peggy?"

"I'm twenty-six."

"So I guess your father was in the Home Guard?"

"That's correct. He fought in the first war, but he volunteered again this time to protect installations in the Cape from the local saboteurs. The girls on Slangkop were tracking Nazi submarines and surface raiders. Between them and the sailors in the radio monitoring station by the beach, they even managed to pick up the *Graf Spee* on its way down to the South Atlantic."

"And these local saboteurs, who were they?"

A man was squeezing past them, a white haired fisherman type in washed out denim, pipe clamped between his remaining teeth. Peggy inclined her head.

"*Wag 'n bietjie*, as we say here." Seeing his confusion, she added, softly: "Wait a moment."

Bradley watched the heavyset old boy negotiate his way to the restroom, muttering more of the Dutch-but-not-Dutch language as he went. Every other word, it seemed, was *fok*.

"*Ossewabrandwag*," Peggy continued. "The 'Oxwagon Sentinel'. Fervent nationalists with strong ties to Nazi Germany who objected to the Union supporting Britain in the war, even though it was the decision of a government led by an Afrikaner like themselves. They spied on shipping and radioed the details back to Berlin to direct the U-Boats. Sometimes, as with my father here, they tried to disrupt the efforts of the South African SSS, the Special Signals Services. Slangkop, you see Sam, was also part of the 'Huffduff' direction-finding network that pinpointed both the U-Boats and the transmitters operated by the OB spy rings."

"You're very well informed," Bradley said.

Peggy looked away, staring instead at her drink.

"I was seeing a naval officer," she said at last. "He was here for a time, but mostly at the main SSS station in Simon's Town. He went back to sea, eventually, and was lost off Normandy."

Bradley cursed inwardly. So many stories like that. So many young women like Peggy, keeping their voices steady.

On an impulse, he laid his hand on hers and, before she could recoil, said:

"I was there. I'm one of the men he saved."

She pulled her hand away and used it to pat at her unruly frizzy hair. But that was a half-smile, half-averted. Was Pride a sin in her religion? Probably.

It was one she might permit herself, he thought.

"But just a minute… That was then. What are these 'OB' guys after now?"

Peggy pulled a helpless face.

"They've gone. By the end of the war, Jan Smuts' government – with the help of the British – had rounded them all up and placed them in internment camps. You won't understand the significance of this, but Afrikaners – Boers – have long memories. When the war ended, they were all welcomed into the National Party. What they are 'after', as you put it, is what the National Party is after: a racially pure state, with non-Afrikaners side-lined and Coloured people stripped of their vote."

Bradley had only the vaguest understanding of the politics, but he knew that the term Coloured, which back home came with its own poisonous history of racial discrimination, was here used to refer to the Cape's distinct population of mixed-race people, who claimed as ancestors everyone from the original inhabitants to the Malay slaves the Dutch had first brought with them. From his limited experience of the country so far, he hadn't exactly noticed them enjoying equal wealth and luxury with the whites but neither, clearly, were they reduced to the status of servants, like the poor black folk. If that was the National Party's plan, he could see why it would fire up Peggy. But she had spoken specifically about wanting to prevent the OB and their crimes. How could she do that if they were gone?

What did she know?

It wasn't the time to ask. Having glanced anxiously towards the open door to the balcony, she was now turned pointedly away from it. Bradley looked. A handsome couple had just entered. The man was fit and tanned, with a neat dark beard and shiny hair. He had on an open-necked shirt and a blazer that was cut to show off his broad shoulders and trim waist. His date wore a navy polka dot tea dress and a floppy-brimmed straw hat that emphasised rather than hid the length of her bare neck and the shortness of her hair.

Mila. Or rather, 'Annie'.

Peggy was watching him now, not the new arrivals. He shrugged.

"I guess we better go say Hi to your 'cousin'."

"You're sure?"

"Sure." Bradley said. "Wouldn't want them to think we were spying on them."

*   *   *

By the time they had reached the bottom of Wireless Road, he had taken her hand to guide her over the stones. On the beach, she employed the excuse of removing and carrying her shoes to disengage from him. But once they were near the waterline, skipping back and forth to avoid the waves, his arm clamped around her like a yoke.

Mila gritted her teeth and forced the smile back onto her silly painted face. In truth she wasn't thinking about Joubert at all. She was thinking about Sam.

He had barely held it together in the hotel bar, barely kept the thunderous cloud from overshadowing his casual greetings.

When Faf had flung out a muscular arm for what was obviously a trademark tough-guy-handshake, Mila had sensed Sam's barely contained urge to twist the squeezing fist over like a stop-cock and run it halfway up the trim, well-muscled back. Even Peggy had noticed it and made it her business to lead him away after the absolute minimum of small-talk.

Mila was used to Sam being protective of her. If she examined her own feelings on the subject, which she rarely did, she had always liked that about him, right from their first encounter, when he had saved her life at the disastrous partisan handover and she had styled him, only half-cynically, her 'guardian angel'. Sometimes, it was true, he became overprotective, in ways that even loyal members of her old resistance group had not. But then it was also true that she was guilty of using his overprotectiveness to manipulate him into taking action alongside her – or into taking separate actions to secure her flank – and that was one reason why she preferred to avoid self-examination.

Had she considered the further possibility? That his overprotectiveness, his devotion to her, stemmed from more than just admiration and a desire to give his own broken life purpose by replicating the others' loyalty, or even bettering it? Of course she had. But every time she thought she'd seen the signs, she also thought she saw them refuted; every time she all-but-invited them, she saw her invitation rebutted.

The awful thing, she knew, was that she might have it the wrong way round. Her single-minded pursuit of Pavel, which was not single-minded at all but tore her thoughts into a *billion* pieces every day, gave each of them the ultimate excuse not to seek any other kind of emotional progress, let alone consummation.

But Sam's behaviour was something new and she understood full well what had brought it bubbling to the surface. It wasn't the situation she was putting herself in now, in spite of his objections.

It was the fact that he knew he couldn't trust her.

She tried to wipe it all from her mind. The beach, the light, the views here were astonishing, in ways that Peggy's sketch could never have captured. Gazing out to the distant fishing boats that clustered beneath the cliffs across the bay, her eye was drawn by closer movement in the translucent rollers. Sleek, dark shapes rushed beneath the surface – then arced gracefully above the wave.

She smiled and almost giggled, in spite of everything. For a moment there, she had supposed the shadows to be sharks. For them to be dolphins instead seemed a good omen.

Faf – or Francois, which was a Huguenot name, he told her proudly – had had an interesting life and was happier to describe it than to ask about hers. For her own part, she was content to hear of his poor childhood in Cape Town's District Six, on the slopes of the mountain. Of his *lekker* cosmopolitan neighbourhood – Cape Coloured, Malays, Jews, all of them better than the *bladdy* British – and the tender age at which he had first gone to sea.

Oh, but not her, he said, backtracking. He could tell she was no Brit. But the *Kakies* from the Freedom War, who had come for his mother and her sisters, putting their farmstead to the torch and dragging them off to the concentration camps... His mother had been a girl then, he said, and all she remembered was a night full of fire and feathers. Why? Because the *Kakies* had ripped into their mattresses with their bayonets, looking for *Boere* treasure. But they had found none because the *Boere* were dirt-poor and starving already with their men away at war, and they died in their thousands – his mother's sisters among them – in the disease-ridden British camps.

Mila was sympathetic. How could she not be, even if she wondered how a man with such hatred of those camps could work for men who had refined the idea into something infinitely worse.

But as the miles passed and their conversation, never as scintillating as the sea beyond the breakers, stumbled into clumsy silence, Joubert began pulling her tighter and tighter against his long, firm body. It was becoming harder and harder to advance along the slope of damp sand, which was presumably his intention. When she turned her face to him, he leaned in for a kiss.

He tasted of the crayfish they had toyed with on the balcony. Or she did. She realised that she had not kissed anyone since those two older men during the war, both of them dead now. She wished she were dead too. Or Faf, for preference.

His hands were on her. With one eye on the incoming waves, she made it seem that he was overpowering her, causing her to totter off balance. He went with her, two steps closer to the sea.

It was enough. The next wave swept in and soaked his shoes and trousers.

"*Ag verdomp!* I knew I shouldn't have bothered dressing up smart!"

She held her shoes and skirt up, kicking playfully at the receding water.

"Wasn't I worth it?"

"*Ek weet nie*," he said as he took off his shoes and wrung out his socks. "We'll have to see."

Oh, we'll see alright, she thought. Not for the first time, she wished that her bag wasn't with Sam and Peggy, currently driving the long way from Kommetjie to Noordhoek in Peggy's father's tiny pre-war car. Her bag and her cosh and her gun.

"Aren't you going to show me the paintings now?" she said in a little-girl voice.

"You bet I'll show you." He stood up again with a grin that was more like a snarl.

It was their third meeting and their first date. Following their chance encounter at the wreck, which had been carefully timed according to Peggy's instructions, they had bumped into each other again this morning, on the road leading down to the Kom. This, Mila was fairly sure, had been engineered by Joubert, since she had told him that she was staying with Peggy near there. The fresh breeze being in a favourable direction, they had strolled around the concrete wall of the pool and chatted awhile, mostly about her sketching, and then he had asked her out properly. When she'd pretended to demur, he had mentioned his employer's collection of European artworks, making it sound as though he pretty much had the run of the place.

"Too risky," Sam had protested when she told him she'd accepted Joubert's offer of a tour. "You'll be in there alone – and unarmed, I suppose?"

"I think I'll have to be," she had said, momentarily unable to meet his eye, or Peggy's.

"Well hell, it's your funeral..."

Three days before, setting off from the Silvermine reservoir, they had climbed the neighbouring ridge, granting themselves a view of the back side of Chapman's Peak. Even with field glasses, however, there had been no determining the internal layout of the main complex of buildings, which appeared to combine the tall thatched roofs and decorative gables of a Cape Dutch manor house and its outhouses with lower, more Mediterranean-looking annexes, much of them obscured by vines. For a couple of hours, they had watched vehicles come and go, mostly light trucks of the type the South Africans called *bakkies*, and always loaded with crates. The only people they spotted were black or Cape Coloured workers.

Even then, lying side by side, there had been the tension between them. There was scant satisfaction to be derived from the hike and less from the reconnaissance.

Now, following Joubert as he hurried off the beach and up the sandy roads that led through the dense milkwood forest at the foot of the peak, Mila wished again that she wasn't so good at forcing Sam to do what she wanted.

Under the tree cover, the vegetation was almost tropical. White stone walls and gateposts on the red dirt road declared that they had reached the Boschkop estate. The wrought iron gates gave every impression of being readily accessible to buyers and other visitors, but judging by the demeanour of the African 'garden boys' stationed there, Mila suspected that they would more likely be turned away with a show of unhelpful incomprehension. Even Joubert, the Head of Security, drew hostile looks as he used his own key for the gate, although perhaps these were reserved more for his guest. At least it didn't seem that bringing women back with him was a regular occurrence.

She wondered what weapons they had hidden in the hydrangea bushes either side of the gate – and whether the fence above the surrounding wall was electrified. But they had already wondered all this and more, without any useful outcome.

It's your funeral, he had said, in that tone. Thinking about it was enough to make her chest heave suddenly. Giving a sniff, wiping her eye, she had to pretend that she was feeling the effects of the long walk, the increasing climb and the heat. Perhaps she was.

"Nervous, *bokkie*?" Joubert leered. "No need to be. There'll be no one in the house."

"Not even your employer?"

"Except him, but he'll be *smoordronk* in his study by this time of the evening."

"And his family… does he have children?"

Something about this question amused Joubert. Mila imagined the feel of the back edge of her hand on the underside of his nose: she could see where he must spend ages in front of the mirror, trimming his moustache there. A scything axe-blow, launched somewhere back in Kommetjie, back in The Hague, back in Czechoslovakia…

"They've gone. That's what he'll be crying about. Boo hoo!"

It was all she could do to muster the few sounds that passed for words. Returning his smile was beyond her.

"OK, Faf. Now I really want to see those pictures."

"*Ag*, you'll get a show alright, *bokkie*, I swear to you."

She had not really thought that Pavel would be here. Not really. If anything, she had resolutely told herself the opposite. Except of course that she had imagined it, pictured it, between nightmares. And now it appeared that her rational self – the part of her she hated most nowadays – had been right again, and the other part of her, the fractured remnants of who she used to be, was receiving its latest lesson in the folly of hope.

Complete the reconnaissance. If possible, obtain intelligence.

Let your rational self, which is to all intents and purposes dead, do what needs to be done to achieve those aims.

As though recalling an instructor himself, and a faint notion of gallantry, Joubert stepped aside to show her into the house.

*   *   *

The southern summer was disorientating. They had put up Christmas trees of all things on the sun terrace of the Boschkop manor house, and there were decorations showing at the few unshuttered windows too. But once the sun began to descend, you were soon reminded that this was not simply an inversion of the familiar north. Sunset was rapid, twilight fleeting. It had grown fully dark by nine o'clock.

At ten, a back door cracked open. A thin border of light showed and went out again. Bradley left the cover of the protea garden and scuttled over.

When she opened the door for him, the first thing she whispered, every bit as urgently as she had whispered to him on the train, was: "Don't react. Don't you dare!"

Crouching next to her in the kitchen, his vision accustomed to the faint glow of lamplight from inside the house and he made out her face. At once, his fists balled and he exhaled several times through his nose.

"It's not as bad as it looks," she said. "It was one wild swing he caught me with."

"As you were subduing him?"

"No," she said, putting a palm to her swollen cheek and wincing. "Before that."

Bradley had been about to reach out careful fingers to turn her chin towards the light. Instead he froze as a wave of fury broke over him. For the moment, he couldn't trust his hands,

"It's alright," she said. "He's out cold now. And tied up. Forget about him."

That was not going to happen, but for now he nodded and handed over her bag. Mila took out the pistol and the cosh, giving him the duellist's choice. He took the cosh.

"Thank you, Sam. For being there. And Peggy?"

"Went back to Kommetjie straight away, as agreed. Who's here?"

She shook her head glumly.

"Not Pavel. Nor Kuhlmann. Only de Klerk, alone in his office, drunk, supposedly."

"Servants?"

"Not in the house. They were given the night off. There are some rooms behind the winery…"

"I've seen them. I think they've gone to bed."

"Good," she said. "I don't want this to be any more disruptive that it has to be. Joubert is out of the picture now, of course, but if we can get de Klerk to play ball…"

Bradley seethed, still angry in more ways than he could count.

"He's the one who killed your husband!"

She sighed. It was almost a groan.

"*I* killed Richard – the moment he forgot his own business and started trying to help with mine. And from what I've managed to pick up, de Klerk is no crime lord. He's frightened. We don't know why but we do know of whom. If we can persuade him to tell us where the others have gone…"

"Maybe we can get there before the balloon goes up?"

"Exactly," she said. She put out a hand and rested it on his arm. "So are you ready?"

He met her eye, the one that was still open at any rate. He knew what that querying, reassuring touch meant, and why she had felt it necessary.

He gave a bitter chuckle and a nod.

No tricks this time, she was saying. No deceptions. No lies to drive us even further apart.

They moved silently through the house, keeping to the shadows. The only lamp that was still lit on the ground floor was on a table in a tall passageway that led, Mila indicated, to the door of the study.

It was a solid-looking door that would have required them to batter it open with the settle bench from the other end of the corridor and even then it might have taken several blows. Bradley saw that Mila was about to knock instead.

But then she paused, both eyes closed. He thought he understood why. Although this was not the last door and Pavel would not be on the other side, what was in there was the culmination of a search, a pursuit, that had taken them from the Scottish summer to the advent of Christmas in the opposite hemisphere. It had been an undertaking every bit as punishing and deadly as an attempt on an unconquered Himalayan peak, and as with any mountaineer, it was appropriate for one to pause and reflect on this before finally stepping onto the summit – even if the true summit was to be found over the next ridgeline, or the next.

She knocked, politely and then more forcefully. From inside there came a tinkling crash, a thud and muffled curses. She tried the door, which opened smoothly to reveal a comfortably appointed, lamp-lit study with a leather-topped desk and deep leather-bound chair. Small framed paintings and drawings lined the walls, interspersed with African carvings: a mask, a headpiece, a beaded club of some kind. On the desk sat a framed photograph of a dark-haired, dark-eyed woman in her late thirties, alongside an intriguing abstract sculpture in plaster or cement and a toppled wine bottle. In the chair slumped a haggard man with unshaven jowls that hinted at a recent loss of weight. The curly hair and close-set, dark-ringed eyes matched the description of M. H. de Klerk.

He raised his head and regarded Mila with that confused look of half-recognition. Bradley wondered if her recent black eye had obscured the resemblance. Then the Dutchman's expression changed to one of shock.

"*O mijn god!*"

"You know who I am?" she asked. "You know who I seek?"

De Klerk nodded, still staring. Then he spoke in good English, albeit with an American accent and the halting delivery of one confronting his guilt.

"I was told that you were dead. His parents, they said, had died in an air-raid. But he always *knew…*"

"Who knew?"

Bradley could hear the agitation in her voice. He began to wish that he had chosen the pistol instead of leaving it for her.

"Poldi, madam. He knew that his adoptive parents were not his real parents, and he always said…"

"What did he always say?"

"That his *máma…*" The eyes widened even more. *"Nee!"*

Mila was unaware of anything but de Klerk's words. Even Bradley took a second longer than he should have done to realise that the man was reacting to something – someone – behind them in the open doorway. As he turned, he knew that it had been a second too long.

In the confined space, the blast of the shotgun was head-splitting. Half-blinded, Bradley launched himself through the smoke at Joubert and brought the cosh down as hard as he could on the hand that held the butt of the gun, striking the thumb. It was a side-by-side piece with one hammer still cocked and he half-expected the man's instinctive reaction to be to pull the trigger again. Instead he yelped, opened his injured hand and made to grab it with the other, letting the gun spin free. Bradley released the cosh and caught the gun with both hands, swinging it around to butt-stroke Joubert in the face.

As Joubert dropped, Bradley saw the second man behind him: another muscular white man. An instant calculation told him that this was one of Joubert's security team who must have returned unexpectedly and set his boss free – because Mila would not have made the mistake of tying the bonds too loose or forgetting a second guard.

Calculation complete, he emptied the shotgun into his chest.

Joubert was more or less unconscious – his second time tonight. Bradley put his boot and his weight on the beardless throat as he turned back to what he already knew must be a ghastly scene in the study.

The blast of twelve-gauge buckshot, too close to disperse at all, had taken de Klerk in the right shoulder and virtually torn it off. Half in the toppled chair, half on the floor, Mila was desperately trying to staunch a pumping arterial wound while de Klerk thrashed and whimpered, his agonised face a blood-spattered grey.

"Tell me!" Mila was screaming at him. "Where is he?"

He clutched at her with blood-red hands.

"Find Rebekka, my wife. Get her away from them!"

"I will," Mila said. "Now tell me where they are."

"At the other house… *O mijn god!*" de Klerk said, and died.

As Mila, bloodied too, turned to him in absolute horror, Bradley immediately took his weight off Joubert's throat.

He would live a little longer after all.

CHAPTER SEVENTEEN

When the young woman's voice broke the silence in the darkened cabin, it was hesitant both with concern and with the resolution to say what needed to be said.

"They'll be waiting for you."

At Peggy's side in the front passenger seat of the little pre-war Austin, Mila gave a mirthless chuckle.

"That's why I need this insurance."

"But even so… simply to turn up and demand your son back?"

"I can hardly assault the place, not with Pavel there!"

"They could still capture you, or just kill you out of hand."

"I'll have something to trade."

"And your friend Sam? Does he think it's a good idea to walk straight into the… the lion's den?"

Mila turned to look at Peggy, but her profile was a silhouette against the haze of the distant floodlights and her expression unreadable.

"Sam has disappeared. If I remember rightly, he said I can do what the hell I like."

She had not told Peggy what had happened. She certainly hadn't told her how they had obtained the intelligence on the location of the 'other house'. But with Sam gone now, it had been all the more necessary to enlist her help in formulating a plan of action.

So she had told Peggy what Joubert had told them, about the ostrich and sheep farm in the vast semi-desert region known as the Karoo, and the group who lived there.

"Van Rensburg?" The young woman's eyes had lit up. "The head of the *Ossewabrandwag* during the war was a man called Van Rensburg, but he and his men are up in the north, and under investigation for high treason. Perhaps this is a brother."

"Then why wouldn't they keep their safe house in the north as well?" Mila had asked. "I gather that is solidly Afrikaner territory?"

"It is also the region most thoroughly swept by our 'Huffduff' for unlicensed transmissions. By contrast the Karoo is virtually unpopulated and of interest to no one."

Recalling their conversation now, Mila let out an involuntary sigh. She was starting to feel very isolated herself – and very alone.

Eventually the head of unmanageable frizzy hair turned towards her. She felt a gloved hand grasp hers.

"The wolf also shall dwell with the lamb, and the leopard shall lie down with the kid; and the calf and the young lion and the fatling together; and a little child shall lead them.'"

At the last words, Mila had to catch her breath.

"Why would you say that?"

"Because you mustn't be afraid." The hand gave hers a friendly squeeze and returned to the steering wheel. "Love holds control over all. Knowing this, as Daniel did, we can shut down negative thoughts, just as God shut the lions' jaws. That's what my religion teaches. You are being led by a little child..."

"Yes."

"Then you are being led by Love," Peggy said emphatically, before adding: "He's here."

Mila almost jumped. But then through the steamed-up windscreen she saw a pair of headlamps flash in the gloom ahead. Peggy's contact: that was what she had meant.

They got out and stepped forward into the faint glow of their own headlamps. A cold sea mist enveloped them, merging with the shredded remnants of the cloud that had descended over Cape Town with the night. The twinkling lights of the city and, in the other direction, the cargo vessels and warships standing off the new basin, were almost overwhelmed by the harsh white glare around the cranes, excavators and bulldozers that were the sole structures occupying the reclaimed foreshore.

The bulbous car in the shadows ahead was a locally produced right-hand-drive Hudson. Two figures in dark hats and coats carried forward a crate and set it on the ground.

"That's it?" Peggy said.

"Fresh off the ship," said one of the men, another South African. "The latest American invention. You best be careful with it."

"We're grateful," Mila said, but the men were already retreating to their car.

"Come on," Peggy said. "Let's put this in the trunk and get out of here."

Mila nodded and bent to take half the weight.

What a strange young woman, she thought. And then, in spite of everything, she burst out laughing.

*   *   *

Fraserburg Road station sat at the junction of two bone-dry rivers, the Gamka and the Leeu. Each name meant Lion, one in the Bushman tongue, the other that of the first Trekboers. Or so said the old man, who like the river beds was so creased and sun-scorched he might have originated from either people, or from the parched ground of the Karoo itself. Even his patchy whiskers matched the stunted scrubland that spared it from being a proper desert. The car he was selling appeared to have had a similarly enigmatic history, having begun life many years ago as a Hupmobile Eight, before its conversion to what must have been a variety of different farm vehicles. But it ran, was cheap enough if overpriced, and came with full tanks and a good map of the local area.

The Broker paid up and got on the road for Beaufort West. Although this was metalled, it was so dust-coated one would be hard pressed to notice. Were it not for the telegraph poles running along the railway line, one might imagine that nothing had come this way since those *voortrekkers* over a hundred years ago. He could tell that there were no vehicles ahead, for by the look of the cloud he was leaving, he would have spotted anything moving within a couple of miles. Nor were there any settlements to be seen, only the occasional unmarked side-track disappearing into the haze.

When he stopped to take a drink of water, strip off his jacket and stow away his cargo, his eyes were drawn by a flicker of light to the south-east, but upon climbing onto the roof with his binoculars, he saw that it was a sign neither of glass nor of water, only the rippling flanks of a herd of springbok in the middle distance.

Like the white horses of the Golden Horn, he thought.

He had been told to look out for the first flat-topped hills and escarpments to the north, but so far the only features on this baking tray of a landscape were distant cone-shaped *koppies* that seemed more like landmarks imported from Edgar Rice Burroughs's Mars. He laughed grimly at the idle notion. The places even sounded the same, as though perhaps they were simply different renderings in different dialects, like the Gamka and the Leeu. *Barsoom. Karoo.*

And would he, on this impossible ambassadorial mission, enjoy strength beyond mere mortals?

He bloody wished so!

Shying away from more serious speculation, his mind gravitated instead to Kipling's poem from the Boer War and he began to chant the infectious marching beat under his breath as he drove the empty miles.

"Seven – six – eleven – five – nine-an'-twenty mile today…
Four – eleven – seventeen – thirty-two the day before…
Boots – boots – boots – boots – movin' up and down again…
There's no discharge in the war…"

And so on, and on.

And no, there really wasn't. Not from this war and perhaps not from any other. No discharge and no clear view of the objective. Not the next objective nor the one after that. Nor the one after that, and after that, and after that...

But eventually... the distinctive dolerite sills, the beginnings of rising terrain, the side track marked only with a buffalo skull on a post. With a heave on the misshapen wheel he turned the Hupmobile north and was soon fighting rocks and ruts as the road wound back and forth. Now there were thin, straggly fences, and thin, straggly sheep, and ostriches, and slowly turning wind-pumps. Much of the land was burned-over and the sandy soil more like ash. Another fork in the road – a ram's skull this time – and he was going down past one of those conical *koppies* into a slight depression in which nestled a complex of farm buildings. The largest was a long shed constructed of rusty tin. Wood was scarce in these parts. But the one that demanded attention was a fine example of a Victorian mansion from the days of the wool and ostrich-feather barons, boasting a rare upper storey and a decorative full-length veranda either side of the imposing front entrance. It demanded attention, and the entrance was especially imposing, because it was flanked by full-bearded men with rifles, bandoliers and high crowned bush hats who looked like nothing if not the ghosts of those dreaded *Kommandos* from Kipling's war.

As the Broker brought the Hupmobile to a halt at the gates, the dust trail caught up and smothered it, swirling around in the lee of the *koppie* until it rose in a vortex that would not have looked out of place on John Carter's Mars.

"Well, I suppose that's one way of announcing that we're here," he muttered.

*　　*　　*

Major Boris Mikhailovich Lebedev of the First Main Directorate of the MGB – and now, of course, of the Committee of Information, with ultimate purview over the *Sovetskaya Koloniya* of embassies, trade delegations and missions – descended the front steps of the Van Rensburg homestead and signalled for his men to follow him. As they did so they drew their pistols, while their host's guards looked on impassively.

218

Seeing the sole occupant extract himself from the dusty vehicle and slip respectfully into his lightweight suit jacket, Lebedev allowed his smooth features to form a welcoming smile – one that clashed somewhat with the demeanour of Kostya, Sasha and Seryozha as they looked over the car.

"A pleasant surprise, Comrade. Our meeting is not until tomorrow. Was the down payment burning a hole in your pocket?"

"I have come early with urgent news."

"Yes? From whom?"

The man looked momentarily taken aback, but perhaps it was the heat.

"From our mutual acquaintance…"

"Our *unmentionable* mutual acquaintance? And what is this news?"

"Well… he was tracking the MERCURY pair as they made their way south to Cape Town…"

That was one way to put it! Lebedev's smile became a knowing pout.

"Of course."

"But contact was broken aboard the train from Pretoria – somewhere not too far from here, as it happens."

"We are aware of this also."

"However, our acquaintance has since established that they completed their journey by other means and subsequently conducted an operation against the Boschkop estate."

"As we ourselves have established…"

"…and that they will undoubtedly be coming here next!"

"Undoubtedly," Lebedev concurred, with a relaxed gesture that embraced the farmyard, house and armed guards. "Our hosts here have been in contact with personnel from Boschkop. We are all perfectly aware of the situation."

"I see. Well then my haste has been unnecessary. But our acquaintance wanted to make sure that you were all forewarned and these are not communications for open channels. Nor would he wish to compromise the… the down payment, as you call it."

The new arrival's Russian was almost that of a native, but the lack of obtuse brazenness in his 'Potemkin front' betrayed his less-than-Russian origins. Lebedev decided to probe the facade.

"That is very gratifying. I must confess, I was not *entirely* sure of our acquaintance's loyalties in this matter."

And then the man stepped closer and Lebedev was forced to revise his opinion.

"I must confess, Comrade Major, I am not *entirely* acting on our acquaintance's instructions."

"Surely that is an unwise position for a Broker to find himself in…"

The man returned the smooth smile.

"Unless a new party is about to declare an interest."

Lebedev took the Broker's arm and gave it a vigorous stroke.

"Then your haste is far from unnecessary. In fact I insist on your staying with us as our guest, until the conference. I will have Sasha bring your car in."

"It's no trouble. If Sasha will get the gate, I can pull it up here…"

Lebedev giggled.

"Here? Oh, I see. No, this is Meneer Van Rensburg's farm. It's not where our actual host resides."

*   *   *

A day later, close to sunset, another characteristically South African vehicle turned off the Beaufort West road for the Van Rensburg farm. This time it was a Ford *bakkie* from the fleet used at Boschkop and it was being driven by another Afrikaner, albeit one with a bruised face and not-so-neatly-trimmed beard.

Next to Joubert on the bench seat, Mila dug her pistol hard into the top of his leg, tilting the muzzle down towards his groin. He might drop his hand from the steering wheel to grab for it, or swing an elbow to strike her, but not before she got off a shot that would add physical emasculation to the spiritual kind he had already experienced – and most likely leave him bleeding out from a femoral artery.

Her nerves were so high-strung at the moment it was a wonder she had not pulled the trigger already.

The men on the gate must have recognised the Boschkop vehicle, for they opened on their approach.

"Drive in there, then stop, gently," she ordered, her heart in her mouth.

Armed guards lurked on the portico of the house. The front door opened and a middle-aged white man appeared between them. He wore spectacles and a linen suit and even from this distance one could make out the familiar shape of his moustache.

"Is that Van Rensburg?" she demanded. She was turning her head from side to side, conscious of the presence of the men at the gate behind them. Now the engine was silent, she heard the gate clang shut again.

"*Ja,*" Joubert said through gritted teeth.

Casting long shadows, several other figures had appeared from the direction of the barn. Burly, bearded white men in work clothes, not visibly armed but some carrying tools and all ready for trouble. A second man came out onto the porch and engaged in conversation with Van Rensburg. He was short and round-faced, with fair, prematurely balding hair, and he kept one hand thrust into the side pocket of his jacket.

"And him?"

"Don't know. Never seen him."

"So it's not Kuhlmann?" She pushed the muzzle in harder.

"*Nee. Ek sweer!*"

"And where will the child be now?"

"*Ek weet nie.* I have only come here once before…"

Abruptly, she pulled the pistol away from him.

"Then you have no value other than to deliver a message."

She heard the fright and resignation in his shaky outbreath. She withdrew the envelope from the glove box and handed it to him. Until the final drive to the farm, he had been kept on ice and had no idea what it contained.

"Take it and get out."

"You're going to shoot me!"

"I'll shoot you if you don't."

When he opened the driver's door, she noted how the gunmen at the entrance tensed, and the little man beside Van Rensburg moved his hand in his pocket. Alone, undisguised, she used only the slightest movements to slide the pistol into the glove box and tuck it out of sight. They were bound to check the whole vehicle over, but much like Joubert it could serve no other purpose now.

She saw that they knew who she was. It was evident in their caution as Van Rensburg sent one of his door guards forward to intercept Joubert. In the corner of her eye she noted first one and then the other of the gate guards move into sight on either side, each gaining a clear view of her in the cab of the truck yet still keeping far enough back not to catch his colleague in a crossfire. Other men – Africans – had appeared from elsewhere around the farmstead and were forming a loose cordon behind the supervisors. She had to assume that their loyalties would lie with their bosses.

Joubert presented the envelope. Through his sweat-soaked shirt, she saw his overdeveloped trapezius muscles tense as he tucked his small, neat head in like a tortoise, expecting the *coup de grâce*. The other man ran the envelope back up the steps to his master.

Van Rensburg tore it open and extracted the photograph. He raised his spectacles onto his forehead to peer at it, then passed it to the shorter man and marched over to Joubert. A brief, heated exchange was brought to a close by a furious slap across Joubert's face that sent him staggering backwards. Bellowing something dismissive in Afrikaans, Van Rensburg strode towards the Ford, the little sidekick fussing in his wake.

However many guns were trained on her, Mila decided that no one was likely to open fire as the boss approached her. She climbed carefully out, keeping her hands visible.

Van Rensburg ignored her and went to examine the empty bed of the truck. He stuck his head into the cabin. Only then did he address her in decent if heavily-accented English.

"You have the wrong house, madam."

"Funny, it looks like the right place to me," Mila said.

"The message you brought is for my neighbour, I think."

His mean little moustache, she saw now, was pepper-and-salt: a bilateral mixture of dark and white, and the white was in the ascendant. She faced up to him, unflinching.

"What was that you just shouted at Faf?"

Van Rensburg looked almost amused.

"A reminder of his responsibilities. *As ek omdraai, skiet my.* 'If I retreat, shoot me'."

Mila adopted a similarly lofty tone.

"'If I fall, avenge me'…"

"'If I charge, follow me' – you know it? Our oath."

She sneered.

"I've heard it before. Fascist play-acting."

Her discoloured eye had reopened fully at last and she had no intention of having it closed again. She'd seen how he delivered the last slap and was ready for this one. Ducking her head to the side, half-skipping back, she let him swing himself off balance but resisted the instinct to counter with protruding knuckles to the side of his neck.

Before Van Rensburg could compose himself for another attempt, the smaller man stepped in and caught his arm in a feeble-looking clasp.

"Menheer… if you please… Miss Slavík, I am Major Lebedev of the Soviet Committee of Information. You have come to ask after your child, yes? He is safe."

She stared. Now even the simplest phrase, in any language, was beyond her.

"Here?"

"No, not here. But nearby."

Van Rensburg had deferred to this Russian, for the moment. But he had been humiliated, which was not a good look for any patriarch and especially not one with several itchy trigger fingers at his command. Mila shook her head to clear it.

"Nearby?"

"Yes. And may we assume…" Major Lebedev held up the

photograph with his other hand. "That these items are also nearby?"

"Yes."

"Then we have the makings of a deal, I should think."

Van Rensburg shook off the restraining grip.

"I'll have her flogged – or I'll give her to my *kaffirs!*"

Lebedev canted his head. Mila looked away from the fuming Van Rensburg to see two heavies descending from the portico, hurrying to their major's assistance.

"No you won't, or not yet," the major gave a genial smile that was backed by thirty years of repressive savagery. "First, we're going to take her to Kuhlmann."

Van Rensburg did not respond. It appeared he had been distracted by an aircraft that was crossing the vast expanse of sky at a considerable altitude, at least a mile to the north. He frowned, then waved a hand and turned on his heels.

"Take her. Kuhlmann will probably kill her for what she did at Boschkop…"

Lebedev watched him go, smirking at the display of disinterest that was meant to conceal the Afrikaner's shame at his diminished status. Even Mila could see through that charade.

But then Van Rensburg stopped to talk to the penitent Joubert and one of his armed men, both of whom came over to the truck, wearing ugly expressions.

"We are to accompany you," Joubert said, unable to meet Mila's gaze.

"As you wish," the major nodded graciously, before turning to Mila and gesturing towards the back of the truck. "Miss Slavík, if you would be good enough…"

She accepted his hand and clambered in. The Afrikaner gunman and an MGB goon joined her, the latter brandishing a Tokarev like the model she had left in the glove box in the cabin. When Joubert got behind the wheel again, Lebedev joined him in there.

The bare boards of the *bakkie* were already thick with dust. Mila soon discovered why. As Joubert headed off between the house and the barn, they began to rattle, bounce and side-slip through sandy grit and ash, all of which took to the air and rained down on them without respite. Mila removed her sun hat and pressed it to her face while Van Rensburg's man pulled up a neckerchief like a Wild West outlaw; Lebedev's just blinked and bore it.

But she needed to see, so she squinted as best she could past the cloth and through the dust. The chaos of a sprawling farmyard resolved itself into some kind of pattern. There were other, smaller barns and outbuildings, mostly of rough mud-brick with corrugated iron roofs. There were kraals of ostrich and kraals of sheep, wind-pumps and troughs, tethered dogs and native dwellings. As they skirted the first *koppie* and took a rough track towards the next outcrop, she recalled what Sam had said to her, before his departure.

"You know what Nazis like? Bunkers. Places to keep safe long enough to destroy everything and then kill themselves. Or maybe with an escape tunnel, if they're feeling less…"

"Narcissistic?" she had ventured, to help him out.

He had nodded enthusiastically.

"You said it! They're all like that. Trust me… the vineyard wasn't it and the farm won't be either."

Trust me…

Yet she had not.

Now it looked as though he had been right. As they rounded the stack of rocks, Mila made out the first of several matching horizontal slabs – but in pale blue-grey concrete that was being swallowed by the shadows as the sun went down across the desert. Asymmetric level by asymmetric level, ninety degree angle by ninety degree angle, the long, low building revealed itself. It was a modernist dwelling in the Bauhaus style, newly constructed, judging by the surrounding building site, and almost completely hidden behind the flat-topped *koppie*. It also looked very much like a bunker.

With a shiver she remembered her first sight of the Radon Sanitorium in the Sudeten Erzgebirge mountains, and the dreadful battle that she and Sam had fought at the end of the war.

But now she was on her own.

Joubert drove into an open car port beneath the house and parked between two other vehicles, a blue Oldsmobile and an older but smarter-looking German 'Wanderer'. Further into the garage, obscured by deep shadow, Mila spotted another dust-streaked *bakkie* much like theirs.

Again Major Lebedev offered her his soft, moist hand.

"I will show you where you can freshen up before you meet our hosts."

"An impressive place," Mila remarked as she climbed down, all the while scanning the structure and the site for entrances, exits, anomalies...

"Our host has uncharacteristically modernist sensibilities — and this is a country where you can build things very quickly."

She followed the Russian up the massive external spiral staircase on leaden legs, each concrete step seeming taller than the last. At the top there was a combined open-plan living space and balcony terrace, conceived on an outlandish scale.

A man had been lounging at a low table and rose promptly when he saw her.

"Ah yes," Lebedev said. "This is one of our best people, who likes to be called *Posrednik* or 'Broker'. He was the one who warned us that you were coming to the meeting of the 'White Spider'."

Mila glanced at him dismissively and ignored the proffered hand. Instead she rounded on Lebedev again.

"Where's my son?"

CHAPTER EIGHTEEN

Anselm Kuhlmann looked every inch the successful Nazi. A lantern-jawed hulk with brilliantined hair and, at this late hour, a blight of black dots on his upper lip and chin, he brought to mind a self-made businessman at a local chamber of commerce: the one the others mocked behind his back. But when he spoke, the choked rasp did not match. He had been gassed in the Great War and had he been wearing his SS uniform, he would have sported on his right upper sleeve the Silver Honour Chevron for the Old Guard.

"How have you done this? This is not possible."

He did not look up from the photograph in his hands. In his leather and stainless steel armchair – one of several that the assembled company had drawn together from around the enormous living space to create an improvised boardroom – he was the model of the dismissive, disapproving boss.

Mila tried to keep her voice level. It was easier in English, which had been chosen as the *lingua franca*. Had she been addressing Herr Kuhlmann in his native German, she would have been unable to prevent her anger from stabbing through.

"It was perfectly possible to acquire the remaining artworks. We had the run of Boschkop for several hours."

He scowled, shaking his head.

"No. This, I mean, this print."

"That was created with a new American invention that will be 'hitting the market', as I believe they say, early next year. A pre-production example was shipped to an advertising agency in Cape Town for use in preparing the publicity material. It is called a Land Camera and comes with self-developing film."

"So this photograph of my Chagal, my Liebermanns, my Picasso sculpture…"

"…was taken a few hours ago, somewhere in the desert near here – but not somewhere you'll ever find without my help."

And then he did look up. For the first time since she'd been ushered in, she met and held his gaze. There was no way of knowing for certain what a man like this would see in her eyes, beyond the offensive audacity of her standing up to him, but she hoped that she had communicated something of her steadfastness. The rest – the hatred, the anguish, the desperation – he would surely take as read.

Behind him, reflected in the huge sliding terrace windows which had now been closed for the night, she could see the backs of the other chairs and their occupants. The MGB major, Lebedev, his head tilted in amused appraisal, his crown thinning. The stiff, awkward and still resentful Van Rensburg, who was clearly courting both the Russian and Kuhlmann himself – an unlikely alliance, in more ways than one.

The Broker, as they called him, who had just returned to his seat after a theatrical stretch and yawn.

Here was the lions' den. Proud males sprawled regally in the centre, leaving the more immediate threats to lurk around the edge. These – leaning at the substantial sideboards or seated in less comfortable-looking chairs – were the foot-soldiers. Kuhlmann's: four of them. Lebedev's trio, again with pockets bulging. Van Rensburg's single bodyguard standing silently by the internal doors with his shotgun. And Joubert, pacing back and forth in the hope of still being seen as a viable challenger and not an outcast.

Unlucky thirteen.

There were no other women, of course. They had not attended the main conference, and while they might have been present at the dinner that had followed it, they weren't invited to this extraordinary session. Yet Mila had been given to understand that there was a Mevrou Van Rensburg, even if she suspected that she was back at the farmstead now. There was certainly a Frau Kuhlmann: she had just met her and was unlikely to forget the experience. Somewhere, presumably, they had de Klerk's widow tucked away as well.

"And we have Poldi," Kuhlmann wheezed.

"His name is Pavel," Mila said. "And I'm leaving here with him."

Lebedev emitted his girlish laugh.

"You will achieve this all on your own?"

In frustration, the Broker slapped both hands palms-down on his legs.

"I told you – all of you. Whatever she says, she'll have the American backing her up, somehow! That plane this afternoon…"

"And I have told you," Van Rensburg said. "My men have the perimeter guarded like a fortress. Herr Kuhlmann has two of his on the roof, on the lookout for parachutes – it is a clear, starry night."

"The American is the least of your worries," Mila muttered ruefully. "In point of fact, he's more one of mine."

This, it turned out, required some whispered interpretation from the Broker for the benefit of Lebedev and Van Rensburg. Mila saw the curiosity cross his face as he explained her apparent meaning for them and she felt a twinge of curiosity herself. From what little she knew of him, she had expected him to be fluent in Russian, but what language was he using to translate for Van Rensburg?

In truth she was finding it impossible to hold onto any emotion beyond that which dominated her every thought and impulse. She wasn't even sure what it was, this emotion, only that it was the most powerful thing she had felt for many, many years.

It had started with a phrase, pronounced in contemptuous Southern German – and the harsh-faced, bun-and-braids *Hausfrau* who had uttered it.

On first entering the house, Lebedev had sought out Kuhlmann's wife, eager to pass over responsibility for their unwanted guest. Having led Mila through the living space and down half a level into a raised raw concrete corridor that was lined with what she presumed were considered lesser artworks, he had called out to the sturdy woman in her unflattering petticoat dress.

"Frau Kuhlmann! Just the person. Miss Slavík is in need of the powder-room before our conference. And I told her she could see her child."

"*Her* child? *I* am Poldi's *Mutti*." The woman's features had fought against one another, settling on an expression somewhere between suppressed distaste and open disgust. "*This* is the *genetische Mutter*?"

Mila could barely recall what words had been spoken after those, or even where exactly in the cavernous rear of the house the woman had led her. All she remembered was standing outside a plain wooden door in a less finished corridor – like a staff corridor, she'd thought – and knowing that it was *Poldi's* room, and that her own long-lost little Pavel lay inside.

"It's late," Frau Kuhlmann had told her. "Past his bedtime. He tired himself out today and will be fast asleep. Still, you may poke your head in and see, if you wish."

If I wish…

But the Broker was bringing her back to the moment, uncrossing his legs and turning away from the other two to address her personally, smirkingly…

"And why would that be, Miss Slavík? Why is Bradley one of your worries now?"

"How is he 'the least of ours'?" Lebedev wanted to know.

She felt that at any minute she might faint. Washing her hands and face had hardly restored her. Her shirt and safari shorts still felt damp and gritty and the temperature in the room, although cooling rapidly, was far from agreeable. She pointed to a low table with bottles and a pitcher of water on it.

"May I?"

And she watched.

Lebedev nodded.

So it was Kuhlmann's hide-out, on Van Rensburg's property, but the Russians were calling the shots.

Filling a glass, taking a drink, taking her time, she decided to answer both their questions at once. She had to meet someone's eye, however, and she chose the Broker's, with a cool, unblinking look of challenge.

"You may all be aware that Mr Bradley and I were passengers on the Blue Train a while ago. *En route* to Cape Town, I woke Mr Bradley, informing him that I had just found our contact murdered, and that the killers had stopped the train to ambush us."

Beginning her story at this point raised many more questions than it hinted at answering, but from their faces, they were indeed well aware of the context. The so-called Broker or the MGB major had made sure of that.

"Were they your men, the killers, Major Lebedev? Or yours, Herr Kuhlmann? Or perhaps yours, Meneer Van Rensburg – I see you have half an army here! Or were you all working together?"

Half-amused, uncooperative faces. Poker faces, they probably thought they were. But they could not resist the urge to glance sideways at their companions to see who, if anyone, was going to respond. They had not been working together. That, presumably, was what this summit conference was all about.

"Of course it wasn't any of you," she told them now. "I myself pulled the communication cord. There were no killers and our contact was not dead. In fact, I made my late-night rendezvous with him, as arranged, and he told me who he really was."

Mila could see the questions occurring to them, one by one. Different questions, perhaps; but a similar anxiety, sown by the way she had just demonstrated how they had not trusted one another to admit to or deny involvement in the assassination that had not happened. The Broker got in first.

"And who was that?"

She took another sip of iced water.

"A representative, he said, of Britain's MI5 Security Service."

"Ridiculous!" Major Lebedev chirped, indicating that he, at least, had known who Monsieur Sept was supposed to be representing.

"What is this stuff and nonsense?" Kuhlmann croaked. "This woman is only here so we can make her tell us where she's hidden the artworks!"

"Herr Kuhlmann, please…"

"That was my first reaction too," Mila conceded, with a nod of acknowledgement to Lebedev. "Our contact didn't expect me to believe him without confirmation, just as I don't expect you to believe me. But let me recount to you how he described it to me. *'Although they're quite active in the other dominions, the Service doesn't operate much in South Africa – apart from sending out a few retired flatfoots to advise the local security chaps on pedantry and speaking nasally. But they do employ what Mr Bradley's countrymen have taken to calling 'walk-on players'…'* That is what he claimed to be – an unrecruited, unaligned accessory – as well as acting in the capacity of representative for certain Soviet parties who wish to remain nameless."

"Wish it or not, that's what they are," Lebedev sniggered. "But I hardly think *they* are playing for the British Security Service!"

Mila pulled a sympathetic face.

"I had the impression that 'Monsieur Sept', as we called our contact, viewed these two roles as perfectly separate." She allowed her gaze to settle on the Broker. "I suppose it's a necessary perspective when one has two masters. At any rate, he advised me not to approach the Soviet agent whom he had ostensibly arranged for us to meet in Cape Town and instead gave me a number for someone with only tangential links to the Party. I'd say that person was most likely also working with MI5. We parted north of Kimberley and made our separate ways to De Aar, where we continued our journeys, Monsieur Bradley and myself to the Cape, 'Monsieur Sept' I know not where."

In the ensuing silence, Van Rensburg cursed and rose to pour himself a tumbler of something stronger.

"It is true the British Security Service has been taking an

interest in patriots like me for our wartime activities."

Mila huffed scornfully.

"I wouldn't flatter yourself. I think you'll find that MI5 have had bigger fish to fry."

"Such as?" Lebedev inquired with an indulgent grin.

"Such as preventing Zionist terrorism in Palestine, by going after those trouble-makers, all over the globe, who have been supplying the bombs and guns. And deterring other factions from arming the other side, which will become imperative with the new United Nations plan for Partition." She fixed the Russian with a steely look. "That might very well see them probing certain aspects of the *Sovetskaya Koloniya* and I doubt either Deputy Chairman Beria or Minister for State Security Abakumov would appreciate the increased scrutiny of their behind-the-scenes efforts."

The grin faded.

Only the Broker still appeared composed, if a little too familiar with the drinks table.

"*Caveat emptor*, eh? Or *caveat venditor*, in this case. But are you seriously expecting us to believe that you conned Bradley like that?"

"Monsieur Sept insisted on it. He was of the opinion that Sam was too eager to follow the trail laid down by our nameless sponsor – and that he might also be too easily manipulated by another American, by the name of Sloane, who is reportedly a figure of some influence within their brand new central intelligence agency. In fact, he suggested that Sam might have had an undisclosed mission all along."

The Broker flapped his hand.

"Very good, ducky... But pull the other one!"

She shrugged.

"You're probably right. Certainly Sam didn't take it well when he found out I'd lied to him, so perhaps he was straight. But ask yourselves what really gets MI5's attention..." She regarded the others in turn, sensing each man's resentment at having his certainties challenged so openly. First Van Rensburg, then

Kuhlmann, then Lebedev. "It isn't pipe dreams of securing communist support to kick the British out and install a whites-only fascist state... It isn't renegade Nazis exaggerating their intelligence prowess in order to trick the Soviet Union into bankrolling a rival organisation to Reinhard Gehlen's... It isn't even Palestine any more, given that the British seem to have decided to let everyone else fight over it now... No, what gets MI5 hot under the collar is the thought of catching someone from their sister service up to no good."

She turned back to the Broker, who was still seated, glaring up at her.

"I think I'm within my rights to ask what *you* are doing here," she said.

A thin, strained smile.

"I brought the money."

"The money from Moscow – to fund this disruptive network of Nazi spies and nationalists?"

"A down payment, yes. You'd be amazed how far a hundred thousand dollars will go in a place like this."

"So you're the delivery man. I can see how this meeting required cash on the table to progress to the next level, whatever that is. A sign of good faith. But why are you *still* here?"

It was Van Rensburg who got there first.

"She has a point. Who's he representing now, eh, Major?"

"I think I can answer that," Mila said. "This man you know as the Broker is actually an MI6 officer who goes by the name of Pendleton. Isn't that right, Pat?"

In this light – embedded in that downcast visage – the Sambian amber was cloudy and almost black. She recognised the effort he made to put a careless expression back on his face before he addressed the others.

"Can't you see? She's trying to make us distrust each other!"

Van Rensburg rounded on him. The piercing blue eyes and twitching moustache were reminiscent of another monster.

"*Are* you a British spy, as she says?"

"That's one of the identities I use in my work as an agent, a

234

middle-man, but it's not a secret, as such. Major Lebedev knows who I am…"

A grudging nod from the Russian, accompanied by the look of loathing for Mila.

"I find this very disturbing," Kuhlmann began to splutter.

Pendleton rose from his defensive crouch and Mila saw that she'd been right about the amount he had already drunk.

"Oh do you? Well, if we're talking secret identities, this Nazi is a bloody charlatan! He claims to run an intelligence network like Gehlen's – 'The White Spider' – when all *Die weiße Spinne* really exists for is to help his fellow war-criminals evade justice, using stolen art as collateral! And all these bloody Boer stormtroopers will be getting out of it is a bunch of Nazi-hunters heavy-breathing down their necks!"

"Enough!" Lebedev had physically to step between the three of them.

"If you're worried about our MI6 friend…" Mila mustered a matter-of-fact voice. "He has a commando knife on his right hip and a .32 Webley self-loading under his left shoulder."

"Thank you," the Russian said with paper-thin civility. He beckoned one of his goons to come and search Pendleton. The weapons, as described, were laid out on the drinks table.

"Bitch," Pendleton spat. "All you ever wanted was to trade for your child and you didn't give a damn what you traded!"

Mila ignored him. *Sotto voce* to Lebedev, she made another suggestion.

"It might be less stressful if Kuhlmann's men also laid down their weapons, don't you think, Major? He's getting quite upset."

As though she had more important matters than this to consider, which was perfectly true in its way, Mila wandered over to the window. There was no gazing out at the view, however. With the lights on, and the reflections of the various moves and counter-moves behind her, all she could discern outside was the murky shape of the man patrolling the terrace.

Her disengagement was an act. In fact her every sense was heightened, almost unbearably, as though the skin had been grated off the nerve endings. It seemed that any second now the men who were cursing and pacing across the floor tiles would recombine, seize her and beat her to death. Or order her shot.

And that could not be allowed to happen, because of promises she had made.

She recalled the weight of the bedroom door as she'd pushed it open. This was a very solid-built house, but just then, like some pharaoh's tomb, that door had held the weight of the ages.

Something that could not have been shame had nonetheless caused Frau Kuhlmann to linger in the doorway, holding the door ajar. It had granted sufficient light to make out the small bed with the small bedside table, a single toy car upon it.

And the small shape in the bed.

Mila had fallen to her knees with such a thud that the child had roused, slightly, from his slumbers.

"*Máma?*"

"Yes, darling," she had whispered, in the Czech language that perhaps had survived in his memories beyond that single, magical word – and then, reluctantly, in German.

A grey-blue eye, half-opened. A half-smile, quickly fading in drowsy confusion.

She had taken his hand.

"Is it *Weihnachten*…?" he had murmured.

"Soon, Pavlík. Go back to sleep..."

It will be Christmas soon, she whispered, her breath making a fading cloud on the cooling glass of the terrace window. And she shivered, despite the heat in here, despite her pounding heart.

If she did not come back for him, would he remember it as a dream?

There, in its essence, was the emotion that powered her heartbeat now, and with it her every word and action.

Peggy would call it Love. But Peggy was a better person than she. Kafka had captured it better. *The knife I turn inside myself – and sometimes not only in myself.*

She returned to her senses to find Lebedev at her side.

"Order is restored," came his snide report. "Herr Kuhlmann

wants his artworks back now."

"Of course. And I want my son."

"You understand that we can use him to compel you to tell us where they are?"

Over his shoulder, she saw his three hoods hovering.

"Perhaps I could propose a different approach," she said, going back to the meeting area.

"We are open-minded men, I think we have shown you that. But it is getting late and our patience is wearing thin."

"I only want one thing from you and you know what it is. That makes me the best kind of friend you can have in this business."

"We are not looking for a friend."

"When you hear what I have to say, you may think otherwise," she said. "All of you."

For this round, when they returned to their chairs, Mila took one too. She asked for a cigarette and Kuhlmann signalled for a guard to oblige her. Finally, tapping ash into an ashtray that looked very much like another one of his modernist artworks, she began to speak.

"Something happened on the Blue Train, something else, I mean. Our contact, Monsieur Sept, told us about the 'England Game'. Let's not pretend you don't all know what that is. Whatever Herr Kuhlmann is really offering you, Major Lebedev, I know it has something to do with that. And you, Pat, mentioned it yourself, on Texel."

As with Joubert, now she had brought him down he could hardly look at her; she had that effect on the men who came to know her.

"So I did."

"At the time, chatting away in the dining car, we found it a rather far-fetched explanation for what Minister Abakumov could want with an old Nazi like Anselm Kuhlmann... As Bradley pointed out, you Russians wouldn't come down here to pussyfoot around if it was just him you wanted – instead you'd whisk him off to some frozen city with a number for a name and squeeze him as dry as the Karoo."

Kuhlmann looked suddenly sick, but Mila just laughed.

"The thing is that Bradley didn't see it. Too trusting, I suppose…"

"See what?" demanded Van Rensburg.

"The explanation. The England Game was neither a brilliant counterintelligence triumph nor an abject intelligence failure. The British incompetence was *engineered*."

"This is preposterous…" Kuhlmann began.

"I'll say," Pendleton chipped in.

"Well, you would," Mila sneered. "But it's not preposterous, as Herr Kuhlmann knows. It's what the Dutch think. Monsieur Sept told me. They're very bitter, he said. Besides fifty Dutch agents executed, there were the resistance networks broken up, the families sent to concentration camps… Some are even convinced that in causing the Allies to doubt all future resistance contacts and their reports, the England Game contributed to the Arnhem disaster, delayed the liberation and led to the *Hongerwinter*. If it could be proved this was done intentionally…"

"But Miss Slavík," Lebedev interjected, ostensibly as the voice of reason. "A pro-Nazi traitor inside SOE or MI6, even if such an unlikely thing were possible, would hardly be of value to *us*…"

"Not as a political ally, no, but as someone who'd be open to blackmail, especially if he was still high up in MI6…" She caught Pendleton's eye again.

And then he grinned, in spite of everything. The sea change was astonishing. Mila remembered his 'Dutch courage' on Texel.

"I suppose he might not be pro-Nazi at all," he said, now playing along with gusto. "One could almost envisage such a person sabotaging the liberation of the Netherlands and the crossing of the Rhine with a view to ensuring that it was the Soviet Union that reached Berlin ahead of the western allies."

"A great man, shaping history at its turning point," Mila nodded. "But if so, there's a problem, isn't there. For you, Major, and especially for you, Herr Kuhlmann."

"The Germans wouldn't know that they were being fed," Pat laughed.

"That's right," Mila said. "They'd be so busy thinking they were such clever little souls to feed the *Engländers*... they'd never even realise that they weren't being clever at all!"

For the moment, neither Lebedev nor Kuhlmann looked capable of speech. It was Van Rensburg who rose angrily to stand, feet apart, fists on hips, in front of Pendleton.

"Broker – whatever your name is and whoever you are – stop indulging this nonsense! This is idle speculation and of no consequence to our affairs."

Pendleton also stood, placing a calming hand on Van Rensburg's shoulder and guiding him back to his seat.

"I'm afraid it isn't nonsense and it is of grave consequence. Even you must see it. If Kuhlmann here wasn't playing the England Game but being played, my sponsors will have to reconsider their investment."

Now it was Lebedev's turn, although being short of stature he did not see the value in standing up.

"Your sponsors? That money comes from the Committee of Information!"

"I think Moscow may need to think twice about what it's buying," Pendleton said.

Mila cleared her throat to interrupt politely.

"There is a further possibility..."

"Oh, here we go again!" Van Rensburg stormed to the drinks table. Finding the bottles empty this time, he kicked it over with a crash.

"I'm just saying... if the traitor *had* found a way to let the Germans know he was helping them. A cryptic message hidden in a transmission to one of the callsigns he knew was compromised, for instance... then perhaps Herr Kuhlmann isn't lying when he claims inside knowledge of the England Game. Perhaps he has the ultimate inside knowledge. And if that were the case..." Mila took a lungful of smoke, expelling it lingeringly across the assembled faces. "Such a person might even be keen to send agents to South Africa to shut him up."

"Now just a minute!" Lebedev was saying. Kuhlmann began

to cough.

It was Pat, incredibly, who had the gall to press her further.

"Yes, steady on, old girl… Giskes, remember, is now working for Gehlen, for the CIA. He'd have passed on anything he knew about a traitor in Mil Six or SOE if he'd known. So the sneaky sod wouldn't be sending out assassins to protect his secret. He'd be running for his life!"

Mila rolled her eyes.

"How silly of me. I forgot to mention something else that Monsieur Sept told me. He said the CIA needed to make a grand entrance into the international intelligence community – and what better way than by snagging and turning a double-agent within MI6?"

She smiled sweetly.

"It's not you, is it, Pat? Only you did mention the England Game to us before, as well as something similar that you knew about in the Balkans. Now it appears you speak Dutch as well… Is that why the Americans set us on the trail that led down here? It certainly wasn't because they thought Kuhlmann had specific knowledge of that operation or the traitor – they know he's just a fantasist, taking credit for other's work while he fleeces everyone he can…"

"Are you going to let her start with this again?" Having been accused, exonerated and accused again in the space of as many minutes, the German had gone bright red in the face as he struggled ineffectually to raise his voice. Finally he leaned forward with a gasp and tapped the breast of his jacket. "You saw the hard evidence that I have here…"

But Mila barely acknowledged him.

"Nor was it for fear that the MGB was *really* going to support their polar opposites, the Afrikaner white-supremacists, or even really send the money…"

This time it was Van Rensburg who shouted her down to restore his credibility within the group.

"I'll have you know the Broker has already shown us the contents of his suitcase – and we have a formal written contract between the Soviet Committee of Information and the *Ossewabrandwag…*"

Before Lebedev could stop him, he had half-risen and gesticulated towards one of the sideboards.

Mila sat back. She could tell from their sidelong glances that she had them where she wanted them again. But still the time wasn't right. On a whim, she asked:

"Incidentally, could anyone explain to me where de Klerk's wife is?"

"The Jewess?" Kuhlmann hissed. "We got rid of that."

Mila nodded to herself.

The final act of a heinous crime. And a promise broken.

"Where?"

"Somewhere out there in the desert,' he said pointedly.

"And that, I think, is quite enough of this," Lebedev's cool tone belied his evident, mounting unease. "Gentlemen, it's time we fetched the boy and compelled Miss Slavík to tell us where the artworks are. Then she can join the late Mevrouw de Klerk."

The lights gave a flicker. New electrics, presumably. Sometimes one could build things too fast.

Mila tensed.

"I can't let you do that," she said.

In the instant that the window shattered, Pat launched towards the far sideboard where the Germans' pistols had been laid out – while Mila skittered across to retrieve his confiscated Webley automatic from the floor where it had fallen off the table.

Three shots in rapid succession from the terrace had dropped or scattered Lebedev's goons, so she selected Van Rensburg's bodyguard at the door and put him down before he could bring his shotgun to bear. Kuhlmann's men were frozen halfway to their weapons, two of which Pat had already trained on them.

One of the fallen MGB men raised head and gun from behind an armchair and a flash from the darkness outside sent him tumbling.

Mila pointed the pistol at Kuhlmann, at Van Rensburg, at Lebedev. They had dined earlier in the other part of the living space and, it appeared, had come to this supplementary session relaxed and unarmed. A smile, a half-smile, began to creep onto her face. Against all odds, it looked like they would be able to enact the final part of the deception – and extract the final piece of information.

Then she spotted the blur of motion in the corner of her eye as Faf Joubert raised his own pistol and took aim at her. She had not thought he had one, but of course it was her Tokarev from the *bakkie*'s glove box. There came the sound of two shots – the first accompanied by the spectacle of the Afrikaner's brains spraying across one of the paintings on the concrete wall there, the second by the crippling shock of a mule-kick to her side.

Unlucky thirteen.

As she collapsed, she saw her own blood spilling brightly on the floor tiles.

CHAPTER NINETEEN

He had done everything that was asked of him.

He had forgiven her for getting him off the Blue Train like that. And gone along with the pretence that she had not told him the truth as soon as they were clear, which of course she had.

He had bitten his lip and allowed her to take off with Joubert. Twice.

He had kept out of her hair and Peggy's hair and made contact only with Pendleton, using the emergency number he had given them in Cape Town.

He had taken the slow train alone to Fraserburg Road, meeting up with Pendleton on the outskirts, and on that sweltering stretch of empty road halfway to their final destination he had wormed into the moonshiner's locker that had been created two decades previously by jury-rigging an Okie flatbed on a Hupmobile sedan.

He had lain cooking in that box, his knee and shoulder killing him, all the way to the farm and after, emerging only later that night in the garage of the Kuhlmann house.

He had conducted an exhaustive recon of the site and its surroundings, tracking all the movements of the men as the perimeter guard was doubled to keep him out. He'd watched the big cheeses hold their afternoon conference and evening meal and, his stomach churning, he had watched Mila arrive on cue.

He had waited for Pendleton's stretch and yawn at the window that signalled she was about to draw all the attention inwards on herself, creating a corridor for action that was completely free of snooping eyes, save the one guard on the terrace and the two up top who were watching the skies.

He had used that corridor of space and time with well-drilled precision – doping Pavel and getting him into the secret compartment in the Hupmobile, doping Kuhlmann's wife and locking in the servants, taking out the three remaining inner sentries with choke-holds and syrettes and taking the place of the terrace guy himself.

He had fused the terrace lights with his knife, getting a bonus flicker throughout the house, and stretched himself out on a lounger with the butt of the newly reassembled Winchester Model 1907 in his shoulder and an extra pair of 10-round mags to hand.

He had taken out the three guys in suits who carried handguns and had seen Mila deal with the frontiersman character by the door. He'd finished off a suit guy who came up for more and joined Pendleton in covering the four shorts-and-braces guys who just had to be Germans.

And then this had happened…

"Mila!" he cried out as he crashed in through the shattered window.

If God wanted to play it like that, so could he. The Model 1907 was barely long enough to call itself a rifle, but it weighed plenty – that was one reason why he trusted the recoil of the self-loading carbine not to throw his shoulder out again. Enough to dump the three big cheeses on their asses with the stock, one after the other, whatever stratagems Mila had originally planned.

Pendleton was quick on the uptake. He unloaded both pistols into the cluster of Germans and used the butt of one of them to chill the two he'd missed.

Everything now would have to be about speed, not stealth.

She was face-down, contorted partly by the pain and partly by the desperate need to get both hands applying pressure to her wound.

"Breathe steady," Bradley said. "Let me look."

He knew it would be bad. There was no nice way to get shot in the guts and that Tokarev round was a killer. Nor, by the looks of it, was it a through-and-through wound. It was low down enough to have missed everything except her large intestine, but if it had ricocheted off her hip and broken up it might have gone anywhere. Anyhow, the intestine was bad enough. If the internal bleeding didn't get you, the infection would.

She had seen it in his face.

"Pavel?"

"Ready to roll," Bradley said.

"Keep me alive long enough to see him when he wakes up."

"You got it," he mouthed. Perhaps the words even came out as sounds.

Inside, he was cursing blue murder. All those syrettes of knock-out juice he'd brought, and not a spare one of morphine... He winced too as another stab of pain lanced through her and he administered everything he'd got, subcutaneously, by the wound.

Pendleton was at his side, where he'd taken the Winchester and was scanning the room. Together they got Bradley's medical kit fully open and packed the hole with antiseptic ribbon. A gauze compress followed, heavily taped in place. She had passed out by now and it took both of them to sit her up to wrap the bandages around her.

"If we want to move fast, we'll need a stretcher," Bradley said.

"To get her down to the car?"

"Yeah. And after that."

"We can't run with her on the veld, with a kid in tow!"

But Bradley wasn't listening. He was grinning, though it would probably be taken for a snarl.

He went over to the biggest painting on the back wall, a tall abstract composition of straight black lines, white spaces and coloured rectangles, almost man-sized.

"A stretcher, I said. And we got one!"

"Give me a minute." Pendleton crossed to the bodies of the big cheeses, two of whom were moaning now. After a moment, he went over to one of the sideboards.

"Pendleton!"

The Englishman rounded on him, eyes blazing.

"Will you just call me 'Pat' for fuck's sake!"

Despite himself, Bradley had to laugh.

"OK, Pat. But please. They'll all be coming."

Together they wrestled Mila onto the stretcher.

"How are we going to get her down the stairs without strapping her to it?" Pat said.

Bradley closed his eyes.

"There's an elevator," he said after a moment. "Must be for the art."

"Well this qualifies…"

"Damn straight it does!"

They were at the garage level in next to no time, yet even so they could already hear commotion beyond the open doors. Running boots. Bellowed orders. Queries called up to the terrace level. Urgent replies.

"Gotta be now," Bradley said. "I'll go in back with her. You drive."

There wasn't room to keep her on the stretcher, which would have to be propped up over the cab. When he settled her on the floorboards, she came around and focused on him. He had never seen her look so deathly pale.

"North by northeast," she said. "Eleven miles."

"The pick-up?"

She shook her head and grimaced.

"Woozy now…"

"Sure, it's the morphine. What's there, baby?"

"The cave." She sounded faraway already. "S-Phone and EUREKA beacon there. Pick-up beyond…"

Pat had flung the Hupmobile into reverse to swing around out of the garage. Suddenly he leaned out of the window.

"Bradley, we can't leave these…"

He meant the Oldsmobile and the other car, the 'Wanderer', as well as Mila's Ford *bakkie*. Climbing out, they both drew their knives and pierced two tyres on each vehicle.

When Bradley got in the back again, Mila was unconscious.

That was probably for the best. As soon as they left the concrete hardstanding, the Hupmobile was bouncing over stones and ruts, sending up clouds of dust in the starlight. Bradley checked his spare mags were buttoned down in his bush jacket and loaded a fresh 15-rounder. No need for the shorter ones now he wouldn't be going prone.

The first men ran out into their path as they rounded the corner of the house to head away from the farm into the bush. Bradley kept their heads down as they passed and maybe even winged one as the shadows came back upright in their wake.

For a moment, it seemed that they'd got clean away.

But then headlights, sweeping obliquely across the scrub, and more shadows... many more shadows. Somehow, the perimeter guards had all figured out where to redeploy. Although Pat was using no lights and Bradley wasn't firing, the pursuers were zeroing in on their trail of dust.

A bullet pinged off the hood. Another came right through the cab.

Van Rensburg's *Boere*, with their rifles, and they were good.

Bradley hammered on the roof.

"We gotta bale. We're sitting ducks!"

Pat took no persuading. He turned the Hupmobile into the next defile – little more than a dry stream bed fringed by burned-out-looking acacia thicket – and they hurried to disembark their precious cargo. Pat slung the boy over his shoulder and took the stretcher and carbine in hand. Bradley took Mila in his arms.

They ran until the gully turned east, and then they ran in the open country, heading for the far-off rising ground that a snatched glance at Bradley's compass had confirmed as north-northeast.

Another snatched glance – soon regretted – revealed several lights, torches, on their trail. There was no mistaking the sound of dogs.

And then the figure looming out of the darkness ahead of them...

*   *   *

Perched on a sun-lounger on the terrace of the Kuhlmann house, pressing a bloodied cloth to his forehead, Hendrik Van Rensburg watched his farm foreman, Andries, appear from the concrete parapet of the spiral stairs and seek him out.

"*Baas!* Word from the *voorlopers*… They found the *bakkie* to the north and are tracking them on foot. Do I have permission to send the others in that direction too?"

Van Rensburg clambered unsteadily to his feet. Despite the fresh night air, he was still feeling sick and suspected that the American had broken his skull. That would need looking at, probably in Beaufort West, where it could be guaranteed no one would ask awkward questions. But not until they'd cleaned up this *fokken* shit-show.

"Send me six boys with strong stomachs," he said. "You can have the rest."

Kuhlmann was dead, throat agape from ear to ear. Likewise the Russian major. And that *doos* Joubert, who'd invented a new form of modern art in the process. It was Kuhlmann's surviving men who'd be no job for the squeamish, as well as Lebedev's wounded examples. As for Kuhlmann's wife, who had brought this whole 'mother problem' down upon them, he had a mind to deal with her himself when she woke up.

Once Andries had departed, Van Rensburg sank down on the lounger again, this time swinging up his feet with a protracted groan. Oh, he'd take it out on Kuhlmann's wife alright, but she wasn't the woman he really wanted to go to work on. If his men could take *her* alive, that would almost make it all worthwhile. Especially if they kept her son breathing long enough too. Then, as his people said, the dolls would dance… As for the American and the so-called 'Broker', well, one could respect men like that for their courage, but one didn't give them second chances.

Watching a dark cloud drift across the constellations, he wondered idly whether their stories about MI5 had been true. Even if they were, there'd be nothing left to find here by the morning, not with farm animals to feed and a desert's worth of holes to dig.

Wag 'n bietjie though… Clouds? On a still summer's night in the Karoo?

Before he knew it, they had spread across the sky and smothered him.

* * *

The man and his dog looked the same. Tall and loping, somewhat knock-kneed, thin as grasses, sere as hardwood. They had the same patchy greying beard and the same all-seeing gaze.

Had he not been clad in similar clothing to the farm workers who were tracking them, Pat would have supposed the fellow had wandered out of the distant past just as silently and startlingly as he had wandered out of the darkness – a first inhabitant, hunter-gatherer and shaman. It was a power and a presence that was there in the way he stopped them with a firm, raised hand, pale in the starlight, and circled them, going one way as his dog went the other, and examined, one by one, their sleeping cargo.

"Poldi," he said. The tone was not one of confusion, or accusation, only concern.

Still cradling Mila, visibly strained, Bradley had tried to explain the situation, or at least a simplified version of it. Clearly this man knew Pavel well enough to know his name. It soon became equally apparent that he had no English.

So Pat, in simple Dutch, had outlined the basics. This was 'Poldi's' real mother: the resemblance was there to see. They were trying for the higher ground to the north. Trying to get away from the bad men at the farm.

That had brought an earnest nod, the bad men at the farm. But also a question. What was wrong with the boy?

"He'll wake, soon," Pat had reassured him.

His mother?

The face that he and Bradley pulled required no translation.

And then the gesture, accompanied by a click for the dog.

Come.

So they had run on, the stranger carrying Pavel with an effortless gait while Pat and Bradley took up Mila's stretcher again. Despite their fatigue, Pat thought their pace was quicker now and the sound of the pursuing dogs more distant. Partly it was the redistribution of their loads. But it was also the confidence of their leader's footing in the darkness. Either his eyes were better attuned or he knew each rock and aloe.

Pat would not have been surprised if that were proven to be the case. Nor, he thought, to find when the sun came up that the stranger hadn't been there at all. He had read those sorts of stories in his youth.

All that mattered was that the daylight did not come yet.

Running on, the poem drifted into his head like an incantation. Gratified that it wasn't the Kipling again, which would have been all too fitting, he decided the deliverance warranted speaking it aloud. The bits he could recall, anyway.

"Where the wave of moonlight glosses
The dim gray sands with light,
Far off by furthest Rosses
We foot it all the night…"

It was, he remembered, called 'The Stolen Child'. Another of Yeats' works, and an early, appropriate one.

"Come away, O human child!
To the waters and the wild
With a faery, hand in hand…"

From behind him on the stretcher, he heard a thin, pained voice complete the verse for them.

"For the world's more full of weeping than you can understand."

"Mila," he heard Bradley gasp.

"Still here. And Pavel?"

"Safe. With us – and with a friend."

"That's good…" Her voice wavered and tailed off into a nauseous retch.

"Jesus," Pat heard Bradley say. Just that. And again. "Jesus."

"Come on," he called back, trying to raise spirits as well as the pace. "We can do it. Foot it all the night!"

And do it they did, even if that bloody Kipling came back more than once (try – try – try – try – to think o' something different!) and their throats were parched from rationing the water, and their feet numb from stumbling over rocks they could not see.

And then they could see the rocks, and the dry grasses and the watching Martian cactuses. Because the sun was coming up on the low horizon.

And they hadn't reached the higher ground, which was catching the first rays and shimmering, tantalisingly close and too bloody far away!

He and Bradley set down the stretcher. They exchanged looks. Each had been carrying old wounds as well as Mila – he his arm from Scotland, Bradley his shoulder and knee – and it was clear they were pretty much all in. Through their gasping breaths and pounding heartbeats they heard the dogs, still behind them but getting ever closer.

While Bradley checked on the girl, Pat stumbled a few steps across the flat, sandy terrain. Almost no cover. Even the bloody bushes were moving away!

Silly sod – that wasn't possible, was it, even here on Barsoom or whatever the Godforsaken place was called?

He kicked himself as the nearest bush resolved itself into an ostrich. The thing was enormous, far taller than a man with its head up. Except it didn't have its head up. Its neck bowed awkwardly and it leaned over to one side, limping, flapping a stunted wing. Was it injured, or performing some sort of mating dance for him?

"Not my type, ducky," he called out. "Sorry!"

But then the stranger came up to him, still surprisingly corporeal and, after such a long march together, really no stranger at all. He laid Pavel down gently, ignoring for the moment his waking protests, and pointed at the ostrich.

"Pretending," he said.

"To be injured?"

"Yes. To be easy kill. To draw you away from her eggs."

"Jesus," he said, echoing Bradley. "The last resort."

"Yes."

And now the man did pay attention to the boy: crouching down, raising his chin, eliciting a sleepy smile. Then he stood up straight and turned back to face the way they'd come.

"I go now. Last resort."

Pavel must have grasped something of the situation. He was getting up, crying in a high, clear voice: "Klaas! Hintsa! No!"

But Klaas was already moving with that unstoppable loping gait, Hintsa at his heels.

"*Tot weersiens*," he called back. "Look to your mother!"

"Where has he gone?" Bradley grunted.

Pat shook his head in wonder.

"To draw them away."

"Might buy us some time, but not enough if we can't find the goddamn cave."

The boy was stock-still, torn between watching his departing friend and going over to the woman on the stretcher whom Klaas had called his mother. No more certain himself – of anything, anymore – Pat went up to him and put a hand on his shoulder.

"Will she die?" Pavel asked in a small voice, in German.

"No," Bradley said firmly. "But she's asleep for now and she can't tell us where we need to go."

He had replied in English. Pat translated for Pavel, before turning back to Bradley.

"Look, I took what I could get from the chaps at the house…" he was going through his pockets, as he had gone through theirs.

"So?"

"There's the 'contract' between Lebedev and Van Rensburg, which our friend will like… And this, which was on Kuhlmann – a record of his good old days on the England Game by the looks of it, on official SD paper, with a bit of luck including that callsign that received the traitor's cryptic message…"

"I'm happy for you. Is there a point?"

"Only this," Pat said, holding up the photo from the Land Camera. "It's the interior of the cave. From the daylight I'd say it's more of a hollow, really. But it only shows the artworks, so that's no bloody use…"

252

The boy plucked it out of his fingers, peering at it, pointing at something.

Pat squinted too. There was enough light now to see the clutter of objects in the picture clearly. Paintings, for the most part. A couple of small sculptures. And in a narrow V behind two paintings, an African carving or something. They had said they'd found African artefacts in de Klerk's study. Presumably Pavel recognised them.

Except it wasn't a carving, or not exactly, and that was why Pavel was jabbing excitedly at it. It wasn't part of the hidden hoard at all. It was an ancient etching on the wall of the cave behind and had only been included by accident. A stylised antelope – an eland, Pat thought – and what looked like it might have been an ostrich…

"You know these?" he asked the boy.

An eager nod. A grin. And a small, grubby finger – no longer pointing at the photo but towards the escarpment rising in the north-northeast.

"Klaas took me there. I can take you. And *Máma*."

CHAPTER TWENTY

The two women in the back of the cave were sleeping. One, dark-haired, swamped in eiderdowns, looked tranquil, perhaps lost in pleasant dreams. According to the note on the back of the painting, she was the wife of the artist, the artist being one 'Max Liebermann'. It was easy to imagine why de Klerk had clung onto this piece to the last – and to wonder what had happened to the woman, for such a private, intimate image of her to have ended up in a Nazi's secret hoard.

The other woman was neither dark nor at peace and they had no bedding to soothe her fitful shivers, save the protective sacking they had torn off the artworks.

As Pat had predicted, the cave was little more than a hollow in the side of one of the dolerite sills that made up the higher ground here. When Pavel had first led them in, her colour had been poor and her dressing oozing blood. They had worked together to change it, using the last of the bandages, and this time, rather than applying more of the penicillin powder, Bradley had set up a simple drip. Throughout, she had drifted between restless unconsciousness and a delirious waking state, making no sense other than to reiterate that the pick-up would be an hour after midnight.

Bradley and Pat had met one another's eyes, struggling to keep up appearances for the sake of the boy.

She would be dead by then.

Powerless to do anything else, Bradley examined the rest of the cave. Besides the small sculptures and the paintings, and the Land Camera of course, Mila and her helpers had stashed two kitbags. He and Pat had confirmed that one was a EUREKA beacon, which formed half of the EUREKA-REBECCA transponding-radar system, and the other was an S-Phone ground set, a UHF radio-telephone that would enable the operator to talk an airplane in.

Such devices had been everyday tools for agents behind enemy lines, as well as for paratrooper pathfinders. Bradley remembered how she'd asked him if he had brought examples with him when he'd flown to her aid that night in the Sudeten Erzgebirge – and how, before finding that he had come sorely unprepared, she had suggested interrupting the signal to send a Morse message. But EUREKA could not respond at all unless the REBECCA equipment aboard the airplane was sending. Added to which, it had a maximum range of 90 miles, and this with the airplane aloft. Mila's pick-up was sitting on the airfield at George on the southern coast, well over a hundred miles away, with mountains in between.

The kicker was that neither device was even necessary by daylight. After all, the pilot and his crew had flown in here before, to meet the Boschkop *bakkie* and deliver the cargo. And they could damn well *see* the landing strip from up here, a paler streak on the scrubland, only a mile further to the north. Pat had put the glasses on it and said it was a peculiar wide stretch of dirt road alongside the foundations of an unfinished structure, connecting only with an intersection of narrower farm tracks, all deserted.

Yet there was no way to summon the airplane early. Just as he had not brought the EUREKA last time, Mila's plan had not included a wireless telegraph set like Pat's Mark III.

Bradley went to the opening of the cave, where Pat was keeping watch.

"Anything?"

"Dust to the south, but heading east. Looks like they're still tracking Klaas."

Fat lot of good... Bradley wanted to say. He'd have rather seen the trails coming straight for them. Not that Van Rensburg,

Kuhlmann or the Russians would have made Mila's fate any less unpleasant or inevitable, but at least he could have gone out killing the men who'd killed her.

The reason he did not say that was also the reason why it was a foolish wish, every bit as *narcissistic* as what he'd said to her about the Nazis and their bunkers.

The boy, Pavel, her son. Their job was wait for the pick-up and bring him safely home. That was all they could do for her now.

Pat got up close and whispered.

"You think he knows?"

"I dunno," Bradley said, shaking his head.

The boy ought to have been sitting with his mother, holding her hand, mopping her forehead, offering her the last drops of not-so-cool water from the bottle, talking to her, *telling* her... Instead, he was over by the far wall, tracing the pattern of another etching with his finger.

Perhaps the reason why he wasn't doing those things was the same reason Bradley wasn't doing them.

"Kid, Poldi…" Pat called out.

The lad replied without looking up from the etching, which appeared to be some kind of spoked wheel surrounded by curious, ill-defined figures. Round and round went the wheel, and his grubby fingertip too.

"Pavel, she called me," he said.

"*Was machst du,* Pavel?" Bradley said. It was pretty much the limit of his German, so when the boy replied – after a fashion – it was Pat who did the translating.

"Klaas told me that in the old days, Ostrich was given the secret of fire to keep hidden beneath his wing. That was why he did not fly. But Mantis saw this and tricked Ostrich into flapping his wings to reach the best plums, high up on a tree. Mantis then stole the fire to give to the first people – and in shame Ostrich said he would never spread his wings again."

"That's some story," Bradley said, thinking of the bird that had tried to lead them away from its eggs. Pat's 'last resort'.

Perhaps the boy was thinking of it too. As his finger traced an inner circle of the wheel and then followed a spoke down to the hub, he went on in a slow, strange voice.

"Only, sometimes, when he thinks no one is looking, Ostrich will open his wing a little – to see the little bit of fire that still remains. But if someone *is* looking…"

"What?" Pat said.

And then the boy did look at them, breaking the spell. His dusty face was tracked with tears.

"I don't know. He will be more ashamed, maybe."

Bradley gave a shudder, as though he'd received a shock of static electricity.

"Maybe he'd be more ashamed of himself if he didn't!" He kicked at Pat to rouse him from his own exhausted trance. "What if someone *is* looking?"

"What do you mean?"

"If you had an airplane, and you had to wait till midnight to go looking for the signal, you wouldn't just be kicking your heels at the airfield. That would drive you crazy."

"What are you talking about, Bradley? It's what they all did, all through the war."

"Yeah, and it drove them crazy, and now the war's over there's no brass telling them what to do."

Pat nodded.

"I'd go up anyway. Once in the morning and maybe once in the afternoon, as long as I had time to refuel before midnight. Up over the mountains and into range."

Bradley dragged the EUREKA bag towards them and started unlacing it, pulling out the wads of raw wool that were stuffed around the various boxes and bundles.

"If we put it up above the cave here, the range should be stretched a little further."

"The beam won't be on target for the landing zone," Pat said. "But we can take the S-Phone for that – redirect them."

Bradley grimaced.

"If it comes to it," he said.

Together, accompanied by the boy, they climbed to the top of the rock pile and erected the spindly telescopic tripod for the aerial, sinking the spikes into the ground as best they could. They connected up the power unit and the transmitter/receiver and looked at one another.

"How long will the batteries last?" Bradley asked.

"Six hours," Pat said.

Bradley looked at his wristwatch. It was ten thirty in the morning.

"Longer than she's got," he said, and flipped the switch.

Pat was holding up the earphone. He recoiled immediately from what he heard, which even Bradley could tell was just a formless snarl of static. He shook his head.

An unearthly cry from down below made them jump. Pavel looked sick.

"Keep monitoring," Bradley said.

With the boy in tow, he climbed back into the cave. Mila had rolled over to vomit, pulling out her drip. She was soaked through with sweat and shaking all over with fever and pain. Bradley tried to get her comfortable again. He examined her stomach – hard and discoloured – and wished he hadn't. There were no dressings or drugs left.

When he raised his head again he saw she was watching him. Her dulled, bloodshot eyes slid to the boy and back again as she bit her lip. Her tears brimmed.

"Sam…" she said in a broken-sounding voice. "I want you to use the Land Camera and take a picture of me for him. Otherwise he won't have anything."

He looked at her – the blue-ringed eyes and pale, shiny skin, the sunken cheeks and bitten lips – and it was all he could do not to cry too.

"He'll have you, Mila. He'll have you."

"Oh Sam," she said, reaching out to take his hand.

"Tone!" came a yell from up top.

Bradley seized the boy's hand and put it in Mila's in place of his own. Without thinking, he leant forward and kissed her softly on her blazing forehead. Then he went back out.

"It pitched up and now it's gone down to a steady note," Pat said excitedly. "A hum – 300 cycles!"

"Wait a minute," Bradley said. "That means he's in radio range. He was already nearby! Send 'SOS' on the transmitter button and let's get moving…"

He stood upright beside the tripod and squinted south, hoping to make out a distant dot in the sky. Instead he saw dust trails, three of them, converging on their position. Whether they had traced the beacon or spotted the aerial pole, the enemy had given up on Klaas and were on their way.

"It's Van Rensburg," he said coldly. "Or Kuhlmann, or the Russian."

"Not the last two," Pat said, unplugging the set and kicking over the tripod.

"Why not? I only chilled them."

"And I iced them, Bradley. As soon as everything went to crap. Operational contingencies. I doubt Van Rensburg will have lasted very long either, with the dent you put in his skull." He frowned, but not with any kind of remorse.

"What is it?"

"This set has a demolition charge on a fuse. If we put it with the pictures, we can brew up something to distract them…"

Bradley started climbing down.

"Forget it – and the S-Phone. There's no time and we're gonna have our hands full."

"I suppose I might have felt rather bad about it…" Pat was saying as they went.

"Icing those guys?"

"God no, blowing up the art."

Bradley almost laughed.

In the cave, he grabbed the blood-stained painting they had used before, setting it out ready again. He handed his Winchester carbine to a wide-eyed Pavel.

"Come on, old girl," Pat said as they lifted her onto the stretcher. "Last lap – not much further now."

As they carried her out past the rock etching that Pavel had been fooling with, Bradley noticed that as well as resembling a spoked wheel it looked like something else.

A transmitter, sending out waves as far as it could in all directions.

*   *   *

Andries had kicked out the window in the rear of the *bakkie*'s cabin so that he could shout to Cobus, behind the wheel.

"*Kyk daar!* There they are, off to the left. To the left, man!"

"*Se voet!* I can't go straight there, we'll rip our tyres off!"

"*Eish!*" With a frustrated cry, Andries planted his feet as wide as he could get them and tucked into his rifle.

Now he could see them clearly through the scope, even if they were bouncing up and down. Bent over in the lead, carrying the front of the improvised stretcher, it was the fellow who'd arrived two days ago and faced up to the *oubaas*. Stumbling along at the rear, that must be the one who'd done all the damage at the house, the one who'd been expected to fall from the sky. Perhaps he had!

On the stretcher, one thin, white arm dangling? It had to be the woman visitor, Faf's companion – as big a dead weight now as Faf himself, by the looks of it. And trotting alongside, with a little rifle of his own… Kuhlmann's son who was not his son, who was the woman's son, they were saying.

How had they come so far like that?

Where the hell did they think they were going?

And where the hell were the other farm vehicles, which had been forming up to follow them not so long ago? It looked like one had forked off towards the *koppie* where the mast had been. And the other? Another puncture? Or pulled over to pour in another can of gas?

What a *kakspul!*

He spared a glance for his companions in the *bakkie*, the two Germans with their bandaged heads. Muttering in their own language, they were busy with a Mauser much like his own. And something else. He saw that they had fitted a complicated sight to the side of the receiver and a launcher cup to the muzzle. That was why they had insisted on stopping by their car on the way out of the farm.

They were opening a wooden box of rifle grenades.

*   *   *

The pursuing *bakkie* sounded like it had spent the night tearing itself apart. It was making such a racket as it lurched across the veld that the occupants probably hadn't even heard what they had.

The airplane, circling around above the high ground to come in from the east.

Bradley could see the terrain opening up beyond Pat's hunched shoulders – and the foundations of the folly that some madman had intended, before the war had got in the way or the money had run out, to build in the middle of this wilderness. Only a few hundred yards now, and the going getting easier with every step...

"We've made it, Mila," he croaked.

"*'unger, thirst, an' weariness!*" Pat crowed ironically. His cockeyed poem again!

They could hear the airplane's twin engine note change again as it lowered its gear and flaps behind them. That was probably why they didn't really register the dulled shot from the direction of the *bakkie*. Not until the veld erupted in front of them.

Bradley hit the dirt – or the dirt hit him. A faceful of grit and dust obscured his view of Pat and the stretcher.

As he rolled and looked for the boy, the huge, cool shadow of the airplane descended right over them. It would be a sitting duck.

Pavel. With his gun.

"Pat *helfen*..." Bradley said. "Help him get your mother to the plane!"

The Winchester was a semi-automatic but if you had numb arms it was a stinker to charge the blowback action with that stiff plunger in front of the handguard. The instant he'd done it, he let rip a couple of rounds at the *bakkie* two hundred yards away. It was essential to throw off their aim now.

Missed. He settled himself and took the time to get a better picture through the iron sights. Windage was impossible to judge – he was lying in a swirl of dust that was being thrown up by the props and exhausts of the airplane as it came to a stop and turned around.

He saw his next shot shatter the windshield roughly where the driver would have been. The *bakkie* came to a halt.

Which was good for preventing them from closing the range. But not so good for denying them a stable, sheltered platform from which to launch the next grenade. This time he heard the thud and watched it fly over. He looked in terror behind him and saw it detonate amid the foundation walls, breaking apart a weathered sign that had borne the words:

ROYAL OBSERVATORY (KAROO).

The airplane, white and silver, swathed in dust, was now pointing towards him. The others must be on it. But it was going to have to come back this way to take off: right towards the *bakkie* with the grenade launcher, which he could tell from the dust trails was about to be joined by two others.

His eyes were full of dust and he couldn't see anything much from down on the ground. He got to his feet and began to limp towards the first vehicle, shooting from the hip.

And then, from somewhere, a rapid-firing machine gun opening up, stippling the *bakkie* and the surrounding ground with pecks of dust… And a hand, grabbing his shoulder, pulling him backwards.

"Come on," Pat said.

In a daze, Bradley allowed himself to be dragged beneath and behind the wing of the airplane, which was already rolling on its take-off run, the purr of its engines turning to a roar. Pavel was there in the doorway, arms outstretched. Pat heaved him up from the rear.

Instinctively he looked for Mila, but right by the door,

obscuring his view of the rest of the cabin, was the housing of a dorsal birdcage turret, in which stood a man in two-tone shoes and a striped double-breasted suit, hammering away with a Vickers K machine gun. Lying on the floor, squinting up in disbelief with his one clear eye, Bradley saw that it was Monsieur Sept.

The thunderous vibrations of the cabin eased as the wheels left the ground.

Pausing to change pans, Monsieur Sept glanced down at him and his features slid into a familiar grin. Then he reloaded the Vickers, revolved the turret with his feet and shoulders, and riddled the vehicles as they took off over them.

"This little beauty is an Airspeed Envoy *Convertible*," Pat yelled in delight, latching the door behind him. "They're quite popular down here. It takes four men four hours to switch it from a commercial aeroplane to a fighter-bomber, although they left the bombs behind today, worst luck. Wanted to save weight for the REBECCA equipment – and a more important cargo."

"Where is she?" Bradley demanded. But he could see. Even with the seats removed and only a single pilot up front, the turret left precious little room in the cabin for anything except the shrouded form on the floor and the boy kneeling beside it.

"It's alright, she's still alive," Pat said. "George in half an hour. Pilot's going to send word to prep the hospital now. Not a big place but it's mostly a sawmill town, so they're pretty hot on traumatic injuries, I understand."

The airplane was in a steady climb, making the slope of the cabin even steeper. Bradley tried to move forward on his knees, but every inch, every rivet, took it out of him. In the end, it was more of a belly crawl he used to get alongside her.

One hand was free, lolling against the fuselage. He reached out and took it.

Did she squeeze back? Later he could not be sure, because that was when he passed out.

EPILOGUE

The Resident flew into Washington D.C. that morning in a privately chartered plane bearing the Chinese tiger emblem of 'Civil Air Transport' – and in triumph.

The war had changed international travel beyond all recognition. Although his wife and daughters were to follow in due course aboard the *Queen Elizabeth* with their possessions, since receiving the notification of his new posting – effective immediate! – his feet had hardly touched the ground. Amazingly, he had departed Istanbul just the previous morning on Pan American's westbound Round-the-World service: the huge, pressurised Lockheed Constellation stopping only at London Airport, Shannon in Ireland and Gander in Newfoundland, arriving at La Guardia in New York before dawn. There he was rushed across the frosty tarmac to the waiting twin-engine transport, to be greeted enthusiastically by its crew, a pitcher of martinis at the ready.

But this was his proper arrival, in his new domain. It was here in the capital that he would be feted, fawned over and formally presented to the real brokers of power. It would be from here that he'd make his indelible mark on the world.

First Secretary to the British Embassy. In reality, MI6's Washington resident, with a brief to oversee and develop Anglo-American intelligence cooperation. He had earned it on merit, functioning at a level far above and beyond the plodders, yet even so he thanked his lucky stars for the fall of the cards. And for friends in the right places.

It could hardly be better. As Deputy Head of Section Nine at the end of the war, he had been perfectly placed to refocus the Secret Intelligence Service's counter-Soviet operations. Then, from Istanbul, as the acting section head of one side and – with scarcely any more acting required! – an unofficial counsellor to the other, he had been able to exploit the growing chaos in Greece and Albania, receiving plaudits from all quarters. But this was the big prize. This would be his chance to score some decisive early victories in the newly proclaimed 'cold war', before it even really got started.

So from the moment the C.A.T. Curtiss C-46 Commando taxied up to the Washington National Airport Terminal, he expected to be treated like royalty. Having been spared the purgatory of the US Health, Immigration and Customs machinery at La Guardia, he assumed that here they would roll out the red carpet, or the secret service version of it.

Instead, a nondescript man in plain clothes beckoned him towards a door that might have gone unnoticed had it not been propped open by a member of the airport police.

"My name's Murphy. Pleased to meet you! Would you follow me, please?"

In no time at all they were through the building and out by a small gate in the boundary fence. Directly outside, a black Buick waited. Another man was loading the Resident's two light suitcases into its boot. Murphy held the rear door open for him.

Waiting for him on the back seat, moving his heavy coat and a heap of files to make room for him, was a long-limbed, cultured-looking fellow wearing dark glasses.

"Sloane, Wally Sloane," he said, offering his hand; then, without further ado as Murphy climbed into the driving seat and the other man beside him: "Take the GW, Mike. Might as well show the poor Schmo what he's missing."

The Resident blinked. After the elaborate niceties of Istanbul, was he that poorly attuned to American parlance that a genial quip could sound so menacing? He closed his eyes and counted very slowly to ten. When he opened them, he was disoriented by the vast expanse of the Potomac, with the Washington

265

Monument rising beyond.

What he's missing?

"Are we going straight to the embassy?" he asked. "I had a mind to see my house first."

When the car looped around to join the traffic flow to the southwest, away from the shining citadel across the water, the weak winter sun swivelled and Sloane removed his glasses. The Resident flinched to see the yellow-tinged eyes glaring poisonously at him. It was like coming face to face with a cobra.

Then the eyes flicked, indicating something out of the window on the right.

The Resident looked. In the middle distance – it was all middle distances here – stretched a long, low building. He couldn't see the shape of it from this angle, but he knew from its position and the signage on the exit ramps that it was the Pentagon.

"Another place you'll be lucky to ever see again," Sloane hissed.

The Resident nodded to himself. By European standards the American car heater was remarkably efficient and his head was spinning already. He needed another drink and wondered if they would let him smoke. It might be an excuse to get a window open.

"Where are we going, then?"

"Way down the turnpike," Sloane said.

"I don't think I follow…"

"Oh, I think you do. Like when the MGB turned up on Texel to silence the Angel. I know that hadn't been your territory for quite some time and you'll claim your job depends on trading unimportant snippets like that, anyhow. But it's what we call a red flag, sport. You see, only you were fed that morsel – and other tidbits, fed to others, have been tracked through you also. We've been adding more red flags every day. Right now, we got people talking to a waiter at Taksim's in Istanbul who looks like he's going to have plenty to say about the last couple of compromised *Balli Kombëtar* insertions into Albania. And then there's the meeting in South Africa…"

The Resident affected a blank look, but Sloane wasn't buying it.

"Remember the England Game? Well, how could you forget! Our walk-ons down there were running their own variation, of course: sow suspicion, so the centre cannot hold. In this case, Moscow Centre. But they improvised and ran a litmus test too. Seems your late buddy 'Dmitriy' got quite upset at the suggestion we might have caught a traitor with a very similar résumé to yours…"

In the front, Murphy snorted.

"Now hold on, Mike," Sloane said. "Nothing's proven, you know that. Specially not as regards actual, full-blown, execute-the-sonofabitch treason. Why, we got headshrinkers theorizing how maybe the guy's just so damn smart he's doing all our jobs for us – on both sides – and making the world a safer place!"

Still ostensibly addressing 'Mike', he thrust out two fingers and gave the Resident a prod in the ribs that fell somewhere between fraternal joshing and physical assault.

"'course we got others who reckon he's an ultra-conservative fruitcake who's plain dumb enough to think the commies will put him on the Throne of England or something – once he's helped them to undo everything we just fought for."

With that, Sloane gazed at him directly again. A tongue protruded from those thin lips; it wasn't forked, but it was tasting the air all right.

"We got Kuhlmann's old report, which he and the SD kept from Giskes and the *Abwehr* – the one with the callsign that picked up the traitor's coat-trailing. Seems when MI6 took over SOE's assets, someone high up ordered the substance of the Dutch Section files destroyed. But there are still logs that show who sent those transmissions. It's not proof, of course, and there's no one left alive from the South African meeting to corroborate it. But it's another flag, sport, whether it comes with a swastika or the hammer and sickle."

The Resident closed his eyes. Twenty, this time. Thirty. Then, drawing on generations of public school self-righteousness, he let himself get red in the face.

"These are outrageous allegations! Do you know who you're talking to? I'm the First Secretary."

His bloody stammer was back. He heard 'Mike' cackle in front.

Sloane was not laughing, nor was he joking; that much was obvious.

"No, you're not. Except in the eyes of Lebedev's superiors. They'll believe you're here in the inner sanctum, supplying them with chapter and verse. But that cable about your promotion never came from London."

And there it was. No old boy network. No immunity. No extraction plan in place. Game, set and m–m–m–match.

They weren't going to let him smoke, either; he could tell that. He certainly wasn't going to reach for his ciggies and have them slap him down. Instead he let out a long, whistling breath and imagined the caustic odour of Gitanes… and the Galata quayside, and the Spice Market. It was all a far cry from these dreary stretches of dead land and wintering trees that rushed past on either side. He might as well be in Russia!

"And my wife and children?"

"What do you think? Oh, they'll be joining you, if you play ball during your debriefing and agree to our proposal for what comes next. You can live a grand old life with them here – once you help us figure out who that 'someone high up' might have been. We'll even keep the FBI investigation off your back, and your people, with a couple of exceptions. But there'll never be fewer than two guns on you, or your daughters."

Sloane held his gaze, his lips finally twitching into an insincere smile.

"Welcome to the CIA!"

*   *   *

Bradley let Scintilia drive him to the ranch near the Rowdy Boys drift on the Hunyani.

Out front, the somewhat dented Humber Hawk that was parked next to the gleaming Cadillac confirmed that Jimmy

Lonsdale had also accepted the invitation, Scintilia said – or at least he mumbled a hesitant mishmash of words to that effect.

"OK, Gerardo." People called him that now, if they called him anything. His former nickname would have been too cruel.

Bradley peered out intently as their car slid into place by the white paddock fence in the shade of the eucalyptus.

They were shown in by a major domo and ushered to a cool, well-lit sitting room that opened onto the veranda. Jimmy Lonsdale was there, but it was Dominic Franzetti, in a floral shirt and Bermudas, who rose to greet them.

The look on his face when he saw the look on Scintilia's came close to genuine concern.

"OK, you're Bradley. I heard about you. You wanna drink?"

"Sure." He took the offered chair across from Lonsdale, who gave him the most cursory of nods. "I'll have a scotch and soda on the rocks."

"*Bene!* I have one too! Sparky?" Trying not to blanch at Scintilia's look of incomprehension, and failing, he flapped a hand. "We get you something later."

At that there was a rasp from Lonsdale that reminded Bradley of the grating sound of the EUREKA headset when it hadn't found a signal.

"Got your fuckin' message…"

He seemed smaller than Bradley remembered. Certainly a lot thinner. But no less dangerous.

"Uh-huh?"

"Vic Parsons' 'ankie, from the Congo."

"Oh," Bradley nodded. That hadn't been his idea, it had been the Omitted's. But he wasn't going to split hairs now. "My condolences."

"That's nice, innit?" Lonsdale looked at Franzetti. "Yeah that's fucking rich, that is."

Franzetti's look went from Lonsdale to Scintilia and back again.

"Africa. It's a wonderful place. But things end badly here. What can we do for youse, Mr Bradley?"

"I came to thank you for the money," he said.

"We ain't given you no money, Mr Bradley."

"Sure you did, Mr Franzetti. Or rather, Mr Lonsdale did. It was there at Ndolo. The last payment Willi Nohl received for arms."

"That weren't our dosh, it was the Russians'..." Suddenly, Lonsdale looked uncertain.

"Oh, I know," Bradley said. "They were using middle-men to purchase arms for the Zionists. But the end-customers never received their last shipment, on account of Nohl's demise – and my condolences there as well, by the way…"

"You never told me we was going into business with the *commies*!" Franzetti exploded.

"I don't s'pose Lucky an' Vito are gonna be queuing up to pin medals on *you* neither…" Lonsdale's breathless counter triggered a coughing fit.

"The thing is," Bradley cut in. "The commies whose arms deal didn't go through were pissed – but the commies we gave the money to were anything but."

"You gave our money to another bunch of commies?"

"A good friend of mine did. All except a small down payment that went astray in South Africa. But I thought it wasn't your money, Jimmy."

"It ain't, 'specially not if the weapons weren't delivered..." He examined his own handkerchief and rolled his eyes. "You really don't want to get on *their* bad side."

Bradley took a last slug of his drink.

"No, I'll tell you whose bad side you don't wanna get on…"

They both stared at him. They weren't used to this.

"Let me put this in terms you'll understand. Then I'm outta here." He tapped several times for emphasis on the table-top beside him. "A contract. MERCURY and me, we've taken out a contract on you two, with our new best friends in Moscow. If you ever interfere with us in any way – and if you ever set foot outside this country again – you'll discover how Soviet 'wet work' makes the Genovese family's look like a fucking paper cut."

270

He set down his empty glass and stood, adjusting his jacket. "Enjoy Africa," he said.

*   *   *

It had been frowned upon, in this most ancient of landscapes and traditional of communities, to tinker with what had come before. But the mistress was no slave to convention.

Now that the gateposts had been properly restored, she had commissioned a local sculptress to carve new finials to replace the eroded examples that had long since grown indistinguishable as pine cones, fish or whatever they had once been. These *metamorphic megaliths*, as the mistress cheekily described them – experimenting with local tastes and tolerances in addition to her English – were modernistic in execution yet harked back to something far older.

In short, they had been inspired by the old master's chessmen that were now the children's playthings: one the thoughtful queen (with toothache!, as the mistress quipped); the other, not a king but instead a stubby, bearded knight upon a stubby horse.

And Miss Robinson, who had introduced the mistress to *Jane Eyre* during her long convalescence and enjoyed many discussions about her favourite book when the children had gone to bed, knew something of who he was meant to be. The old master, who had been, in a manner of speaking, her husband – but also a St John Rivers, Jane's rescuer in the book, with a large heart, but with a mission that left no room for passion.

Here above the property, silhouetted against the golden afternoon light that dusted Loch Fyne and the summits beyond, he would forever challenge all that came this way, while behind him his glorious sun hastened to its setting.

It was the end of the novel that had given the mistress the idea, and Miss Robinson who had helped her choose the inscription.

His is the sternness of the warrior Greatheart, who guards his pilgrim convoy from the onslaught of Apollyon.

A suitably masculine-sounding tribute to a great British man –

penned by a great woman and reinterpreted by two slightly tipsy, lesser ladies of Eastern European background who had been confused and then amused by the Christian name, St John, and its even more ridiculous British pronunciation. Now it was the sign for where to find the ever-growing children's sanctuary.

Arm in arm, they finished their walk and continued down towards the house.

"And how, I wonder," Mila said. "Have the children been behaving without their governess? I do hope we haven't upset Mrs Macrae by our absence again!"

"Their *plain, Quakerish* governess…" Ava muttered. But Mila was having none of it.

"Hardly! And you can't tell me you haven't been making a little more of an effort now our house guests are here."

Ava blushed. She did not mind. They were nearly at the brick archway to the garden and she knew it suited her well.

On the patio below the terraces, hunched over a cricket bat that was sized for a child of nine or ten, Mr Pendleton was surrounded by a gang of Mrs Macrae's 'wee beasties', each apparently intent on putting another lump or bruise on his uncharacteristically pale, hairless legs.

With gratification, Ava saw that even Little Hans was joining in the fun, though not as uproariously as Rat and Maggot, who were taunting the terrorized batsman.

Mila's eyes, of course, were on the bowler.

"I don't see why I have to roll my trousers up to act as the stumps," Mr Pendleton was pleading. "I don't remember that being part of French cricket!"

"Och, but it's part of *Scottish* cricket," Mrs Macrae cackled, setting a fresh pot of tea on the table for the two more civilised-looked visitors. Having heard Mila's stories, or at least a heavily edited smattering, Ava knew that neither Mr Jones nor his sometime assistant were even halfway as civilised as they made out to be, although she suspected that Mrs Parker, the former Corporal Jenny Simmonds, would have to mellow once her baby was born.

And Mila? Had she mellowed? For the moment her concentration was wholly focused on the boy with the hard rubber ball.

"Right then – make it a good one, Pavlík!" she called in her customary medley of German, Czech and English. It was her special way of communicating with him, often in private whispers, stroking his hair at the fireside, but now designed to engage him in the general din. "You can hardly miss those knobbly knees!"

"Had I the heavens' embroidered cloths…"

"Yes, Mr Pendleton?" Ava giggled.

"Pat, please… I would spread the cloths over my shins."

"That's not Yeats!"

"Tread softly… ouch!"

Mila clapped and jumped in delight.

"You got him, Pavlík. Well done! You're in next…"

"Stay where you are! You'll have to bat from there, you little fiend."

Pat handed over the bat and limped across the patio to Ava. She blushed again, more deeply this time.

His face all kindled, and his full falcon-eye flashing, she thought.

"Miss Robinson… Ava? Please deliver me from these monsters immediately. Take me for a stroll around the gardens."

"I have just been for a stroll, Mr… Pat."

"Then come and feed me scones. Look, my tormentor is already scoffing the last of them, no doubt employing her usual excuse of needing to recover her strengths."

"She was dreadfully ill, Pat. All through Christmas in South Africa, and then with peritonitis when she finally sailed back here."

"I know," he gave her that smile as he settled her and took the seat next to hers.

The words, both regretful and wonderful nonetheless, popped into her head before she could stop them.

No woman was ever nearer to her mate than I am…

"Can't have been too easy hearing about what the communists

got up to in Czechoslovakia, either," Jones said. "Have you heard from anyone since the coup – brothers, old acquaintances?"

Mila shook her head.

"Well, that's for another day," Jones said. "The latest bloody mess is this business in Berlin…"

One hand resting contentedly on her bump, the other frozen in the act of reaching for another scone, it was Mrs Parker who spoke for all of them.

"Sir – beggin' your pardon and all, but do put a sock in it!"

"Thank you, Jenny," Mila said warmly, before twisting around with care to watch the children at their game. Despite the lingering discomfort from her wound, she appeared immensely contented, her long mission fulfilled. Satisfied with tranquillity, Ava thought, not without irony.

And mellowed? Perhaps. For now. Certainly the old mistress, as Ava had known her, would never have permitted even those few, frustratingly incomplete tales of the madcap chase they'd been on this past year; nor sat back, laughing, as the others offered completely contradictory versions of events that could have no possible connection. These included the discovery of a Nazi hoard in South Africa, the release from prison of an artist in the Netherlands, the disproving of a commonly held belief about ostriches burying their heads (an unconscious bias more likely to be demonstrated by recently created and even more recently terminated Soviet intelligence committees, they joked), and the move-by-move account of a game of chess with a masked man in Vienna which, Pat said, he'd let the masked man win. Listening to this, chipping in now and then with pantomime boos and cheers, Mila had acquired, it seemed, a newfound ability to take pleasure in the inconsequentiality of it all.

Perhaps Pat had said it best a little while ago, although of course it had been impossible to define the context: "We spent so long selling stories to people, it's nice that it no longer matters if anyone believes us."

Mila had nodded. She was still nodding now, slowly, wistfully to herself.

Then a toot from the top of the driveway brought an instant sparkle to her eyes and a whole different level of satisfaction to her features.

"It's Darroch," she said as she got to her feet. "He knows I've banned him from even attempting to drive through my new gates."

"Oh, can I give you a hand…?" Ava made to rise too, but Pat's hand was on hers to stay her.

"He's brought Mr Bradley," Jones said quietly. "He's been in America for debriefing. Only flew in this morning."

Ava nodded. For the moment, she was too absorbed even to notice that Pat had not removed his hand. She watched Mila skip across the patio and disappear through the arch.

By the time she reappeared above the garden wall, halfway up the long curve of the driveway, she was running.

AFTERWORD

This concludes the Chasing Mercury series, as well as Mila and Bradley's adventures (for the moment, at least). Please leave a rating and review on Amazon – one line is fine! – and keep in touch at www.bypaulphillips.com/chasing-mercury.html

As before, *The Safehaven Complex* draws speculative links between real events, employing generous dramatic licence. It is certainly true that 1947 saw the birth and 1948 the untimely demise of the Soviet Committee of Information – and that while Beria and Abakumov continued to compete for Stalin's favours, evidence against each was mounting. By 1954 both had been executed.

It should be noted that the portrayal of the management of the Mauritshuis is completely fictional and there is no suggestion that anything in the present day collection is other than what it appears to be.

Printed in Dunstable, United Kingdom